Pleasure Workers
The Trophy Wives Club Continuation

Annette Mori

Also by Annette Mori

A Window to Love
The Book Witch
The Book Addict
The Dream Catcher
Free to Love with Ali Spooner
Unconventional Lovers
The Organization with Erin O'Reilly
Captivated
The Termination
The Review
The Ultimate Betrayal
Locked Inside
Out of This World
Asset Management
The Incredibly True Adventure of Two Elves in Love
(Affinity 2014 Christmas Collection)
Love Forever, Live Forever
The True Story of Valentine's Day
Vampire Pussy...Cat
Nicky's Christmas Miracle X3
(*It's in Her Kiss*, Affinity's Charity Anthology)

Pleasure Workers
The Trophy Wives Club Continuation

Annette Mori

Affinity
Rainbow Publications

2019

Acknowledgments

First and foremost, thanks to Ali Spooner for agreeing to this collaboration and allowing me to add to her Trophy Wives Club story. Ali is a delight to work with and I always appreciate any opportunity I have to work with such a talented author. A huge thank you to all of my beta readers: Gail Dodge, Carrie Camp, Ameliah Faith, Dana Holmes, Elle Hyden, Gayle Teller and Maria Siopsis who made great suggestions to improve the initial draft. As always, I have to acknowledge Erin O'Reilly who is a constant support and encouragement to me. I am honored to call her a friend and have her support me in my journey.

I would also like to express my gratitude to Affinity Rainbow Publications and the wonderful trio (JM Dragon, Erin O'Reilly and Nancy Kaufman) who continue to provide feedback to tighten up manuscripts that need assistance and publish my unconventional work. I am eternally grateful for the opportunities they give me to let my stories see the light of day. My other family members who are also very supportive, include my nephew, Aaron and his wife, Chelsea, my older sister Val, and my father who struggles to read my books with one eye. I always enjoy working with the beta editor Nancy Kaufman who helped tighten our stories.

Thanks to Angela Koenig for her magic as the final editor to tighten the story even further. She is a delight to work with. Inevitably, there are those pesky final errors that slip through and I am thankful that the final proof editor, Alexis Smith, caught those before the book went to print.

Thanks to Nancy Kaufman for the final cover. Nancy is also a promoter extraordinaire. A huge thanks to all the other readers and fellow writers who have sent personal e-mails, written reviews and posted nice things on Facebook (you know who you are). The Affinity authors are an especially supportive group and often share posts or send words of encouragement. Finally, my wife, Jody, continues her support even when it interferes with our time.

Dedication

To Ali Spooner who is the absolute best writing partner and person to collaborate with.

And, as always, to my beautiful wife who I love with all my heart.

Table of Contents

CHAPTER ONE

Alejandra Cortez stood on the edge of the dusty side road, coughing as dirt invaded her lungs. The wind kicked up the particles that tickled her airway as they weaved their way inside. Covering her mouth with her hand, she made a vain attempt to keep the tiny intruders from taking over. She squinted at the distant truck rolling down the sparsely traveled lane. Maybe she'd catch a break and the truck would take her a fair distance down the road. She wasn't sure what direction she should go, but east sounded as good as any other. Certainly, that would be far away from border patrols or anyone who hated Mexicans. An increasing number of people saw her and her family as a blight on their pristine white land.

Alejandra didn't feel like her name ever fit her. As soon as she earned the right to make a stand, she'd declared to her parents her preference for Alex. That name seemed to fit a whole lot better for reasons she'd never shared with her very Catholic parents. When she was growing up, her mama had wanted her to learn a more fitting vocation than handywoman, something more suited to a woman, like nursing or teaching. Both were professions that contributed to society. Alex tried to remind her mama that even if she managed to get an education, she couldn't possibly work for a hospital or a school without a valid social security card. The real reason was she didn't have an affinity to medicine or education, but preferred to follow her papa around and learn all about fixing things. Papa was her hero. Juan could fix everything. He could do anything. She wanted to be just like her papa and she was good at it too. She took to plumbing, electrical, painting, and all manner of machinery, like a duck to water. Her mama had given up well before Alex hit puberty and seemed resigned to what was clearly Alex's preference.

The wind kicked up again and the dirt swirled around her, causing another round of uncontrolled coughing. As the truck approached and pulled onto the shoulder, the dirt tornado expanded. Her need to expel the foreign material from her lungs took on a new level of desperation. She was a desperate woman with no job, very little money, and no idea where to go. Not that she'd collected very much while living in Nevada, but for the second time in less than a year, she'd had to go on the run with little more than what she could carry in a pack on her back. A memory surfaced from the last conversation she'd had with her papa. Alex liked giving her papa shit, so she'd joked with him on the afternoon right before everything came crashing down around her family and forced her into her current situation. That had been nearly eight long months ago.

Her papa kept blowing his nose and complaining loudly as he tinkered with the small motor Old Man Hartford had brought in for him to fix.

"Hey, Papa, you should really find some triactin." Alex handed her papa a small screwdriver, anticipating his need.

"Triactin?" Her papa scrunched his face. "Is that a new remedy, Mija?"

"Uh huh." Alex laughed. "Try acting like a man." She leaned back and held her stomach while laughing without restraint.

"Very funny, Mija. You should become comedian and stop following your old papa. You not laugh so hard if you catch this cold from me."

"Sorry, Papa. I couldn't resist. Mama always says how much the men complain when they get a tiny sniffle and how the women endure so much more. She says that's because it is expected of us."

"True, your mama endure a lot to bring your enormous body into world. At nine pounds, I thought surely she give me a son."

"Do you regret she could only give you one child and it was a girl?"

Juan reached over to pat Alex. "Never. You my pride and joy. So beautiful and talented. You take over family business when I die. It will expand. You not make the mistakes I have. I do not have good judge of character like you and mama."

Alex sobered quickly. "I'm sorry I couldn't handle all the work. I wish you didn't have to hire anyone else and then we wouldn't need to trust someone outside of the family."

Juan shrugged. "Price of success and fulfilling American dream."

"I suppose."

The truck skidded to a stop and Alex brought her face to the passenger side window as she peered in. The gapped-tooth smile of a man with a deeply lined face studied her. He seemed harmless enough. Besides, at nearly six feet tall with well-defined muscles, Alex could easily fight her way out of a tight situation if she needed to. The man looked like a strong wind could blow him over, but it was always the small wiry ones she'd had to watch out for. The men who knew a hard day's work and spent the day in the hot sun were not to be taken lightly. Even though the owner of this beat-up jalopy appeared to be in his 70s, he was one of those hard-working types she'd known from hanging around her papa's friends. Most of the men worked the farms. She made a split-second decision and tossed her ratty old pack into the back of the open truck.

"Where ya headed, young man?"

"East." Alex wasn't about to correct his error. Sometimes she was mistaken for a guy. She could live with that, especially if it kept the assholes from hitting on her. She lifted her baseball cap off her head and pushed her fingers through the perspiration that had collected in her short thick locks.

When she pulled on the silver handle to open the door, the truck groaned and squawked at her, almost as if trying to communicate that, like its owner, she was old and this sprite young'un ought to treat her with gentleness and care. Folding her tall lean body inside, Alex cautiously closed the heavy door and winced at the loud clang. The vinyl seats were covered with gray duct tape in an attempt to patch up the numerous cracks and tears in the upholstery. No air conditioning. Well, beggars couldn't be choosy.

"Thanks for the ride. However far you can take me is fine with me."

The old man's eyes narrowed as Alex pulled the seat belt across her chest. "Oh, I'm sorry. I thought you was a fella. I suppose I shoulda looked closer. You sure don't have a man's face or uh, body." He coughed. "You ain't got nothing to worry about though. Been married to my wife for nearly sixty wonderful years. You know you shouldn't be out here hitchhiking. There's a lot of crazy people running around in the world today. Some that ain't so nice."

He offered his words of wisdom and Alex thought there was something sweet about him. She knew how shitty some men and women could be. This wasn't the first time someone had mistaken her for a boy, albeit a pretty boy, they had said. She'd gotten her full lips and high delicate cheekbones from her mama. Her papa had contributed her smoldering brown eyes that some had described as bedroom eyes. She was glad to have inherited them from her papa. Many a woman had fallen prey to her expressive eyes.

The low rumble of the engine played in the background instead of music as the old man pulled his ancient truck onto the rough road. Alex noticed a large hole where a radio may have resided long ago. She settled in as the engine's sound lulled her with the familiarity of riding inside an old jalopy.

"I'm pretty good at taking care of myself. Been doing it for a while now." The reality was that she hadn't always taken care of herself. She'd depended a whole lot on her family. It wasn't until she had to go on the run that life had handed her a crash course in how to be an adult. Before that she'd led a sheltered life in her sleepy little town, following her papa around and taking the evening meals with her mama and papa. She hadn't even felt the need to move out of her family home.

"Name's Henry," he grunted. His cheeks looked like an alien was moving around inside, before he turned his head toward the open window and spit out a sunflower seed.

"Alex."

Henry shook his head. "Just like my granddaughter. Had a perfectly good name, but said Georgiana don't fit her. Makes us call her George. I don't like it much cause it makes me think of those Bushes from Texas." He cackled. "You a lesbian, too?"

Alex raised her eyebrow. "If I answer honestly, will you still give me a ride?"

"Course. Love my granddaughter. She can't help how she was born. God don't make mistakes, ya know."

Alex smiled. "In that case, yeah."

Henry eased his truck back onto the road. "You single?"

Alex laughed. "Why? Is your granddaughter?"

"As a matter of fact, she is. But you ain't her type. She likes em a bit frillier. You know, them lipstick lesbians."

"Too bad. I don't have a type. I like them in all shapes, sizes, and styles. Never met a woman I didn't appreciate."

Henry grabbed a handful of sunflower seeds. "Me too and then my wife tamed my wild side. When you meet the right one, she becomes your type for life." Nodding, he shoved the seeds into his mouth. He pointed at the bag, offering some as they traveled along the road kicking up more dust.

Alex declined his offer. "If you don't mind me asking, how far can you take me?"

"How far you need to go to get away from whatever you're running from?"

Alex stiffened in her seat. "A couple of hours on this road should do it. Maybe to a truck stop where I might be able to catch a longer ride. How'd you know?"

"I been on this planet for a lot of years. I reckon I know about stuff sometimes. It's the way people look around or carry themselves. I can tell when someone's a good person and hasn't had a fair shake in life. Never been wrong before and I don't 'spect I'm wrong now. I got just the place to drop you off. I might even know a trucker who will give you that lift."

"Thanks, Henry. You remind me a little of my papa. Maybe my luck is changing and this is a sign."

Alex turned away and looked out the open window. She didn't want Henry to see the tear that had formed and think she was soft or something. She suspected he knew but ignored her sudden flash of emotion. Yes, he was a lot like her papa. She was going to find a way to bring them back, no matter what it took. She figured Henry might see the resolution in the setting of her jaw, so she forced herself to relax and smiled at him.

†

Holy shit. Henry screeched into the truck stop, his tires leaving their mark along with the pungent smell of burning rubber.

"Henry, I still have a lot of years ahead of me. Are

7

you trying to kill us?" Alex placed her hands on the dash bracing herself as the truck skidded to a stop.

Henry pulled on the door and jumped out. "Come on, Alex, Rosie's getting ready to leave. Guess I got to jabbering too much and lost track of time." He began running toward an eighteen-wheeler starting to ease out of the parking space the big rig had recently occupied. He was waving his hands madly in the air.

Alex thought for an old man, he was very quick. She was afraid the truck couldn't see him as the sky was growing darker. She jumped quickly out of Henry's old beater and joined him in his waving routine. She winced when she heard the squealing brakes. A minute later a compact woman with short-cropped salt-and-pepper hair jumped down from the cab. She placed her hands on her hips and frowned.

Alex didn't ever like to feed into stereotypes, but diesel dyke was what popped into her head and she mentally chastised herself. For an older woman, she was certainly attractive enough, but then again as Alex had told Henry, she didn't have a type. All women were appealing to her. Nothing compared to the sheer beauty of a woman reaching climax as she threw her head back in pure ecstasy. Alex lived for those moments, although she'd had to discover those opportunities outside of the tiny town where she'd grown up and lived most of her life before she went on the run.

"What the hell, Henry. I almost mowed you down," the woman said. As if the woman all of a sudden registered there was another person standing next to Henry, her eyes roamed across Alex's body. Alex felt like the woman was leaving no stone unturned as she checked out every inch of Alex's tall frame. Her eyes spent a few extra seconds on Alex's breasts and then a slow smile emerged on her face.

"Who's your friend, Henry?"

"This is Alex. She's a sweet young gal who needs a ride east. I didn't want her accepting a ride from some low life, so I thought you might give her a lift."

"I sure can. Come on, sweet thing. Grab your bag and I can take you as far as Atlanta. Name's Rosie." She took several steps closer and held out her hand. "Very pleased to meet ya."

"Um, I sure am appreciative of the ride, ma'am, but can you not call me sweet thing? I'm a bit more sour than sweet." Alex took Rosie's hand.

"Fair enough if you don't call me ma'am. I already feel old. I'll look forward to the company and the energy of someone on the younger side of life. Thanks for bringing a nice woman I can pass the time with, Henry. You give my best to your wife. Oh, and tell that adorable granddaughter I said hello. If only I was thirty years younger."

"You old cougar. You know she had a crush on you," Henry teased.

"Now you know you don't have to lay that bunch a malarkey on me. I'd be eager to give this handsome little gal a ride. She's definitely brightened my day." Rosie winked and her blue eyes twinkled.

Alex got a mental picture of Rosie's sapphire eyes darkened in arousal and she considered whether there was enough time or opportunity to finagle a way for her to experience that, versus simply imagine the scene. She was good at two things—sex and fixing things. Her papa always said she should capitalize on her talents and not dwell on the things she wasn't very accomplished at. Especially cooking. When she was barely ten, she'd attempted to impress him, with disastrous results. He'd kindly informed her she best leave the cooking to her mama, who was the only master in the kitchen they'd ever need. If Alex took away that joy, her mama wouldn't be utilizing the talents God bestowed on her. Juan insisted God had decided on a whole different set for Alex. Alex mused that if only her papa had known about her other skill set, he might not have encouraged her so much to find her niche in the world.

Alex's mama had different ideas about cooking. She had decided the importance of passing down their culture and her gift was more valuable than the numerous messes she'd have to clean up. Her mama never gave up and taught Alex how to make homemade tamales and a decent breakfast burrito. If that was the only authentic meal she could make, so be it. That skill might come in handy one day if she was trying to impress a woman. Besides, she got to spend time with her mama and that made them both happy.

Alex showed Rosie her gleaming white teeth as she offered her most seductive smile and then ran back to Henry's truck to retrieve her bag. Maybe this woman would appreciate being on the receiving end of her touch.

Pack in hand she grinned at her new friend and said, "Ready whenever you are."

Turning to Henry she felt a rush of affection and dropped her pack, then pulled the wiry man into a bear hug. "Thanks for the ride, Henry. I won't forget you and your kindness. Will you give me your contact information? If you don't mind, I'd like to keep in touch and maybe someday find a way to repay you for picking up a stranger and giving me a reason to have hope for mankind after all."

"Dontcha worry about that, Alex. I was happy to have you come along when I saw ya on the side of the road. I'll give you my address. I like the idea of getting a letter from you. Knowing you've settled somewhere and things are looking up for you will make this old man's heart soar."

Rosie pulled a pad from the front pocket of her shirt and handed it to Henry. She began patting her pants pockets until she found a ballpoint pen that Alex figured she'd shoved into the back pocket of her jeans.

Henry grabbed the pen and started scribbling his contact information. "I guess you're always prepared, Rosie." He winked. "Ya never know when you're going to meet the one, huh? It'd be a shame not to have paper and pen to get their number."

Rosie smacked Henry on the arm. "Now ya know that ain't why I carry those things. Gotta jot down if my cargo has a problem on delivery. Boss man always wants the details and I write down exactly what the customer says, word for word."

Henry chuckled and handed Alex the paper he'd ripped off the pad, and then gave Rosie back her pad and pen.

"I know, Rosie. I just like to tease ya. But ya know ya ain't getting any younger. When ya gonna settle down with a nice little gal who can have a meal ready for ya when ya come home from a long stint in the big rig."

A sad smile crossed Rosie's face. "Maybe someday, Henry, but I gotta convince the one I've had my eye on for years and so far, no luck."

"I'm rootin' for both of ya." Henry waved and returned to his old beater.

At least Alex had got to say a leisurely goodbye to this man who reminded her so much of her papa. That wasn't a luxury she'd had when they took her mama and papa away. She tried not to let the melancholy get to her as the memory flashed before her eyes. A warm hand on her arm interrupted the sadness Alex felt. She quickly painted a smile on her face as she followed Rosie to the large eighteen-wheeler waiting on them in the middle of the truck stop.

Alex looked up at the enormous vehicle with the bright yellow paint job. It reminded her of one of those cartoon suns—all bright and shiny. She liked the smooth round surface over the top of the cab and thought the rig matched the owner perfectly. Rosie had a broad smile on her face just like a ray of sunshine.

The next adventure was around the corner for Alex. She could feel it in her bones.

†

"So, what's your story, darlin'? Not that I don't think you can't take care of yourself" —Rosie let her eyes once again roam over Alex's body— "with those rippling muscles and your impressive height, but why are you hitchhiking by yourself? Henry was right to bring you to the truck stop and catch me before my long haul to Atlanta. No offense, but there's a lot of ignorant rednecks lookin' to fuck up, um..."

"A Mexican dyke?" Alex shot Rosie a wry look. "Hey, don't worry about it. There isn't a lot of love for brown people, what with us all coming from shithole countries. I'm used to the slurs."

"Somebody chasing you or something? You don't have to worry about me. You can consider this truck a rolling sanctuary city. I don't believe in that stupid wall or sending people back who lived their whole life here."

"What makes you think I wasn't born here?" Alex's jaw clenched and her tone had a clipped edge to it.

Rosie shrugged. "Look, I don't mean to rile you up or anything. I'd be sensitive too if the President started talking about the Irish like he talks about Mexicans. My grandparents came from the Emerald Isle. Immigrants who worked their asses off in the factories. None of us ever went to college, but I make a good living driving a rig. It suits me."

"Fixing things suits me, but it's hard to get a job without references. I've only ever worked in the family business and then on a kind of ranch in Nevada." Alex turned away and looked out the window. "I liked it there. Got to use some other skills, too, until...well turns out that no good deed goes unpunished. Felt bad about not giving my notice, but hey, it was time to leave."

"I can tell you're a good person, so if you're running, I suspect the jerk chasing you is some asshat that got his knickers in a twist for some shitty ass reason."

Alex returned her gaze to Rosie, giving her an appraising look. "Thanks. I appreciate you giving me the benefit of the doubt. So, who's the woman that captured your heart but hasn't seen the light?"

"A friend. She's Catholic and they don't get divorced. Married to a real son of a bitch. I've wanted to kill the bastard so many times but she won't let me intercede. She's afraid he'll take it out on their daughter. She's a grown woman now, so I don't understand why she won't let me help. Wish the fat bastard would keel over and die of a heart attack. I bring him food sure to clog his arteries every chance I get. The stupid asshole thinks I'm being nice."

Alex chuckled. "Keep it up and maybe you'll get your wish. Does she love you back?"

Rosie shrugged. "I think so. We haven't been, uh,

intimate with each other, but yeah, I know she loves me in that way. I catch her looking at me sometimes and I know it's longing I see in her eyes. Some days I want to make love with her so bad, it nearly kills me not to touch her."

"So, then how do you, ya know, take care of your urges? Surely you aren't keeping yourself from having sex because she's a devout Catholic. Remember those skills I told you about, well I might as well confess that my last employer was Stacey's Ranch. They do a pretty good business and you'd be surprised how many women ask about having a sensual experience with another woman. I could help you release some of that tension. It's the least I can do since you're giving me a ride and all."

Rosie laughed. "No thanks. I'm an old—fashioned kind of gal. I can't ever see myself making love with a woman I'm not in love with. You're a very handsome, tall drink of water that I'm sure most lesbians would jump at the chance to bed. But, I'm not one of them. I'm not giving you a ride so's I can have myself a quick fuck, but thanks for the offer. Stacey's Ranch, huh? Never heard of it."

"Well, you know prostitution is legal in some parts of Nevada. The Ranch is like a high-end spa that offers a few extras. Fifteen percent of their business is middle-aged women wanting to check out whether they've been missing out on something all their lives. They aren't sure if they're a lesbian or even bi-sexual, so Stacey's is a safe place to explore. I was developing quite a clientele until one night someone followed one of my regulars. Her husband started beating on her. I wasn't going to let the bastard continue using her as if she was his own personal punching bag."

"Let me guess. He took one look at you and called in a few favors with his redneck buddies."

Alex nodded. "Worse. His brother was an INS agent. I got lucky because someone found out they were coming for me and tipped me off before they could make a grab. So now you know the whole sordid story even though I didn't want to tell you."

"Look, I didn't mean to pry. There's a lot of that going around and it was an easy assumption to make. Sorry about that. I'm no better than the rest when I start making guesses based on the color of your skin. Are your parents still alive and do they live in the States or were they rounded up as well?"

Alex turned away again. She looked down at the white lines in the middle of the highway after Rosie had changed lanes and began to pass a slower eighteen-wheeler. She tried to let them hypnotize her into a state of calm. She didn't want to open that old wound. So far she hadn't made enough money to pay the exorbitant fees to help them cross the border again and start a new life somewhere else.

"I'm guessing they're in Mexico right now and not doing so well. Can we talk about something else?"

"Sure, sure."

CHAPTER TWO

Alex didn't like the uncomfortable space they'd somehow created, especially after talking about their lives so freely before Rosie had broached the sensitive topic of her parents. She liked Rosie and genuinely wished life would take a new twist for her. She wanted karma or fate to intervene and put Rosie together with the object of her affection. It didn't seem fair to keep them apart, but then life wasn't fair. Bad things happened to good people and good things happened to those without any redeeming qualities in her humble opinion.

Alex broke the silence. "Hey, you hungry? If you find us a good place, I'll buy dinner."

"You don't have to buy dinner. I'm the one that ripped off that huge piece of gauze. Maria always says I'm too nosy for my own good. She says I should keep that big nose of mine outta someone else's business. I kept at it until I learned the whole sordid story from Maria. Sometimes, I wished I hadn't, but in this case ignorance wasn't bliss. If it weren't for me in her life, Maria wouldn't ever feel what it's like for someone to love you unconditionally. I don't like that she stays with her bastard husband, but I accept it's her choice to make."

"But that choice affects you. Don't you get a say?"

"Nope. Not if I love and accept her and everything about her, including her deep faith. She believes that once she made a vow, she wasn't going to break it. No matter what."

"I don't think many Catholics adhere to every last teaching of the church. That would be antiquated. Surely she doesn't drink the entire tall glass of Kool-Aid. Or I suppose I should say wine? There wouldn't be much to hope for then. Because the two of you would never be able to come together, regardless of her marriage."

"I don't think it's about being Catholic, although that's a big part. It's more about the vow. We've talked and she'd have no problem being with me if she wasn't married. Most people pick and choose what they feel is important about the lessons organized religion teaches. Maria's no different."

"Hmm, I suppose morality is unique to different people. It doesn't matter if you're Catholic, Protestant, Muslim, Atheist, or Jewish. We're all products of the influences in our lives. The subtle and not so subtle messages from family and friends. My mama is a devout Catholic, but she'd leave my papa in a second if he ever laid a hand on her. My abuela was a trail-blazer. She didn't leave grandpapa, but she did wake him up in the middle of the night and smacked him with her cast iron fry pan. Told him if he ever hit her again, she'd do much worse. She said he should consider himself lucky she only decided to bean him one on the head. I think he was terrified of her after that, but sure enough he never hit her again."

Alex marveled at how Rosie managed to get her to talk about her family, but this time it wasn't the painful memories.

Rosie smiled. "You ever tell them?"

"Tell them what?"

"That you were a lesbian." Rosie chuckled. "A lesbian prostitute."

Alex bent over laughing. She was laughing so hard tears were coming out of her eyes. "Are you fucking kidding? No, I never told them. Although, I may have underestimated them. When I get the chance, I plan to rectify that. Except I don't think I'll fess up about my short stint in prostitution. And prostitute is such an ugly term. I prefer pleasure worker. Besides, I wasn't using those talents when I lived with my parents. Well, not exactly," she amended.

"Not exactly?" Rosie asked.

"I lived in a tiny town of less than a thousand people. I'm almost positive I was the only dyke there. But I used to borrow my papa's truck and drive the thirty miles to Laredo. There were plenty enough women there to, uh, explore my interests. For a short while I even had a steady girlfriend, but when I wasn't willing to introduce her to my mama and papa, she got pissed and dumped me. I didn't get any complaints from her or the others, but that was different than making a vocation out of my talents."

Rosie smiled. "A vocation, huh?"

"Yeah, that's a relatively new thing for me. I can't

imagine I'll be able to find that kind of work where I'll eventually land. Can you imagine somewhere in the Deep South having lesbian pleasure workers? Glory be, I'd get so many, 'Bless her hearts' I wouldn't know how to handle it."

"Maybe," Rosie said. "But you know Southern women have as many needs as those Nevada housewives. There's a lot more rich socialites dying to throw money at someone who has talented hands, or knows how to handle a tool with precision." Rosie chuckled.

"Point me in the right direction and I'm there. I need to make some big cash and fixing things besides women's neglected pussies doesn't pay very much."

"I like that. A woman's neglected pussy. I'll have to remember that. 'Cept I don't think noting Maria has a neglected pussy, and I'd love to fix it, will endear me to her."

"Nope, I wouldn't recommend that, my friend. Now take us somewhere I can get a juicy burger I can barely put my mouth around. Oh, and after that a big slice of apple pie."

†

Alex appreciated when Rosie suggested they stop at Russell's, a truck stop in Glenrio, New Mexico. The place was almost on the border of New Mexico and Texas and Alex preferred to barrel through Texas. The state held both fond memories as well as the most excruciating ones. She'd decided to head west when she'd left Texas before, and that hadn't quite worked out the way she'd wanted it to. Now she was on the verge of heading back to the state that still caused her to shudder in fear. Texas was like a foreign country. She felt better about stopping in New Mexico for dinner, the people seemed different here. She knew that was an overgeneralization and there were good people in Texas. She'd had first-hand experience of that growing up, but she couldn't shake the bitter taste the asshole INS agents had deposited in her mouth those final days in Texas. She never wanted to return. Passing through the place was hard enough, but stopping for a meal would have put her over the edge.

"I believe Russell's has everything you told me you have a hankering for. We could travel up the road a spell to one of the places in Texas—"

"No! This is fine. I'm pretty hungry and mostly I'm not too particular about food anyway. A burger and fries from a fast food restaurant would hit the spot just fine. I'm thinking this place is several steps up from the international chain, so lead the way. I insist on paying. Please just say thanks."

"All right." Rosie looked like she might say something else and then thought better of it.

Alex knew her response was a bit too forceful and that probably piqued Rosie's interest, but Alex didn't want to relive the last days with her mama and papa before they were taken from her. The INS agents never cared how they ripped a family apart.

The two women found a booth and Alex slipped her tall frame into the old-style red vinyl upholstery. It was the kind of fabric her leg might stick to if she was wearing shorts that didn't cover a significant portion of her thighs.

"This place is interesting. I love the old cars. The pink Caddy with the Elvis...uh, not sure what to call it. Life-sized ceramic figurine? I don't think sculpture adequately describes the art. But then again, maybe that's what it is, a sculpture, just not a bronze version. I suppose it reminds me of the painted velvet canvases. You know sculpture art for the indiscriminating taste."

"Maybe I can find you a miniature in the gift shop. A reminder of this adventure." Rosie laughed.

A gum-chewing waitress, complete with a beehive hairdo, stepped up to their booth and Alex thought, *how cliché.*

"Hello ladies, what can I getcha?"

"Burger and fries for me and then a slice of apple pie if you have it," Alex answered. "Can you make the burger medium rare without getting into hot water? Every once in a while, the cooks will say no because they're afraid of e-coli."

The waitress smacked her gum loudly. "No, we can do that. It's your choice if ya wanna pee out your butthole, not mine." She winked. "Just kidding. Beef is high quality here, ya don't have ta worry none."

Rosie pushed the unopened menu toward the waitress and said, "I'll have the same thing, but you can cook mine a little more. I don't want anything squirting outta my ass tonight. Medium please."

"Got it."

The waitress pushed the pen back onto the top of her ear and walked away continuing to smack her gum loudly. Alex had to turn her head to keep from laughing. A gum-smacking waitress with a beehive hairdo, and a pen sticking out from behind her ear, was just too much, especially with the retro decor of the place.

"Tell me about this Stacy's Ranch. Wish I'd known about that back in the day, 'fore I met Maria. I know it don't look like it now, 'cause all you see is a broken-down old trucker, but I used to be very handsome and popular with the ladies. If you know what I mean."

Alex leaned back into the vinyl booth, resting her

head against the rounded back of the seat. A satisfied smile appeared on her face before she lifted her head and brought her eyes back to Rosie's.

"At first, I didn't know what kind of place it was. I thought it was some fancy resort. Once I hooked up with this woman in Laredo who was staying at this posh hotel. I think it was called the La Posato." Alex shook her head. "Anyway, I'd never been to such a fancy place. I just thought the Ranch was a lot like that hotel, only on a much bigger scale. Not to contribute to the stereotypes, but I assumed from my experience at La Posato that most of the housekeepers in the big hotels and fancy resorts were Latinas. I figured I could talk my way into a job."

"Didn't they require working papers? I had to give the trucking company ID to prove I could work in the United States. They're real picky about that these days."

"I know that now. Guess I was a bit sheltered growing up. I'd been working with my papa since I was old enough to hold a wrench. It was a family business. I don't think he ever knew the rules. Didn't even ask for ID when he hired that double-crossing pendejo."

"So how did ya get a job then?" Rosie asked.

"Well, I strolled into this fancy office ready to tell them that if they hired me, besides cleaning the rooms thorough enough for a person to lick the floor, I could fix any plumbing or electrical problem they had. I knew I'd be able to save them a ton of money. People who came to see papa always whined about the cost of repairs. I would hear them complain that licensed electricians and plumbers made more money than most professions these days. They were happy that papa was so cheap."

"I don't think convincing some hotel you're a great

worker makes anyone ignore the rules."

"True. The human resources lady was nice. She gave me an application to complete. When I didn't fill in the space for a social security number, she asked about it. I can't say why I trusted her. I guess you could say she had kind eyes. She asked me how long I'd been living in the United States. I answered her honestly."

"Can I ask the same thing?"

Alex laid her long arms on the table. "I've been here since I was barely one. I can't speak Spanish. Not really. A few words here and there. Mostly the bad ones. If they send me back..." Alex took a deep breath.

"I don't have a fancy college degree, but I listen to the news. Can't you get that DACA status thingy? I know there's still a lot of controversy and it ain't guaranteed or nothing, but maybe that's an option."

Alex grinned. "That's what she said, but she couldn't hire me until I had that all squared away. I was walking out feeling pretty low and this beautiful young woman came bouncing into the office, plopped herself on a chair and tilted her head in my direction. She had this mischievous look on her face and eyeballed me like I was some prized heifer."

Rosie's eyes lit up and Alex thought she was riveted to the story. She considered whether she should have tried to pursue another line of work. Could someone make it as a professional storyteller, she wondered.

"And?" Rosie asked.

"Ariel was her name. She asked the HR lady if I was a new recruit. Then she said, 'The ladies are going to love her. When can she start? I have a particular customer looking to party this evening. Can I show her the ropes and she can join me?' The pieces started clicking into place for me. My eyes must have looked like huge alien saucers."

Rosie laughed. "Didn't the name Stacey's Ranch clue you in? I can't imagine the place actually looked like a ranch."

"I didn't see the name. The place is huge, you know. Sits on twenty acres of pristine landscaping. I swear it looked like some high-class resort."

"Okay, so go on. How did you get around the requirements for the proper documents? That takes time, don't it?"

"Yeah, it does. After the initial shock and realization of where I had landed, I started to get excited, only to have my bubble burst. The HR woman began to explain to Ariel the barriers to Stacey's Ranch hiring me. Ariel told me I could bunk with her until we sorted out the paperwork and she'd slip me money on the sly. She came up with a plan to pay me under the table. Officially, the customers would book with her, knowing they would get both of us or sometimes just me. The owners and HR knew what was going on, but they looked the other way. Especially after I came across one of their maintenance guys screwing up the wiring and I fixed it for them all neat and clean."

"Wow, that's quite a story. You never got your social security number then?" Rosie asked.

"Almost had it, I think. The court date was set up and everything. I couldn't let that fat bastard continue using Mrs. Collins as a punching bag. I was about to give her a Nuru massage. Learned that special skill from Ariel. Mrs. Collins came in every week for this sensual treat. Before I stepped into the room, I heard the commotion. When I saw her cowering in a corner, without a stitch of clothing on, and him kicking her with his cowboy boots, I saw red. I only had a robe on myself. I didn't even wait for security. I pulled his fat ass off of her and started swinging. Broke his ugly nose. I don't remember much later, other than Ariel patching up my knuckles and making me ice them. I hope Mrs. Collins finally got the nerve to leave him. She was a sweet woman."

"They couldn't hide you until you got your papers?"

"Nah, I didn't want to bring the authorities to the Ranch. They'd already gone well out of their way for me. Ariel took the day off to drive me a good long distance from the Ranch. We both cried when I told her to git. I assured her I could catch a ride from someone. She was a good friend. Now here I am, telling you my life story, or at least part of it."

The waitress returned carrying their burgers and both women tucked into the food. When Alex took a large bite of her burger the red juice spurted out landing on the plain white ceramic plate. She nodded in appreciation. They'd cooked the burger just the way she liked it. She grabbed the paper napkin and absently wiped her mouth. It didn't take long for both women to quickly devour the American classic meal.

CHAPTER THREE

Danna Nichols had delayed going home for as long as possible. She'd eagerly accepted a late client. The woman couldn't afford to ask for time off and risk losing her job if she was going to win the nasty child custody case her ex was mounting against her out of pure spite. Meeting with her after hours satisfied both their needs.

Living alone in the large house after her husband, David, had passed away six months earlier put a huge spotlight on how Danna felt. At least when he was alive, she had a companion to attend the various events popular in her circle of friends. Now, she garnered those well-meaning looks of pity from everyone except Lindy, who was a force to be reckoned with and had practically dragged her out to lunch and dinner.

After pulling into the large garage and parking next to

David's pride and joy, a cherry red Porsche, she entered her empty house. Her high heels tapped along the wood floors until she reached the master bedroom where she carefully removed them and set them on the shoe rack in the walk-in closet. She tossed her purse on the bed before she began undressing. She began to remove her silk blouse when she heard the faint sound of her cell phone tucked inside her purse.

Danna hurried to the purse and rummaged in the bag to retrieve her phone, quickly pressing the button to answer. "Hello."

Lindy's confident voice burst through the speaker. "Danna, what are you doing tomorrow?"

"What I normally do during the day" —Danna chuckled— "meet with clients."

"Cancel your afternoon appointments. You're coming to the club. You said you wanted to get in shape, well, no excuses now. You'll start with a fitness assessment and trust me, you're going to love the fitness instructor. In fact, after you get that assessment and a massage with Marley, I highly recommend a different kind of session with Luna. She's the fitness instructor."

"I've heard you speak of Marley before and a massage does sound good, but I don't know about the rest. I'm not sure I want to be naked in front of some buff exercise guru."

"Trust me, you'll forget all about your vulnerabilities the minute Luna works her magic. Live a little, Danna."

"All right. I might just need all that club of yours has to offer after lunch with my mother tomorrow. Maybe I'll engage in this risqué behavior in the hopes that she'll find out and shun me. It's taken me forty years to rebel.

Although, her constant calls since David's passing wore me down. I finally agreed to have lunch with her. Why is it so hard to stick to that rebellion I so desperately want to engage in?" Danna slumped on the bed.

"Your mother would drive the sanest person crazy. Frankly, I don't know how you haven't moved thousands of miles away from her by now. I thought my mother was bad, but mine is an amateur compared to yours."

"Send me the address and I'll be there. It'll give me an excuse to cut my lunch short. Being late for an appointment is gauche, don't you know?"

Lindy laughed. "I can't wait to get your impressions of the club."

†

The exclusive restaurant where her mother had insisted they meet for lunch instantly grated on Danna's nerves. The music was a bland, soft, background noise that seemed to emphasize old world stuffiness. A tall thin man with pursed lips greeted her the moment she entered the dining area. His stiff rigid posture had her imagining that he might really have a rod up his rectum. She stifled a giggle.

"Good afternoon, Mrs. Nichols. Your mother is already seated. I'll escort you to the table."

"Thank you, Nathan."

Danna noticed the dry martini sitting in front of her mother and she wondered if Nathan had set it on the table the minute she sat down. Probably. He knew where his best tips came from. As she reached the table that was decorated with a pristine white tablecloth and fine china, Danna leaned down to kiss her mother on her cheek. She knew her mother would not bother herself to stand and greet Danna with a warm hug.

"You're late." The disapproving look on her mother's pinched features set the tone for the lunch date.

"I needed to wrap up with a client. Besides, I'm only ten minutes late."

"A client who undoubtedly won't be paying you for your services, so why do you need to make me wait while you attend to the riffraff?"

"And you wonder, Mother, why I haven't made time for you since the funeral. If you're going to bring forth that tired old argument, I think I'll simply cut this lunch short and let you drink a few more martinis to dull your sharp tongue."

"Sit down and don't be impertinent," her mother ordered.

Danna sighed and took a seat across from her mother.

"I saw your old roommate the other day. She hasn't changed a bit. Flaunting that French hussy of hers in a disgusting display of bad taste. She had the audacity to walk arm in arm with her, not making any attempt to hide the nature of her relationship. That might fly in Europe, but not where grace and good manners prevail here in Atlanta."

"I wouldn't necessarily label what you're doing right now grace and good manners. Thanks for letting me know she's in town. I'd love to catch up with her and her wife."

"Don't be gauche, Danna. Just because it's legal now, doesn't make it right."

"The Supreme Court disagrees."

"Oh, I'm sure the new court will come to their senses and turn that decision around. Thank God for President Trump. We needed a strong leader to take us back to a time in our country when high morals prevailed."

"Mother, we will not ever agree on this, so let's please move on. How's Father?"

"Oh, you know your father..."

As Danna's mother droned on, Danna continued to look at her watch waiting for the moment when she could make a graceful exit. There was only so much she could endure when it came to spending time with her mother.

†

Danna was thankful for how much Marley's talented hands had managed to relax her. After meeting Luna during her fitness assessment, Danna was feeling extra self-conscious about those unnecessary pounds stubbornly refusing to leave her curvy frame. Luna looked like she'd just stepped out of a special magazine layout for elite athletes. Surrounded by the beautiful women at the Trophy Wives Club, TWC for short, including Marley, Danna felt like a frumpy middle-aged housewife.

While she was in the shower prior to her scheduled massage, Danna kept poking at the places on her body where the flabbiness had grown. She vowed to do something about how she'd allowed her loneliness and depression to take hold in the form of thirty extra pounds. Six months and already she felt overwhelmed by the need to nip the weight gain in the bud.

Marley was skilled at both massage and conversation. As they made small talk, Danna could feel herself relax until Marley grazed her nipple and she was unable to hide her reaction. She tried not to feel self-conscious, especially since she had also agreed to a session with Luna. Lindy had been so matter-of-fact about the club offering intimate touch.

She'd mentioned that many of her circle of friends planned on taking advantage of those services. That didn't mean Danna was a lesbian. She knew Lindy wasn't; even if Jay-Dub was not meeting her needs at the moment.

†

Danna knew she was being ridiculous when she hesitated to remove her robe, even though Luna stood before her in all her naked glory. She was surprised by Luna's gentle touch as she coaxed the robe from Danna's body and her hands lazily followed a path down her front.

"You have nothing to be ashamed about. I know you have a goal to lose some weight and tighten up a bit, but you should be comfortable knowing that you're a beautiful woman exactly as you are. If you're entering into a diet and exercise program, that choice should be about feeling healthy, not about reshaping into something you believe is more attractive."

Danna laughed. "Says the Greek goddess who looks like she was chiseled from stone."

"If I admit that I'm a little nervous because you're my first official client, will that allow me to step off that pedestal you have me on? I need you to relax or you'll give me a complex." Luna brought her mouth to Danna's neck and her hot breath sent a pleasurable tingle through Danna's body. An involuntary moan followed as Luna's hand began exploring other sensitive spots.

"Toys or no toys?" Luna whispered. Her mouth was inches from Danna's ear.

"Um, I've never, uh, actually..."

"I'd like to introduce you to a new experience, then.

I've been told I'm quite proficient."

"Okay." Danna's excitement grew, thinking about what was on the horizon. She'd never let herself completely surrender to someone. There was always a part of herself she held back. She didn't want to do that anymore. She'd earned the right to receive pleasure and she was going to squeeze every last drop out of this experience.

Luna never broke their physical connection as she trailed her one hand over Danna's body while smoothly stepping over to the nightstand and removing a harness and a mid-sized dildo.

"I hate to stop touching you, but I need to be prepared for when you'll want and need this little toy a bit later on." The sweet scent of tangerine filled the air as Luna began coating the toy. "Girl scouts aren't the only ones that are always prepared. I find that after I'm done fucking you, the hint of tangerine mixed with a woman's own juices is quite pleasing when I go down on you."

Although Danna felt the loss of her touch immediately, she had a visceral reaction to hearing Luna state in a matter-of-fact tone that she planned to taste her after using the toy. Coupled with the almost erotic dance Luna was performing as she completely coated the dildo, Danna was bursting with the need for Luna to touch her. Danna had never had a lover place their mouth anywhere near her clitoris. She was more than eager for this new experience.

It didn't take long for Luna to return to Danna and position her onto the bed as she began to increase Danna's level of arousal with feather-light caresses to her body. Danna felt the brush of the dildo and her anticipation skyrocketed as Luna expertly found every erogenous area of

Danna's body. Finally her fingers, lips, and tongue found their way to Danna's hot core. Sucking lightly on Danna's clit, Luna was met by Danna's hips bucking to meet her as she sought a harder and more intense contact.

Danna completely let go and began moaning and asking for more. Never had she been so vocal before.

"Oh, God, that is positively heavenly. I think I'm ready. Please, Luna, I'm about to burst. I need more."

"I'm surprised by how wet you are. I probably could have foregone the lube." Luna easily slipped the toy inside and began a slow movement of her hips as the dildo pushed further into Danna's vagina with each deliberate thrust.

The increased rhythm caused Danna to lift up and meet each insertion. She felt the fullness of the toy and was glad Luna had not chosen anything larger. The thickness and length were plenty big enough to create the perfect friction against her sensitive spots.

Danna continued to moan loudly, too excited to care who heard her. She cried out as she felt the glorious release. *So this is what the fuss is all about.*

CHAPTER FOUR

Rosie had been kind enough to let Alex lie next to her in the cramped space of the big rig when they stopped for the night. Her toes touched the side of the rig as she tried to stretch out. The long-haul trucks were undoubtedly not designed for a person as tall as Alex, but she made the best of her accommodations. She was lucky to have something over her head to keep out the elements. Ever since leaving Texas many months ago, a solution had presented itself on every step of her journey. She'd never had to live on the streets or create a makeshift camp. For a pseudo Catholic who didn't believe in God, she thought someone was up there looking after her.

There was no way Rosie could have made the long journey to Atlanta, which was her final destination for this particular long haul, without stopping for a few minutes of shuteye. When they had almost reached the city limits, Rosie laid out a plan to help Alex ease into a new life in the city. Alex had decided Atlanta was as good a place as any to begin again.

"I got a friend that can put you up for a few days while you look for a job. She might know of a place to try that doesn't look too closely at work papers."

The emotion of saying goodbye to Rosie caught up with Alex and she began to respond through choked words.

"Rosie, I...I don't know how to thank you. For everything. Listening without judgment and getting me this far away from Nevada and the INS agents. I'm not sure how rabid they are in the South, but the West and certainly, Texas, are two places it doesn't help to have technically been born in Mexico. Maybe a big city is where I need to be, a place to blend in a little. That same woman that took me to the fancy hotel in Laredo was from Atlanta. And she told me the city was becoming more multicultural every day."

"You'll like my friend. She's got a gentle spirit. Likes helping people out. Drove a truck like me, until she retired last year. Drinks a bit too much and tends to hang out in bars most evenings. I keep telling her she's looking for love in all the wrong places, but she don't know any other way to meet women. After the woman she's been in love with forever up and left without as much as a 'goodbye' or even 'kiss my ass,' she's planted her butt on a barstool nearly every evening. I'm not gonna change her though. I wouldn't even try. Just accept her for who she is. Under all that gruff is a kind and compassionate human being. Mind if I give her a call to come pick you up?"

Alex lifted her shoulders in compliance. She didn't have anywhere specific to go and the couple of days for her to gain her bearings would help. "I'd appreciate that and the chance to have a roof over my head while I look for work."

Rosie pulled her phone from her back pocket to make the call.

"Hiya Betty... I'm good. You?... Yeah, the reason I called is I got a friend here who needs a place to stay for a few days while she gets herself established in Atlanta... Yeah she's cute, but way too young for you. And if I'm not mistaken a bit too, uh, well she ain't on the girly side." Rosie winked at Alex who smiled back at her and held her hand over her mouth to keep from laughing too loud. Rosie handed the phone to Alex. "She wants to talk to ya."

"Okay." Alex put the phone to her ear. "Hello... Um, sure, we can do that... Yeah I do all right sometimes." Alex began to laugh. "You got yourself a deal." Alex handed the phone back to Rosie.

"All set, then?... Yeah same place I always stop at. I'll hang around til ya get here... Thanks, Betty, you're a peach. Too bad I ain't your type either and of course my heart will always belong to someone else. See ya in a little while."

After Rosie ended the call, she looked at Alex expectantly. "Well?"

"Well, what?"

"What were you laughing about?"

"Betty wants me to be her wing woman tonight. I'm supposed to reel them in for her. She says if I'm not going to make her heart go pitter patter, I might as well help her snag someone who will."

"It's not like you won't make her heart leap around in her chest. Girl, you'd do that to just about anyone, even someone more inclined to go after a pair of painted lips.

Shoot, if I was twenty years younger and not so in love with Maria, I mighta taken you up on your offer."

"I'm going to send good thoughts out to the universe so you and your woman finally come together. I don't think I've ever been a good Catholic, so I'll not be praying. But sometimes sending those positive thoughts out, and asking for what you need, does the trick."

"Considering life's given you a shit sandwich, I'm impressed by your optimism."

"Sometimes, Rosie, it's the only thing left to hang onto. If I don't have hope that life will turn around for me and I'll be able to reconnect with my parents, I've got nothing," Alex quietly responded.

†

Alex was looking out the window as the tiny smart car pulled alongside Rosie's big rig. The car looked absurd compared to Rosie's rolling home.

A short woman with close-cropped salt-and-pepper hair that was mostly salt, emerged from the compact vehicle. Her body reminded Alex of a barrel. She looked like a sturdy woman, but there was a pleasant expression on her face that gave her a kind of softness. Alex thought both the car and Betty were incongruent yet perfectly suited to the way Rosie had described this woman. Alex wondered how someone could go from all that vastness to a tiny piece of metal. She chuckled to herself as she got the vision of an eighteen-wheeler spitting out the little car from its exhaust pipe.

"I know what you're thinking. She's quite an anomaly, kinda like me. Now there's a great word, anomaly. Yeah, I ain't as stupid as I look. Some words seem to fit, even when they come out of a redneck trucker. I read a lot. Not quite what you expected?" She grinned.

Alex chuckled. "Well not to be crude or anything, since apparently I'm in the presence of a well-read long-haul trucker, but those smart cars are like an eighteen-wheeler's little turd."

Rosie bent over laughing. "Good one. I'll have to remember that." Rosie opened the door and jumped down, gathering Betty into an embrace.

Pulling her bag along with her, Alex stepped down and waited patiently for the formal introduction. She smiled at Betty who was unabashedly looking her over.

"Well, she sure is a looker. I mighta changed my type for her, if only I was thirty years younger." Betty stuck out her hand. "I'm Betty."

"Alex."

"She thinks your car looks like something my rig would poop out in the morning after coffee."

Betty smiled good-naturedly. "It gets good gas mileage and I never have trouble finding a place to park."

"Good point, but don't you miss traveling in something a bit roomier?" Alex asked.

"Nope, when I retired, I didn't ever want to take a long trip again. Driving in the city is a whole different experience. Come on, kid. Let's get you settled into my place. It isn't a mansion either, but I got a guest room with a bed."

"Oh, I don't need much. I could crash on a couch, or even the floor, and be perfectly happy to have a roof over my head," Alex said.

"That's 'cause you don't have old bones like me and Rosie here. When you get older, a bed is a must. I sure got tired of crashing in my rig. Don't know how you do it, Rosie. I got myself a nice cushy pillow-top mattress and I'd never go back to sleeping on some glorified cot ever again."

"I gotta head out, but I sure am glad I could help you. You mind if I give you my number? I wanna know how things end up for you. Maybe we can reconnect when I cruise back into town again." Rosie retrieved her ever-present notepad and pen from her pockets.

"Please do give me your number. I'd like to hear how things turn out for you, too. And I'd love to get together when you're in town. Maybe grab lunch or dinner."

Rosie scribbled her contact information on the paper and handed it to Alex. "Now don't you two go drinking and driving tonight. I can't very well park this big rig by the bar and come pick you up." She winked.

"Don't worry. I always call myself a cab if I have more than two," Betty answered.

"I got this. I can be the designated driver. I don't care for hangovers, so I always stop after one," Alex answered. "Besides, how else am I gonna keep my girlish figure." She slung her arm over Betty and laughed.

Rosie cuffed Betty on the shoulder. She shuffled her feet and Alex removed her arm. She took a step toward Rosie and held her arms out as Rosie strode into them to give her a goodbye hug.

"Thanks, Rosie. I'll call. I promise."

Rosie returned to her rig and waved at them before climbing inside.

Betty turned and then walked over to her car. She appeared to scrutinize Alex, looking between the car and Alex. "I never thought I'd be picking up the Hispanic butch version of Xena, Warrior Princess. Sorry you're going to have to fold your tall body into my toy car. Good thing my place isn't too far away." Opening the door, she climbed inside.

Alex followed and imagined that to the outside observer this might look extremely comical. "That's okay. I'm sure I can make do for the short ride to your place. I really appreciate you helping me out. I've had such a rash of good luck lately, meeting Henry, Rosie, and now you. I won't ever let myself forget America is filled with wonderful people and I refuse to let the asshats drown out those voices."

"That's a good way to look at the world, kid. I hope you don't mind being my wing woman tonight. With you attracting all the beautiful ladies, I'm sure to get lucky. All I need is one. Preferably one who'll stick around. Course I probably shouldn't expect too much. Most of the ladies are far too young for me. I wish there was a place I could meet someone my own age."

"I suppose the bar is not the best place to find a life partner. Have you ever tried online dating? I don't know a whole lot about it myself. Never really got into the technology craze. I've always been much better with a tool belt versus a computer. Papa didn't have much use for one either."

Betty seemed to ignore her comment. "Do you need to freshen up or anything? Not that I think you look bad."

Alex wasn't sure if Betty was as incompetent with computers as she was, or if she'd tried online dating and had a bad experience. She lifted the ball cap from her head and pushed her fingers through her thick locks. "Well, I wouldn't turn down a hot shower and a chance to do something with this mop besides stick my ball cap back on."

"Sounds good to me. Might grab myself a beer while you're getting ready. It's a lot less expensive to have one at home."

"I meant what I said before. I'm happy to be your designated driver. You can let loose all you want. I'm sure I can make the seat go back enough to not feel like my knees are up against my chin. One beer is good enough for me."

"I think I'll take you up on that offer, but I need to cut down on my drinking." Betty patted her stomach. "I already look like a beach ball. I don't need to be adding to my belly."

"Too much alcohol isn't good for anyone, so cutting down probably isn't a bad idea. Just don't stop doing the things you like because you feel like you need to match up to some version of health those women's magazines always promote. No one looks that good without clothes, and very few women I've met have an airbrushed flat-as-a-pancake stomach. It doesn't exist."

Betty looked at Alex skeptically. "I'll bet you come pretty damn close."

"Don't be so sure. Curves are nice. Men don't have them, but most women do and that's a very good thing. Don't know why women gotta body shame each other, including themselves. Even lesbians do it." Alex shook her head. "I don't think there's a body type I'm not attracted to. As long as it's female."

"You are quite a breath of fresh air. Bet you have a knack for making every single person you come in contact with feel special. Since you're traveling by yourself, I guess you don't have someone waiting at home for you."

"No, and the time isn't right for it either. Besides, I can't see myself settling down into domestic bliss anytime soon. Maybe down the road after things settle and, never mind, I'm blabbering."

"It's okay. You don't gotta tell me."

†

Alex was glad Betty's small duplex was only a ten-minute drive from the bar. Sisters. That was the name of the pub. She liked the name. It always reminded her of the 1970's song, *We Are Family*, by Sister Sledge. The song was still popular nearly forty years later. She'd always enjoyed dancing to it when they would play it at one of the gay bars in Laredo. The tune was a crowd pleaser that instilled a sense of community and family in everyone.

A part of Alex had longed for siblings. She had an unusual Mexican family because it was just her and her papa and mama. Alex supposed that was a blessing in disguise considering how an unforgiving border now separated them. A border that was only going to become less porous, not more. She'd find a way, though. Somehow there had to be a loophole or something. If not, she'd simply bring them back across the border. Illegally if she had to. They could disappear in one of those sanctuary cities.

Alex was suddenly famished. She'd turned down Betty's offer of a beer before dinner because she didn't want to drink on an empty stomach. The sun was nearly down for the evening, tucked safely away before it would rise again the next morning. Her papa always said that, like little girls and little boys, the sun needed to sleep every night so it could shine brightly the next day. Alex, always the curious child, had asked her papa what happened on gray days. Did the sun have nightmares that made it sleepy the next day and not able to shine brightly? He'd smiled and said sometimes the sun had a bout of insomnia. She'd nodded like that made perfect sense to her. Tonight the sky displayed an amazing array of color against the red bricks of the pub. The fully extended umbrellas continued to shade customers who preferred sitting outside, drinking their beers and munching on appetizers or other pub food. Her nose caught the scent of fried food and her stomach grumbled.

"I smell grease. Time for a cold beer and whatever they dunked into that large vat of bubbling hot oil," Alex said. "I know it's not good for me or my body, but damn it's mighty tasty."

"At least you're still young enough that burning it off is a bit easier. It looks like that couple is heading inside. They're probably ready for the music and action that happens in the upstairs bar. Great timing. We can snag their table." Betty made a beeline for the square wood table and pulled out the wrought-iron chair. The scraping of the metal over bricks could be heard above the pulse of the music coming from inside.

Alex thought the pub looked and felt like a living, breathing, entity, complete with a pulsing heart as the bass punctuated the rapidly darkening evening. The twinkling lights that were strung almost haphazardly above the outside patio lent an air of casualness to the place. A fun gathering spot for the lesbians in Atlanta. She liked it. Maybe she could get them to give her a job.

"Do they have wait staff who will come out here and take our order?" Alex asked as she looked around for someone who might come to the table and clear out the remnants of the previous couple's dinner and drinks. Two empty beer glasses, baskets topped with crumpled napkins, and a few stranded fries laying in globs of ketchup, sat on the table.

"They do, but it'll be quicker to order at the bar. I can do that. How about I get us a couple of beers and some mozzarella sticks? Maybe some sliders. They have both beef and chicken sliders. The Grand Slam Sliders with blue cheese, bacon, mushroom and arugula are a house specialty." Betty's chair scraped against the brick again as she began to stand.

"That sounds perfect, but please, let me buy. I'm not destitute yet. It's the least I can do." Alex quickly rose to make her way to the bar and order for them both.

"Okay, I'm gonna let you, 'cause I know a little something about pride." Betty sat back down and smiled at Alex.

Alex maneuvered between the throngs of women talking and milling about inside the pub. She could hear the steady beat of the music from above where Betty had claimed the real party was occurring. Alex sensed that was definitely not Betty's scene and she probably preferred the quiet of the patio. They could hear the loud music but it didn't blast out her eardrums or prevent a person from having a conversation. She'd almost made it to the bar when she noticed the long queue and a frantic woman trying to placate the women waiting in line. She appeared to be trying to sell bottled beer instead of what was on tap. She glanced down at something behind the bar.

"Fuck," a voice from the floor yelled.

Alex moved closer to the bar and peered down at a blue-haired woman fiddling with a severely leaking keg.

"I don't know how to fix this damn thing. I'm not a plumber or whatever. Can't Janice call the distributor to fix it? Is there such a thing as a keg technician?" The young woman was squatting with a wrench in her hand and a disgusted look on her face. "I'm going to smell like I bathed in beer."

"Um...can I take a look?" Alex called out. "If you need a new washer, you might be out of luck. Could be damaged or missing rubber seals. If the line needs tightening, good fortune might shine for you."

The young woman stood and held out the wrench. "Be my guest, tall dark and sexy." She grinned.

"Mind if I climb back behind the bar with you?" Alex asked.

The blue haired woman smiled. "Not at all. Terry, let this gorgeous hunk back here to save the day. Name's Chancy, and I am so pleased to meet you."

Alex went with the most obvious and easiest fix, hoping that would take care of the problem. There were several places she suspected Chancy had attempted a fix, but not tightening the correct nut. After a few quick twists, the golden liquid stopped spilling from the top.

Chancy was leaning her hip against the bar and watching Alex with a predatory grin as Alex stood up and handed back the wrench.

"I think you're good to go."

"Oooh I just love a woman who can handle a tool," Chancy purred.

Alex chuckled. "Enough to give me a job?"

Chancy looked over Alex's shoulder and pointed to a woman gliding down the stairs and making a beeline to the bar with a frown on her face. Her long light brown hair with golden highlights curled up on the edges and touched her delicate shoulders. As she came closer Alex noticed her light amber eyes, the color of a pale ale.

"Chancy, what's going on?"

"Um, problem with the tap." Chancy pointed to Alex. "She fixed it for us. Wants to know if we have any openings here."

The amber eyes swiveled in Alex's direction and traveled up and down her body. "How are you at leaky faucets, temperamental wiring, and flickering lights we don't want to flicker?"

"I can fix almost anything with the right tools, ma'am," Alex bravely declared. "I don't have my own tools, but if you have a decent toolbox, I'll prove it to you."

"Come with me and if you can fix my little issue, you got yourself a job." The woman flicked her fingers in the air, beckoning Alex to follow her.

"Um...I don't want to be rude or anything, but can I order some food and drinks for me and my friend before I start fixing things."

The woman smiled. "Chancy, take her order and it's on the house if she does a good job."

†

Alex was not about to let this opportunity pass her by. She needed to let Betty know what was going on. She hoped Betty would understand her need to abandon her while she proved her skills to the woman she assumed was the owner of Sisters. Underneath the gruff exterior, Betty was a sweetheart. She waved her hand and told Alex she was happy to devour her sliders and eat all the mozzarella sticks while Alex played the big butch heroine. Alex had chuckled at her comment. She'd fix every last problem no matter how long it took or how tasteless those sliders would be after she finished. She needed this job. Her knotted stomach wouldn't allow her to eat anyway while this test of her skills teetered on the edge of a cliff.

After she gave Betty a brief update, Alex followed the beautiful woman up the stairs and noted the party wasn't exactly in full swing yet. The night was still very young. She was amazed there were any lesbians out this early in the evening. Pounding bass music seemed to keep the small swarm of dancing women moving rhythmically to the beat. Alex felt the sexually charged energy as she moved amongst the dancers, gathering a few appraising looks. She needed to focus and keep her raging hormones from taking a side trip. She hoped the first test was far away from the cluster of women. She got her wish.

Thankfully the bathroom wasn't crowded yet. There was only one woman standing at the sink, and Janice briefly acknowledged her with a smile. The music seemed blunted inside and Alex felt a sense of relief to be out of the melee of the central party zone. Someone had prominently displayed a crisscross of bright yellow tape across one of the stalls. Since there were only two options for the women, Alex sensed this would be a huge issue for the owner once the party started to swell with new customers. She thought if the yellow tape didn't exemplify a crime scene now, this would soon be a reality if Alex wasn't able to fix whatever problem was behind the tape.

"Won't flush properly and the plumber says he can't come until next week to fix it. I wasn't happy. Damn redneck assholes. They probably don't have a fucking thing to do tonight or tomorrow, but decided they would make things more difficult for the local lezzie bar. Pisses me off, but every single plumber told me the same thing. I hate being beholden to those asshats."

"Okay, I'll see what I can do. I'll need that toolbox and I sure hope it's a big one," Alex quietly murmured.

"I thought we had a person who could fix things and then she up and left. She did make sure we had every God-damned tool imaginable. You know, one of those dykes who love shopping for tools. God, I'm being rude. I haven't even introduced myself. I'm Janice, one of the owners of this fine establishment. I'll get the toolbox."

Alex held out her hand. "Nice to meet you, Janice. I'm Alex."

Janice shook her hand. "I sure hope your fixing skills are as fine as you. You'll be a big hit behind the bar as well." Janice let her eyes roam up and down Alex's body again. She shifted her focus to the woman who hadn't exited yet and then she pivoted as she left the bathroom. Alex wondered why Janice had been so forthcoming while there was another person in the crowded room who clearly overheard every word.

She was standing in front of one of the sinks washing her hands as she turned her head and announced, "So far one bathroom has been okay, but wait until later when the beer starts having its effect on everyone. Trust me, you will definitely be the heroine to this crowd. I wouldn't be surprised if Janice kisses your feet. No one wants to cross their legs to keep from pissing themselves. That will surely happen if a line causes them to wait too long."

"I'll do my best." Alex removed the tape and examined the broken toilet. She prayed the toolbox really did have everything she would need.

Janice was struggling with a huge metal box when

she walked back into the bathroom. She glanced briefly at the woman who was now leaning against the sink, then refocused on Alex.

Alex rushed over to Janice and took the heavy box from her hands. When she flipped the latch, she breathed out a low whistle. "Whoa, this is impressive."

"It better be. It cost an arm and a leg," Janice responded.

Alex knew it was a risk, but she decided to take a chance. "I can fix this toilet, but in exchange, I want a job. No questions asked."

Janice narrowed her eyes. "You running from the law or something? I don't need any trouble." Alex thought it odd that, once again, her eyes traveled to the woman at the sink who had turned around and was smiling at Alex. They seemed to know one another.

Alex crossed her arms across her chest. She needed this job and decided it was worth a chance to have not one, but two people know a tiny bit of her story. Besides, she'd always been a good judge of character and lesbians didn't rat each other out, especially over questionable immigration status.

"Not exactly, but I might not have proper papers. No job, no miracles with this toilet. Good luck dealing with a throng of unhappy dykes who won't want to drink too much if they have to wait to pee."

"You are a cocky little shit. I like it. Okay, as long as you haven't killed anyone. You have yourself a deal."

"I promise no one's dead, although the asshole who beat up his wife deserved—"

Janice held up her hand. "I don't want any details. I'd like to plead ignorance if it comes to it."

The other woman was now leaning against the wall and chuckling. Alex thought she saw her nod at Janice.

Alex stuck out her hand. "I'm going to take your word and your handshake to seal the deal."

Janice took her hand and shook.

"Give me twenty minutes and I'll have this toilet working again. I don't do well with an audience."

"I can't shut down the bathroom for twenty minutes." Janice's voice squeaked in panic.

"I meant that I don't work well with my future boss looking over my shoulder spraying all her nervous energy on top of me."

Janice laughed. "Okay, I'm leaving and will return" —she turned her wrist to look at her watch— "in twenty minutes."

Alex hadn't realized the woman at the sink was still in the bathroom. "Nicely done. By the way, I'm Selene, the other owner of Sisters. I'll leave you to your, uh, tools." She winked and left the bathroom.

Alex blew out a huge breath and then dragged the large toolbox into the stall to begin fixing the toilet. She made sure she closed the door even though the space was small. She didn't appreciate an audience while her future teetered on a very precarious edge.

CHAPTER FIVE

Carrying the heavy toolbox, Alex left the bathroom exactly eighteen minutes later. She moved through the small crowd and walked down the stairs to find the owners. Alex couldn't wait to sink her teeth into dinner. Her stomach had grumbled as she tightened the final bolt. Selene was laughing at the bar while Janice scowled at the co-owner.

Selene draped her arm across Janice's shoulder and said, "Stop worrying. I get the sense our Latino Amazon will be a far bigger asset than a potential liability." As if sensing Alex's approach she turned and shifted her attention, locking eyes with Alex. "Ah, here she is now. Everything flowing correctly?"

Alex nodded. "I sure hope you aren't planning to renege on our deal."

"Wouldn't dream of it," Selene said with a big smile.

"Can we ask you to take a look at a few other minor problems and then maybe help Chancy out behind the bar? She's a cutie, but not very strong." Selene gave Alex another appreciative glance. "I'll bet you could bench press your body weight. Chancy has to make twice as many trips to the back storage to replenish supplies and I wouldn't want her to injure her back."

"Sure, lead the way."

Janice seemed to relax a bit and approached Alex. "I think your food is up. How about you eat first. I did promise your food would be on the house if you managed to fix our plumbing issue."

"Thanks," Alex quietly replied.

"You can put the toolbox behind the bar for now. How'd you hook up with Betty if I can ask? She, uh, well she's a little bit older..."

Alex smiled. "She's a friend. We aren't sleeping together, if that's what you're asking. She's a nice woman who offered to help me out. I've been blessed on my journey to Atlanta. Although, honestly, I've never been one to put artificial barriers between two consenting adults. Judgment has no place in my world. If she wanted sex, I wouldn't have a problem giving her what she desired."

"Betty's a regular here and she has a good heart." Janice raised her eyebrow. "I wouldn't want someone to break it. I'd like to see her find a woman more suited to what she's looking for. It's not a judgment, I just don't see the two of you establishing a long-term relationship."

"Got it. Don't break her heart and stay away from her bedroom lest she misinterpret the signals."

"You staying with her?" Janice began to move toward the outdoor patio.

Alex followed Janice as she continued to fill in the gaps. She supposed this was the oddest interview she'd ever encountered, but then that seemed par for the course. She hadn't really interviewed for her previous job either.

"She offered to put me up for a few nights until I got settled here."

"I assume you don't have your own transportation. How about if you stay at the bar? We have a small place you can crash at. That way if we have an emergency and need your expertise, you'll be right here to fix it for us."

"Okay. You still don't quite trust I won't screw Betty over. I get it. You don't know me, and you don't like my perspective on sex." Alex grinned and shook her head. "Lesbians, sometimes we gotta make things so complicated. Look, I don't have enough stuff to fill a U-Haul, so why would I ever consider combining sex with a long-term relationship. I have too much legal crap to navigate. It wouldn't be fair to drag someone else into that."

"Betty's the type to help someone like you out. She'd probably offer to marry you so your legal troubles went away. Just don't cause any problems in the bar with your player tendencies. Lesbians can be nasty when they think you've taken them for a fool or encroached on what they consider their territory. And we don't need any drama at Sisters."

"Okay, got it. No sex with the customers either. What about with Selene?" Alex joked.

Janice gave Alex a withering look.

Oops. Alex held up her hands. "Sorry, that was a joke. I'm sufficiently chewing on my big fat foot right now. I should have figured it out. You and Selene are more than business partners, right?"

Betty was chuckling as they approached the table. "Seems I can't leave you alone for one second. Hey, Janice. Alex is a good kid. Don't you worry about her. Selene may look, but I know for a fact she would never touch. I've only just met Alex, but I believe she has her own moral standards that include not being a home wrecker. So wipe that jealous look off your face."

Alex kept her eyes on the ground. Damn, she'd needed this job and now she'd blown it by running her mouth like that. She should keep her views to herself. Maybe if she got another chance, she would stay quiet and do her damn job. The less people knew about her, the better.

"I'm sorry," she mumbled, not bothering to look up. "I promise not to cause trouble if you'll give me a second chance."

The food arrived and Alex sat heavily not chancing a look at the owner. At least she would have a good meal before pounding the pavement to seek another job.

"Stop acting like a whipped puppy. I liked the confident young woman I met before. A deal is a deal. But, if you ever make a move on my wife, I will slice your tits off and feed them to my German Shepherd. Bring those meager belongings to the bar tomorrow and I'll give you a key to the place. Oh, and when you're finished eating, we have more chores for you. I plan on getting the better end of this deal we shook on."

Alex looked up at Janice who grinned at her. She could see the attraction. Janice was a beautiful woman when the worry slid from her face and she replaced it with a smile. Alex thought Selene and Janice undoubtedly made a stunning couple. Janice waved her hand in the air and then disappeared back inside the bar. Alex grabbed for the sliders they'd ordered and took a big bite.

"I guess I'll only have you as a roommate for one night. Too bad. I was looking forward to ogling you." Betty laughed. "Even though Janice probably gave you the lecture, I still want you as my wing woman after you finish fixing all their problems. I don't care what she said, I'm counting on you to flirt and reel them in. This kind of golden opportunity doesn't come my way very often. I plan on taking advantage of it. If you have to blame me, go ahead. Besides, your kind of sex appeal oozes from your pores without any effort. She can't very well fault you for something you don't have much control over."

A young woman strolled to the table and asked, "Hey, Betty, who's your friend?"

Betty cupped her hand over her mouth and whispered, "See, what'd I tell you?" She looked up at the young woman. "Let her eat, before you pounce, Erica. Besides, Janice and Selene just gave her a job. She's the new fix-it woman. So, I'm sure you'll have plenty of opportunity to get to know her later. Now skedaddle so's you can go back and report the news to your gaggle of friends over there whispering and giggling."

"I thought you wanted the women to come over to our table?" Alex asked.

"Those are little girls. I do have an age limit. Try to target that magnetism to women over fifty please."

Alex laughed. "Okay, I'll be sure to card everyone I meet." Alex looked around at the crowd and didn't see anyone who looked anywhere near fifty. She turned serious. "Betty, if you don't mind me saying so, I don't think you're going to meet the right person here at Sisters. Maybe you should try something else." Alex thought she might as well throw the suggestion out there again.

Betty took a deep breath. "Maybe. I have a computer. Even signed up for the Facebooky thing. There are groups out there you know, for older lesbians. But it all seems so fake to me. I get to talking to some nice women and then I find out how far away they are. It's discouraging. When you get to be my age, you don't want to move across the country after you've settled. I like it here. I have friends at Sisters. Even the young ones are nice to me. I'm like their mother, you know. I've been around the block and can be a shoulder to cry on. When they get all stupid with each other and start sleeping around, I listen to their woes. Toss out some advice here and there. At least I feel useful."

"I'm not saying you have to stop coming here and socializing with the women you've come to know. Just don't expect to find your Mrs. Right here."

"Yeah, but maybe one day, someone just like me will stroll in. It could happen."

"I guess so and I hope it does, Betty. I really do." Alex grabbed a mozzarella stick and dunked it into the sauce. "I'm not letting you gobble up all these gooey pieces of fried goodness."

†

Alex pushed the covers aside and climbed from the bed. She ran her fingers through her short hair as she stood naked in front of the dresser. She tried to tame the disarray on top of her head to no avail. Giving up, she rummaged around in her bag and plucked out her ball cap. Grabbing a pair of boxers and a tank top, she quickly put on the clothing because she smelled coffee. She didn't think strolling out to the kitchen in her birthday suit was appropriate. Alex never liked wearing clothes to bed. Even clothing that wasn't restrictive was irritating to her. The boxers or T-shirt tended to bunch up in the middle of the night.

Betty was at the stove with a spatula in her hand, flipping pancakes. "Just brewed a pot of coffee. Help yourself. Breakfast is almost ready."

"Do you need any help with anything?"

"Nah. This is the last pancake. It's still early. Janice said to bring you over at eleven. That should give you plenty of time to shower and have breakfast."

"Thanks, Betty. Now that I have a job, can I pay you for putting me up and taking me to the bar today?"

Betty waved the spatula in the air. "Nah. You've been good company. At least for one night. I suppose you'll be too busy with your new job and fending off the ladies to pay me much mind."

"I wouldn't exactly say that. I'd like to make sure we keep in touch. You never know when I'll be one of those people who can benefit from your many years on the planet." Alex picked up the pot of coffee and filled two mugs, bringing them to the table before sitting in one of the empty chairs.

"You calling me old?" Betty brought the stack of pancakes over to the table and set them down.

"Never. Wise, not old. That looks great."

Betty turned and grabbed the plate of sausages and added the meat to the table. She pointed to the glass container with the light brown liquid inside. "Maple syrup is on the table. I have this special blackberry flavor, too, if you want. I can grab that from the fridge."

"No way. That would be blasphemy. Maple syrup is

the only way to eat pancakes and sausages. What can you tell me about my two new bosses?"

"You've probably already figured out Janice is the worrier and the one to run the day-to-day business side of the bar. Selene is the big idea person. She has the marketing know-how and also is the one to smooze her way past any possible hiccups. Atlanta is a cosmopolitan city but don't let that fool you. We still have our fair share of asswipes to deal with. Selene is better at that than Janice. She has more finesse, shall we say."

"Got it. Have they been together long?"

"About five years, I think. Why?" Betty's face scrunched up.

Alex lifted her hands in a placating gesture. "Don't worry. You were right. I would never get in the middle of a couple." Alex frowned. "Well, not a lesbian couple who loves and respects one another."

Betty sat back in her chair. "I'm thinking there's a good story behind that qualifier."

"I never thought about what I did for a living before. I'm second guessing myself now."

"Fixing things? It's not like you were some pool girl, servicing the woman of the house while her husband was away." Betty forked three pancakes and put them onto Alex's empty plate.

Alex winced. "Um, no, I wasn't a pool girl..."

"Okay, spit it out. What's got you looking like you just ate a piece of rancid meat."

"Well, uh, would you think less of me if I said I used to be a sex worker?"

"You, a prostitute? Oh, hon, did it really get that bad for you and you had to give some old, fat, businessman a blow job to keep from living off the streets? Damn, I hate what happens to kids that are kicked out of their homes or find themselves in a situation where there aren't options for them. It's those damn immigration people that did that to you."

"Not exactly. Um, I had a special clientele at the Ranch. I've never had to live on the streets and the Ranch was about as posh as you can imagine. I'm still a gold-star lesbian in every way. I've never had sex with men for money. Women, yes. Mostly women who were curious, but some were married."

"I never heard of a lesbian prostitute. Damn. I'm not sure how to feel about that. I ain't wired to want to have sex with someone I don't love. Although, I gotta admit, I fell in love a whole lot when I was younger." Betty grinned. "I suppose I shouldn't judge people."

"Sometimes the married couples would come together. I never, uh, serviced couples. The married women who came seemed eager for our services and I never asked questions. Just gave them what they wanted and they paid me well. Getting paid to give pleasure to a woman was hardly work for me. I've only been good at two things in my life. Fixing stuff and sex. I didn't want to break up any marriages or anything."

"Hey, don't beat yourself up over this. I just never heard of that before. It might take me a little bit of time getting used to."

"It wasn't even illegal. The brothel was near Vegas."

"So what happened?"

"I suppose I did get in the middle of a married couple but I couldn't let her continue to be his punching bag. You said I wasn't a home wrecker but I was. Sometimes morality has a lot of layers to it. I don't regret my actions at all. I'm sorry if you think I was wrong for busting up that marriage. She deserved better than him."

"Do you think it's the same when it's a wrong match between two women?" Betty seemed deep in thought as she caught Alex's eyes for a second then looked away.

Alex paused and then said, "Yeah, I guess I do. If I saw one woman beating on another, I wouldn't feel bad about breaking them up either. It happens, you know."

"Yeah, I know." Betty pushed away from the table. "Eat up. I gotta take a shower now." She stood and started to walk to her bedroom.

Alex looked at Betty's empty plate and wondered if she had upset the kind woman. Did Betty think less of her because of her line of work at the Ranch?

"Betty, I'm sorry. I've disappointed you."

Betty turned around and her eyes had the kind of sadness Alex suspected matched her own. When they'd taken away her parents, she'd felt impotent and couldn't do a thing to stop it.

"No, kid, it isn't you I'm disappointed with. It's me."

†

A kind of uncomfortable silence filled the space in the short drive to the bar. It felt like a pair of underwear riding inside her crack. Alex wanted to pull it out and stop the discomfort. She didn't know if now was the time and place for that. Alex kept looking over at Betty, trying to find that elusive conversation starter to chisel away the granite that covered her stony expression. Somehow, the earlier conversation had hit a very sore spot for Betty and she desperately wanted to make things better.

Fuck it. Alex was not going to get out of the car without ripping off whatever bandage Betty had wrapped around herself to avoid this conversation. "Look, I'm sorry about whatever I said that made you so...sad...mad...not really sure how you're feeling. If I know one thing, keeping shit all bottled up is not good for the soul. Sometimes, it's a whole lot easier talking to a stranger, or rather an almost stranger. I'd like to think we've started on the path to friendship."

Betty pulled into a parking space near the bar and put the car in park. She scrubbed her face with her hand and turned an anguished look at Alex.

"I shoulda done something when I knew Alice was feeling the brunt of Tam's frustration. Tam and I were drinking buddies, and every once in a while, Tam wasn't a very nice drunk. Alice was on the receiving end of a bad night of drinking. She'd start spewing her frustrations about how everyone else was at fault for whatever wasn't going right in her life and then smack Alice around. I'd go over and try to smooth things over. Help out ya know. Then I fell in love with Alice and Tam figured out my feelings. She uprooted Alice and took her to Oklahoma. I don't know how Alice is doing because she was afraid I'd make things worse for her if she kept in touch. I don't even know if she's still alive. She left without telling me anything."

"Wow. Not sure what to say to that. A lot of lesbians can't believe that women would beat on their partners. That isn't true. I sure wish people would be more open about it. It's more underground with lesbians because they're too embarrassed to admit another woman can be capable of that kind of violence. You should try to track her down. See if she's okay and get her some help. Do you think Rosie would help? Maybe she goes through Oklahoma on one of her long-haul trips. That way you wouldn't be putting Alice in danger."

"It hurt me real bad that she left without saying anything. I thought she trusted me. I mighta let that hurt get in the way of trying to find her. We have some mutual friends at the bar. I suppose I could ask. They might know."

"You want me to try to find out? That way your name is completely out of it. If you and Tam were buddies, and she was a regular at Sisters, I'll bet I could ferret out the information without even breaking a sweat."

Betty offered a weak smile. "I'll bet you could too. All you'd have to do is turn those bedroom eyes on someone. Now git. You're gonna be late for work after getting settled into your new place if ya don't stop jawing at me. Janice will be immune to those smoky brown eyes of yours. Selene might not be, but she doesn't run the day-to-day like I said before."

Alex laughed. "Right. No using my charms on Janice. Oh, and not on Selene either. Janice will 'slice my tits off and feed 'em to her dog.' Besides, if Selene isn't the one who'll save the day, why take the chance of riling up the one who makes all the decisions about my future employment at Sisters."

"Yup. Good assessment of the situation."

Alex opened the car door and stretched after she'd unfolded herself out of the tiny tin can as she liked to refer to Betty's smart car. She waved at Betty before entering the bar and yelled back, "See you later tonight, right?"

Betty smiled and nodded. Alex thought she'd managed to chip off at least some of the granite that had formed on Betty's face this morning.

†

Alex carried her duffel on her shoulder and walked into the bar. The bar had a more subdued feel to it in the morning before the lunch crowd descended on the place. Selene was sitting at one of the tables with a cup in front of her talking with Chancy. Janice waved her over to the bar.

"Is that all you have?" Janice asked.

"Uh, yeah. I travel light. It's a necessity." *Damn, why did I have to add that? Now they're going to think I'm one foot out the door with even a whiff of trouble.*

A small wrinkle formed in the center of Janice's forehead. "If you're going to bail on us in two days' time, you might as well march your ass right back out the door."

"Sorry. I've had to leave in a hurry before and wasn't able to take much with me. That's the truth. I'll always be honest with you. I'm committed to this job but sometimes factors beyond my control..."

"Well, you're a miracle worker with those tools, so we plan on doing everything in our power to make sure those influences stay put. That shit needs to stay outside of this bar. Selene is the expert on greasing palms and smoozing her way into the good graces of those influential twatwaffles. I've no patience for them myself. Selene has taken a shine to you and I'm smart enough to know we need your talents. Hopefully you'll be able to settle in and acquire some more belongings. Maybe you'll become a hoarder like the rest of us stupid lesbians. You'll need to have something to fill a U-Haul when the right woman comes along. Follow me. You can dump your bag and then we need you to take a look at the refrigeration for the kegs. It's not staying cold enough. There's nothing more disgusting than warm beer. This isn't Ireland or the U.K. Yuck. The Brits and Irish can drink their beer at room temp. Not me and not our customers. I know I'm being an arrogant American, and it isn't exactly warm, but I still don't like it regardless of the claim that ice cold destroys the flavor."

"Oh, I'm with you on that one all right. I don't think I'll ever want to visit Europe for just that reason. Nothing like a cold beer on a hot day. Could be they don't care because it rains all the time over there and doesn't get sticky hot like here. I've never been to the Northeast or Northwest where it's cold and rainy. Maybe they like room temperature beer."

"They don't, because it sucks," Janice answered as she motioned for Alex to follow her up a set of stairs in the back.

The fully furnished studio apartment had a futon that apparently folded up into a couch if she wanted. The kitchen was miniscule and the bath even smaller but Alex didn't mind. It was a place to crash. She didn't plan on cooking here anyway. Not while she could walk downstairs and grab a bite to eat at the bar. Janice had told her she was entitled to all the free meals her stomach could handle. That suited Alex just fine. She was young enough that unhealthy pub food wouldn't make her all soft as long as she continued to remain active. Hauling cases of beer and other heavy items to the bar would surely keep her in shape.

"Let me toss this bag in the closet. None of my clothes are fancy enough to hang anyway," Alex said.

"I know it isn't much, but at least it's a roof over your head. And it's free."

"Free is good." Alex grinned.

"There's a small dresser where I'm sure most, if not all of your clothes will fit." Janice pointed to the three drawer, light pine, dresser tucked away in the corner close to the futon.

"Okay, then if you don't mind, maybe I can empty the duffel real quick."

"Need any help?"

"Nah. It'll only take me a few minutes." Alex quickly unpacked several pairs of boxers, a few exercise bras, a couple pairs of jeans, T-shirts, and her favorite khaki shorts. She always appreciated having the zipper pockets to store her cash and license.

Before Texas had changed their laws requiring proof of citizenship, she'd gotten her license as a teen. For a little while she could drive legally, but then in 2008, even a renewal required papers. When she'd learned about the relaxed licensing laws in California, Ariel had taken her to get a new license. California was close enough to make the trip. Alex really wanted to have a valid driver's license for when she'd eventually be able to afford a car. That hadn't happened because she'd had to go on the run again. She wondered if her California license would do her any good in Georgia with the pressure to round up all the illegals. At least she could use it to purchase alcohol. There were so many laws she had to keep track of in the different states.

Alex hadn't looked into the Deferred Action for Childhood Arrivals (DACA) program when she had the chance because she had worked for her papa and didn't think she needed a work permit. She wasn't sure if that decision had been a good or a bad one now. The DACA program was in serious risk. Nearly 500 dollars was a lot of money to gamble away, especially with her future so unsure. She stuffed a twenty in her pocket and hid the rest under her clothes in the drawer. Even though she didn't have a large nest egg from her work at the Ranch, it was everything she owned. If she needed to move on quickly, she would need every cent she'd earned.

"Ready?"

"Yeah, thanks. Lead the way. My stuff is safe up here, right?"

"It is. No one but Selene, Chancy, and I even know this little studio apartment exists. Chancy lived here until she got on her feet. She's a good kid who's had a very hard life. Her parents are the scum of the earth in my humble opinion. Kicked her out at fifteen and she lived on the streets for a long time. We gave her a job to get her away from the drugs and other shitty influences. She might have done a little hooking to try to make ends meet, but she managed to stay away from the pimps and drugs. That didn't keep her from getting her ass beat until we came along. She just turned twenty-one six months ago. Now she's been able to make a decent living with all the tips the women toss her way. She's very popular with the ladies."

Alex followed Janice back down the stairs. She thought about her situation and how having sex with women was probably a whole lot different than Chancy's earlier life. No doubt Chancy had to give hurried blow jobs down back alleys to fat, sweaty men. Alex shuddered at the thought. She wasn't sure how she felt about prostitution. Back at the Ranch most of the women enjoyed their job. She knew she had. But, was she contributing to a culture where women were regarded as nothing more than a sex toy for the entertainment of men? She had to admit that most of the

Ranch business catered to men. Still, she knew her experience was a far cry from the streetwalkers the men used and abused on a daily basis. There were too many layers to the issue and she wasn't about to be the one to peel them all down to get to the core nugget.

CHAPTER SIX

Danna's experience with Luna wasn't at all what she expected. Sure, she'd fumbled around before, but it never made it past the make-out stage. On the one hand, she'd never felt so good. Both Marley and Luna's touch had awakened a craving in her that had always been missing. Yet, something was still absent for Danna. Emotion. She needed to feel something for her partner and that was not present with the purely physical experience she'd had with Luna. Great as that had felt, it wasn't enough for her. She wanted the whole enchilada.

She wasn't sure whom she should talk to about her jumbled emotions. Although Lindy had convinced her to try out the special offerings at TWC, she wasn't sure Lindy would understand the tumultuous inner dialog she was having with herself. For the first time in her life, she had to consider that maybe she was a lesbian. It was one thing to have those sexy workers at TWC scratch an itch that husbands were ignoring, but it would be quite another to completely replace the back scratcher with a model not generally accepted in her high society circle of friends.

A certain amount of exploration was acceptable in her youth, especially at the all-girls boarding school she had attended. Wellesley College hadn't been any different. Developing close friendships with the other women who attended the elite college was not only acceptable, it was almost expected. Add alcohol to the mix and the perfect rationale was served up on fine china.

Danna debated whether to find out the phone number for her freshman roommate, Tanya. They weren't close friends in high school. When their mothers heard about the two Atlanta debutantes going to Wellesley College, they had insisted both girls team up and room together.

Danna sighed. Tanya. *Was Tanya her first love?* Maybe. But that ship had sailed a very long time ago. Danna hadn't been brave enough to explore a real relationship, even after that one drunken night. Proper Southern ladies simply did not fall in love with their female roommates and ride off into the sunset. She couldn't handle anything greater than an especially passionate kiss. Danna had pushed her away. She'd tried to convince Tanya it was the best thing for both of them. Things were tense at the end and she'd always regretted not keeping in touch and fixing the awkwardness that blanketed them for the remainder of their time at Wellesley.

Although Tanya had done her duty and married a Harvard grad, the marriage lasted a mere six months before Tanya had slammed down her foot. She wasn't going to let her mother run her life anymore. She'd moved to France to be with "her one true love."

Danna had moved on too. She'd married David and settled into Atlanta society. Her identity was lost the minute she'd married David. She wasn't Danna the pro bono attorney, but rather the wife of a car dealership mogul. She hadn't even tried to fight her mother or David to become her own person.

Danna envied the strength it had taken for Tanya to defy her parents. It had royally pissed her off when she'd had lunch with her mother who had made that acerbic comment about Tanya's return to Atlanta. Calling Tanya's wife "that French hussy" was cruel and uncalled for. The lunch had reminded her why she hadn't spoken to her mother since David's funeral. Now the gossip about Tanya had Danna pining to speak with someone who might understand what she was going through.

†

Danna was sitting at her favorite cafe drinking a caramel latte and picking at her croissant. The morning was pleasant with a small breeze and the delightful smells emanating from the cafe. Not only did the rich aroma of freshly brewed coffee reach her nose, but she could distinctly smell cinnamon and other tell-tale signs of freshly baked goodies. It reminded her of when her nanny would let her stir the ingredients for snickerdoodles, her favorite cookie.

She nearly spilled the coffee down the front of her silk blouse when she saw the very person she had been thinking about. Tanya was positively glowing as she exited the cafe's competition two doors down. An attractive woman had her arm looped inside Tanya's and was whispering something in her ear. Tanya threw back her head and began laughing.

Without thinking Danna waved her hand and called out, "Tanya."

Those sharp hazel eyes turned toward Danna and the corners of her lips turned up in a genuine smile. The woman, who seemed to be holding on for dear life, shifted her curious gaze to Danna.

"Oh, my, God. Danna? You look fantastic. I see the years have been especially kind to you."

"I was going to say the very same thing. You look happy." Danna sighed.

Tanya grabbed the woman's hand and was pulling her along as she took several steps in Danna's direction. She looked like she was evaluating what to say next. "I suppose that's surprising to someone like you who probably has a rich husband, two point five kids, and a lifetime membership to a country club." She turned her head in the direction of her companion. "Honey, this is my old roommate at Wellesley."

Danna realized Tanya must have interpreted her sigh as judgment. She wanted to correct that misperception.

"Husband's dead. No kids. And an exclusive spa for women only is more my style. Especially when a very attractive woman pays special attention to my more sensitive spots—after I'd already received a glorious massage. Country clubs are overrated and filled with fat old men."

"Oh, uh, Danna, I'm a tactless idiot. I'm really sorry for my gaffe. I didn't know your husband passed away. I suppose the gossip only flows one way. I'm sure your mother ran right back and told you I was in town. I assumed you were like everyone else, judgmental and stuck in proper

Atlanta society, which definitely is not very accepting of me and my wife."

Danna smiled. "Honestly, I've been wanting to call and talk to you. I've been a bit confused lately and didn't know who else would be able to give me some perspective. As for Atlanta's high society, you'd be surprised at how far we've come. Do you remember Lindy Jackson? She's Lindy Freemont now."

"Married to a judge, right?"

"Yes, and owns the Trophy Wives Club. That's the exclusive women's club I was talking about. The one that offers special attention to those neglected society folk you think are so stuffy. Let's just say the young women Lindy has working for her definitely know their way around a vagina."

Both Tanya and her wife erupted in laughter.

"You're shitting me," Tanya said.

"I swear, I'm not." Danna crossed her index finger over her heart. "Will you and your wife please join me? You probably already had your morning coffee at Sophie's. The Perky Bean surpasses Sophie's in the croissant competition, although their coffee is not quite as tasty."

"Well, you would know, being born and bred here. I'm sorry, Danna, I was being an ass earlier." Tanya sat in one of the empty chairs and pulled her wife down to sit next to her. She gestured to her wife. "This is Martin. She definitely appreciates a light and flaky croissant."

"Hello, Martin. I'm glad to finally meet you. I can't believe I ran into you today, Tanya. I've been meaning to call. I wasn't sure who else to talk to about my recent, uh, come to Jesus meeting with myself. I know we've lost touch. You probably have a very different perception of who I am based on our college days, but things have evolved for me..."

Tanya arched her eyebrow. "Realized you're a lesbian, huh? I wondered how many years it would take. That is if you were ever to allow yourself to go there."

"Direct as always. I'm so glad that hasn't changed. After David passed, Lindy took me under her wing and brought me to her club. I think she believed I was a lost lamb needing something. She was right. The experience at TWC was eye-opening for me. I allowed myself to simply melt into the delight of those special services and, well," Danna leaned in and whispered, "I had my very first orgasm and the pieces of the puzzle clicked into place for me. Now I don't know what to do. I want the cow and the farmer's wife. How does one go about meeting other more mature lesbians? I've thought about checking out the local lesbian bar but I don't think I'll find a life mate there."

"Probably not. Although, it might get you a little more comfortable around other lesbians. I say go for it. Besides, stranger things have happened. I met Martin at a bar. Granted it was twenty years ago, but still."

Danna nodded. More to herself than Tanya and Martin. The smiles on their faces seemed to suggest they approved. Danna took a deep breath. "I suppose I'll make the jump and hope there is a soft landing. You know, saying those words out loud just now...I feel like a huge weight has been lifted off my shoulders. I do hope we'll be able to stay in touch. Other than a few of the workers at TWC, you're the only lesbians I know."

"That you know of. Not everyone is out and proud. You'd be surprised. You weren't the only overzealous girl at Wellesley who seemed to enjoy a random make out session. Some were eager to participate in something a bit more than an experimental foray into the wild and wicked lesbo ways." Tanya wiggled her eyebrows. "I have it on good authority Eleanor is living with a woman and they aren't sisters."

"No way. She was way more stick-up-her-rear than me."

"Yes way. And you didn't exactly have a rod up your ass, more like a tiny twig. Welcome to the dark side."

Danna laughed. "I've missed you, Tanya." She really did miss her old roommate.

Martin coughed and pulled her wife close. "Hey, get your own hot lesbian. This one's mine," she joked.

Danna looked longingly at Martin and Tanya. "You two look perfect together. I'm so glad you found one another. And, yes, Martin, I plan on it. I simply needed a little push."

CHAPTER SEVEN

Alex was feeling more settled after methodically taking care of all the minor repairs at Sisters. The condenser was shot on the refrigeration unit keeping the kegs cold and that was stressing out Janice. There wasn't much Alex could do about that until the part came in. She'd jerry-rigged a solution that marginally worked. The beer wasn't ice cold, but it wasn't room temperature either. As she schlepped another case of bottled beer into the other refrigeration unit that wasn't causing them problems, she noticed the two attractive women who'd come into the bar. Alex got her fair share of looks, but one of the women seemed to particularly focus on her and that was unnerving. She didn't need the attention.

She stacked the beer on top of the two cases she'd hauled out earlier from storage. Alex felt an intense need to escape from prying eyes. She was particularly unnerved when she heard Chancy reveal her first name. She paced in the back room like a nervous lion in the zoo and mumbled, "Shit, shit, shit."

She felt a hand on her shoulder and jumped.

"Hey, are you okay?" Chancy asked.

Curiosity got the better of her and she decided to ask Chancy about the woman who seemed more than a little fascinated by her. She motioned with her head toward the bar. "Who was that woman you were talking to?"

"Oh, that's Marley. And Luna's the one who made a beeline for the dance floor. Luna comes here more than Marley. She's sexy as hell in those leathers, huh?"

"Yeah, I guess. What do you know about them?" Alex wanted to ask Chancy why the hell one of them was watching her so intently. "They aren't cops, are they?"

Chancy began laughing. "Hardly. Marley's a massage therapist. Mrs. Freemont offered her a job to manage this upscale spa. For women only. Luna works there too as some kind of fitness guru."

"Interesting."

"That's not even the best part. I'm kinda seeing this smokin' hot older chick who goes there. She told me about how the spa offers 'special' services to ladies needing extra attention to their hoohah. Apparently, their hubbies aren't cutting it and lesbian sex is all the rage now. Didn't you hear? They actually published some study about lesbians having more orgasms. Well, duh?"

Alex laughed. "Hoohah. That's a new one. You're fucking with me, right?"

"No, honest. But you can't tell anyone. We were sorta talking in bed one night and she let it slip. I'm not supposed to know anything about it. She'll kill me if she knows I confided in you, but you're not the type to go telling stories. I can trust you, right?"

"With my life. I won't say a word. You know, brothels are legal in Nevada, but not here. How do they figure they're gonna get away with it?"

"Mrs. Freemont is the owner and her husband is Judge Jay Dub Freemont. He's very powerful around these parts. Ain't no way he's gonna let his wife end up in jail with some big dyke claiming her as her bitch. Helena says he doesn't know what goes on upstairs. I don't think he'd be pleased, so that's why everybody has to exercise a lot of discretion. I sure wouldn't want to be in the shoes of the person who let that slip and ended up cutting these women off. I'll bet Jay Dub would be mighty pissed if he had to get involved, but he'd do it for his wife."

Alex relaxed against the bar. "Maybe, but sometimes the husbands get off knowing about their wives' extracurricular activities with women. As long as they aren't boinking the pool boy. The Judge can envision her getting all hot and bothered with a beautiful woman, while he has his little affairs. Everyone wins. How many people are working at this place and do they all participate in the 'special' services?"

Chancy shrugged. "I don't even know if Marley and Luna are involved or just their staff. Helena didn't tell me who she...uh...asked to give her hoohah special attention."

"Okay, I better grab some more beer for you. It's a thirsty crowd tonight and I don't want the boss to think I'm slacking."

Alex picked up another two cases and brought them out to the bar. She caught Marley's eyes and held her gaze for a few seconds, nodding briefly to her. Marley was stunning by anyone's standards. The smile formed on her lips without Alex realizing it until the woman returned with her own smile.

With the drag show starting, Alex was momentarily distracted before she returned to surveying the bar. She needed to concentrate and see what Chancy might be running low on. After several more trips to the back room, she wiped her brow and leaned against the bar to take a quick break and talk with Chancy.

Feeling like someone was watching her, Alex turned around. Standing in front of her were the two women she'd been discussing earlier along with her boss.

"You need something, Janice? I think Chancy is set for beer, but maybe I ought to bring some coolers or cider from the back to get them chilled."

"No, you deserve a five-minute rest. You've been nonstop since you started. I've never met someone who doesn't pause to take a breather. I was glad to see you talking with Chancy. I brought some friends over who wanted to meet you."

"Janice always hires the sexiest women. I'm Marley. It's good to meet you." Marley held out her hand.

Alex never let women fluster her, but for some reason Marley was having an odd effect. Blushing, she offered her own hand in response. "Um, Alex." Marley's hand was soft and warm. She imagined the oil she used for her massages must keep her hands supple.

"Luna, aren't you going to introduce yourself?" Marley turned to her companion and smirked.

"I think you just took care of that for me," Luna answered.

Alex looked directly at the tall, regal woman who had such a commanding presence. She couldn't help admiring how she exuded the kind of confidence Alex rarely came across in her recent travels. Most of the women at the Ranch had that certain air of self-reliance, but that had been an entirely new phenomenon to Alex. None of them was the least bit hesitant about loving their vocation. They were not about to let anyone shame them into submission or guilt over sex work.

"Nice to meet you, Luna." When Alex took Luna's hand, she felt the calluses and surmised Luna must do a fair amount of weight lifting. Her grip was firm, but not bone crushing. The message—she didn't have anything to prove. And neither did Alex.

"We should probably let you get back to work, but maybe you can join me for a drink sometime. Janice does give you a day off every now and then, doesn't she?" Marley smiled.

"Don't you dare even think about poaching Alex. I heard you needed someone with her skills," Janice interjected.

Marley arched her eyebrow. "Skills?"

"Yeah, she's the best fix-it gal we've ever had. I'm exercising the 'finders keepers' rule. I found her, I get to keep her. She's saved us thousands in outrageous repair bills. Not to mention the ladies love the additional eye candy when she restocks the bar."

"Careful, Janice. No one likes being considered someone's property. Proper incentive to stay is usually the right answer. I trust you're paying her for what she's worth." Marley winked.

Alex laughed. "I'm doing just fine. Where else can I

get a place to stay, decent pay, and be surrounded by beautiful lesbians in all their glorious variety? I never met a lesbian I didn't think was beautiful."

"Ooh and a smooth talker, too. Well, perhaps you'll get everything all squared away here at Sisters and have so much free time you'll want to consider picking up a second job." Marley pulled a card from her pocket and handed it to Alex. "If that happens, give me a call."

Before Alex could answer, she saw Selene making a beeline to the small group. Selene wasn't the type of person to let anything rattle her but Alex could tell something was amiss.

"Hey, Alex, can I get you to take a look at something?" Selene asked.

Janice shot Selene a questioning look. "What's wrong?"

"Settle down, honey. It's just a little problem with the toilet." Selene placed her hand on Janice's arm to hold off an over-the-top reaction.

"The one Alex just fixed?" Janice's tone was sharp as she directed her cool gaze at Alex.

"No, no, the other one. And you need to take it down a notch because I think it just needs a new flushing thingy."

Alex covered her mouth to hide her amusement. "You mean a tank lever."

"Sure, the thing that's attached to the handle when you flush. I picked up the lid and the chain isn't attached anymore. I wasn't about to stick my hand in there," Selene clarified.

"Easy fix. I'll take care of it. Nice to meet both of you. If you'll excuse me, I have a toilet to fix."

†

While Alex was fixing the tank lever, Luna came into the bathroom and approached her and struck up a surprising conversation. It seemed that neither Luna nor Marley had been scared away by Janice's warning to keep away. Alex felt a swell of pride after the conversation. Luna had wanted to know about her background and Alex had shared enough to pique her interest without coming right out and stating she was undocumented. Luna had clearly insinuated there was a job waiting for her and all she needed to do was say yes.

Alex had a lot to think about. She wouldn't mind the extra money that she could send to her family once she tracked them down. Sisters didn't have a lot of repairs left after she'd spent numerous hours fixing everything and checking on all their systems to make sure nothing was about to break.

After Luna left, Alex began humming and made fast work of replacing the tank lever. She quickly washed her hands then placed her tools in the back room. Nearly skipping down the stairs, she returned to the bar and noticed the empty beer bottle in front of Marley. Smiling at the beautiful woman, she offered, "Let me replace that for you."

"Thanks." Marley's gleaming white smile was instantaneous. She handed her empty bottle to Alex before waving and then walking away with Luna. They looked cozy as they headed to the dance floor. When Luna leaned down and whispered something into Marley's ear, Alex wished she had super-sensitive hearing. Especially when Marley turned her head back in Alex's direction.

"Someone's got a crush," Chancy said.

"How much do you think it costs to join that club of theirs?" Alex asked.

"A helluva lot more than either one of us have, that's for sure. I think it's twenty k and that doesn't include any extras," Chancy answered.

Alex whistled. "Wow. It's pretty tempting considering a part-time position at their spa, but Janice gave me a job when I desperately needed one and I'm indebted to her. If nothing else, I'm very loyal."

"Marley's right, though. I don't think Janice is going to need you as much in the near future. You've already got this place mostly shipshape and you've only been here for a couple of days. I know Janice. She'll want what's best for you. If you can make some extra dough at their fancy spa, I say go for it."

"I sure hope Helena was telling the truth about that 'special' treatment."

"Really? Why?"

"I have experience with that. I took a chance and told Luna a little about my past."

"No shit? When did you talk with Luna?" Chancy grinned.

"No shit. She came into the bathroom when I was fixing the tank lever and we had a brief conversation. After you let slip what Helena said during your pillow talk, I thought what the hell. I guess it doesn't hurt to leave my options open, just in case something happens. I told her about working at a place in Nevada where it's legal. I gotta admit, that was the best job I've ever had. I like fixing things, but there's nothing quite like satisfying a woman. They taught me some special techniques like Japanese Nuru massage."

"Damn. Wish someone would offer me a job like that." Chancy's eyes clouded with darkness. "I've got related experience, just not with the right gender. I'm a real fast learner, though. Think you could teach me a few tricks? Then maybe I could ask Marley if they're looking for someone like me. Do you think a few of them women would go for the punk rocker look? Helena sure seems to dig it."

Alex scrutinized Chancy and then answered, "They might. You do have a certain amount of adorable going for you."

"Oh, can I keep you? Charming never goes out of style."

"Well, you might want to be careful about how you spread that adorable around. Some women get possessive and jealous."

Chancy frowned. "Good point. I don't know how Helena would feel about me working there and being one of the staff who participate in the upstairs activities. Right now I'm the one scratching that itch of hers and I wouldn't dream of taking money for it. Did I mention how smokin' hot she is?"

Alex smiled. "You did."

†

Alex had her head under the sink with a wrench in her hands. Laying on her back to get the right angle was better than crouching and trying to see underneath the tight space. She could hear someone approach but she decided she'd wait for them to say something. She had a nasty drip to fix and didn't want to waste time in an idle chat with whomever was standing there. Alex groaned. If it was one of her bosses, she decided they might consider her rude or insubordinate if she stayed underneath and asked one of them

83

to hand her the smaller wrench. Sliding out from under the sink, she met Selene's curious gaze.

"We had a lot of shit to fix, huh? Neither one of us knows a phillips from a flathead. I don't think our previous fix-it gal was very good but she did look mighty sexy in a tool belt. Of course nothing compared to you."

Alex sighed. "Do you have a problem that requires my attention right this second, or can I finish on this leak?"

"Oh, no, nothing urgent. I wanted to talk to you about something else."

"Okay." Alex set the wrench on the floor and sat up.

"I'm worried about Betty. Have you heard from her?"

"What? Um, no. I haven't been a very good friend. I've been too tired at night to do anything but relax in my loft and fall asleep."

"Betty's like clockwork. She comes in practically every night. Sometimes I wish she wouldn't. She isn't going to find the love of her life here at Sisters. I know I own this joint, but I would not recommend it for finding a life partner. A temporary lover, sure. Women hook up all the time and I'm not judging..."

"I get the picture. I didn't know she came here every night, but you're right. She hasn't been here since Saturday night. Want me to find my way to her place and check on her?"

"Oh yeah, that's right. You don't have wheels or a cell phone. I don't know how you survive," Selene joked.

"Never really needed them before. They were both luxuries Papa said wouldn't enhance our life one bit. I was planning on buying a secondhand car, nothing special, when I lived in Nevada, but then my plans shifted."

Selene raised her eyebrows but didn't comment.

Alex continued. "Papa always said food, a roof over your head, an occasional Corona, and the love of a good woman were all a man needed in life. Fancy cars, cell phones, computers, and everything else were, in his opinion, a waste of space and a way to throw away good money."

"If you know where she lives, I can drive you there and check things out. I worry about Betty. She's got a good heart and, well, I'd hate to lose a good customer." Selene grinned.

"Yeah, Betty was a lifesaver. I'd like to make sure she's okay."

"Why don't you come to the office when you finish here and we'll head out? Oh, and Alex, I know we aren't paying you a ton, but I sure hope you stick around. Speaking of lifesavers, that's what you've been to us. I suppose if you want to work at that new spa, we shouldn't stand in your way. From what I've heard it's a classy place. Maybe you could consider working part-time here and part-time there."

"Hey, don't worry. You and Janice gave me a job when I needed one. I won't forget that. I won't leave you high and dry no matter what enticing carrot they stick in front of my nose. Remember, stuff like fancy cars and cell phones don't impress me."

†

Janice was dealing with the beer distributor and she sounded irritated. The order was all wrong. Alex was glad Janice hadn't been the one to approach her about Betty. She respected Janice, but she was more tightly wound than Selene. She paused mid rant with a curious expression on her face. Selene quickly filled her in on the reconnaissance mission to find out where Betty had been the last couple of days. Janice didn't exactly smile at the news, but her face relaxed a bit with Selene's explanation.

Betty's place wasn't very far away. Alex could have walked, but Selene seemed anxious to check on her. Their first clue that Betty wasn't home was the absence of her compact car. Alex decided to knock on her door anyway. It was possible she'd done something like lending her car to one of her friends or a neighbor in need. That would be something Betty would do. Alex rapped on the door and waited a few seconds. After no one answered, she took a few steps to the right and tried to peer in one of the windows through the partially open blinds.

"Maybe she met someone and is on a date," Alex suggested.

Selene shook her head. "I don't know..."

"Hey, just because she's a bit older doesn't mean she couldn't have met a woman who is interested in her."

"I know you're probably right. It must seem awfully snobby of me to question her, um, allure to a potential partner. I'd feel a whole lot better if I saw the whites of her eyes. Do you think I should call the police and have them do a welfare check?"

Alex shuffled her feet and looked down. She'd rather not call attention to herself and having the police involved made her especially uncomfortable. "I...uh...could you maybe call when I'm not around?"

"Okay. How much trouble are you in? I trust that you haven't killed anyone, but Alex, do we have to worry about someone trying to track you down? You aren't on any ten-most-wanted list are you?"

Alex laughed. "No, nothing like that, but police aren't

exactly warm and fuzzy to us Latinos. Sprinkle a little dyke on top and I'm a target for every macho dude looking to prove himself. Keeping a low profile usually works well, until I have to defend some fair maiden's honor. Then, I simply can't help myself. I'm like a bee to honey. Trouble calls to me in those circumstances."

"All right. I'll check back later tonight after the bar closes. Either something is terribly wrong or Betty really did get especially lucky." Selene chuckled.

"If you have some paper and a pen, maybe we can leave her a note for her to call you. If you let me borrow your fancy cell phone, I can call Rosie. She might know something."

"Who's Rosie?"

"Another angel who helped me out by giving me a ride and hooking me up with Betty. She's a long-haul trucker. Knew Betty before she retired. She's got a big heart like Betty. Maybe they keep in touch."

Selene smiled. "I'll bet you never have trouble finding some woman who will loan you their cell phone."

Alex tilted her head. "Come to think of it, no, I don't. I suppose that's another reason not to own one. Besides, I don't like the idea that some government person can track my every move. Nobody's laughing at me now with those social media sites selling all your private info. Next thing you know, they'll be telling everyone that all the phone carriers have been selling their information for years. No thanks. I'll stay off the radar."

"Paranoid much?" Selene arched her eyebrow.

"More like realistic and observant. I read, you know, the newspaper. They still have them. Speaking of observant. There might be nosy neighbors ready to call the cops on two women loitering on Betty's doorstep. Can we go now?"

"Yup, paranoid."

"You should take that lily-white body of yours and walk in my brown shoes."

"Doesn't keep the women from fawning all over you." Selene held her hands up. "Just saying."

CHAPTER EIGHT

Danna hovered outside of the bar debating whether it was a good idea or not to enter. The light bulb had gone off after her session with Luna. David had been a good husband, but not a very talented lover. Danna sighed. Maybe the problem had been her all along. She hadn't wanted to fall into the same trap as all the wives who bitterly complained about their husbands. David had wanted to try many things to please her, but nothing had worked. Plus, his physical appearance had turned her off in the end. He'd let himself go and the wide expanse of his belly on top of those chicken legs was not an attractive sight. Add his ridiculous comb over and puffy jowls, the result of too much drink over the years, and she'd barely been able to have sex with him in the last couple of years of their marriage.

Danna tried to remember if she'd ever been

physically attracted to David. When they'd first started dating and he was active on the tennis court, he was fit and trim. His sandy blond hair and bright blue eyes fit right in with the other men at the country club. He could have had his pick of any of the young debutantes of Atlanta. Her mother had been over the moon when they started dating. She would croon about how handsome, smart, and nice David was. She never ceased to emphasize how lucky Danna was that he'd decided to court her over all the others. Danna had fallen into step and accepted her fate. She would marry David and become another respectable lady in Atlanta's high society. The prominence of both their families ensured that neither went outside of their circle. It felt like a modern day arranged marriage and Danna supposed that, looking back, that is exactly what it had been.

Danna had grown to love David, but not in the way she had hoped. They'd never had heart-pounding, rip the other's clothes off, sex. When Luna had given Danna her very first orgasm, she began to wonder if she might be a lesbian. Talking with Tanya had bolstered her confidence.

Now she was second-guessing her curiosity with the famous lesbian bar she'd overheard Luna and Marley talking about. She shook her head and muttered, "Stupid old woman," as she turned to leave.

"Danna?" Luna approached in full leathers. Tossing her shiny black hair back from her face, she smiled.

There was no denying Danna's immediate reaction to Luna's beauty. The minute she saw Luna approach, she was like one of Pavlov's dogs. The drool did not escape her mouth, but the wetness made itself known in a decidedly lower region.

"Hello, Luna. I, uh, heard you and Marley talking

about Sisters and thought I might check it out."

"Well, you're going in the wrong direction." Luna smiled. "Come on, I'll escort you inside."

"You don't have to do that. I'm sure you don't want a middle-aged woman cramping your style."

"Nonsense. Besides, you should be more worried about people thinking you aren't free to accept offers. For those that don't know me by reputation, I'll be sure to clarify you're free as a bird." Luna winked.

Well, it's now or never. Danna accepted Luna's offer and walked inside the bar with her. Her eyes darted around, trying to take in every detail. She heard the faint sounds of pounding bass upstairs and decided that wasn't her cup of tea. How would she enter into a conversation with anyone over that racket? Yet, maybe that was the point. No conversation, just raw sexual energy played out on the dance floor. Maybe she shouldn't toss that option aside too quickly.

Danna decided a drink was something she desperately needed to settle her nerves. "Can I buy you a drink, Luna?"

"You don't have to do that. Now that I'm working at TWC, I have more money than I need."

"I admit you've rescued me from chickening out. I wasn't going to go inside. I'd like to say thank you with a drink."

"I don't normally consume alcohol except on very rare occasions. I'll just have water."

"I won't comment on you being a cheap date," Danna joked.

"I'm not much for dating, but I suppose I could make the person treat me to expensive food or perhaps some other form of entertainment to make up for my aversion to putting alcohol in my body."

"Yes, Luna, you deserve for someone to wine and dine you, without the wine, I suppose."

Danna swiveled her attention to the cute bartender with the multi-colored hair. *Not my type, but she is an attractive young woman.* Danna's assessment of the young woman behind the bar was a surprise as she realized she'd admitted she might have a *type.* When the tall woman with short dark hair and expressive brown eyes walked behind the bar, her biceps bulging with the weight of what she was carrying, Danna's eyes followed her. She noted how well her jeans fit over what she suspected was a nice firm behind. Visions of that ass, bare and moving with a rhythm on top of her invaded Danna's thoughts. She wanted to meet this woman. The realization that this woman was exactly her type didn't seem to disturb her. She supposed she was getting used to the idea she might be more attracted to women than men.

"What can I get you, pretty lady?"

Luna chuckled. "Chancy, you flirt."

Danna reluctantly turned her attention away from the other woman. "Oh, um, can you make a mojito? Or margarita if you don't have the ingredients for a mojito. And, may I also have a bottled water. If you have a Pellegrino that would be perfect."

Chancy's face screwed up. "I can make a killer margarita or mojito, but I'm afraid we don't get too many requests for either and we never get any requests for a Pellegrino. Sorry, all we have is plain bottled water, but Luna don't care for bubbles anyway."

Danna flushed. "Oh, right, I'm sorry. I sound very pretentious right now. Old habits."

Luna touched her arm. "You're fine. Chancy, you go

ahead and make my friend that killer mojito." Luna motioned with her head in the direction of the woman who had turned to leave after leaning over and putting the drinks inside of a refrigeration unit. "Alex still happy working here?"

Chancy laughed. "God, you're not even going to try to mask your intentions. Yes, she's very loyal to Janice. Just between you and me, I think she has exactly the skills you're looking for. When things settle here with the repairs she's been doing for us, you might want to approach again. I don't think she has much of a social life."

Luna arched her eyebrow.

"I know," Chancy continued, "just look at her. You should see how many slips of paper she gets in a night. So far, she hasn't acted on any of it. She's a little guarded about some things. In other areas, she's been surprisingly open about her previous work life."

Danna was suddenly very interested in the direction of the conversation. She had a keen desire to know if Lindy or Marley had offered this Alex person a job. If that was the case, she wondered if she might schedule a special session with her. "A possible new recruit?"

Luna grinned. "Maybe, but apparently not until she gets everything at Sisters in top shape. She's some kind of fix-it goddess."

Goddess is right. She certainly is that. "Oh." Danna could not keep the disappointment from her voice. "I suppose even though TWC is brand new, eventually, you'll need someone mechanical to attend to the building and equipment."

Luna threw her head back, laughing. She lowered her voice and whispered in Danna's ear, "You're hoping she'll help with our special services."

Chancy shifted her gaze between Danna and Luna. "Are you two a couple? I've never seen Luna with a date."

"No, no, Danna's too classy for the likes of someone like me," Luna answered.

"Not true, but I don't think anyone can tame this one," Danna quipped.

"Oh, I don't know about that. The right one doesn't seem to...never mind. You should send Alex over to meet Danna here, I think she's smitten."

"Yeah, well, she'll need to stand in line, then. I better get to fixing that perfect mojito before Janice tosses me out on my ass for slacking."

Chancy turned around and began gathering the ingredients. She started to gently muddle the mint, lime, and sugar she'd just dumped into a glass. Danna definitely approved of her technique. Clearly this young bartender did in fact know what she was doing. Danna returned her focus to the imposing woman who approached Chancy.

"Mmm a mojito. Wish I could have one of those." Alex pushed her hand through her hair wet with sweat. "You running low on anything else?" She absently lifted her T-shirt and mopped the sweat from her glistening face.

Danna was riveted to her flat stomach.

"Nah, relax for once. I can get you something non-alcoholic to drink." Chancy lowered her voice and continued her conversation with Alex.

Danna strained to hear whatever Chancy was saying to Alex when she heard Luna's name and then Alex turned around and looked in their direction. A quick smile from Alex was nearly Danna's undoing. She had to find a way to meet this woman. Maybe she could speak with Lindy and have her talk with Janice. Surely they could work out a deal to share Alex's talents. Danna desperately wanted to feel Alex's hands caressing her body. She wasn't sure the woman would consider working for TWC. Even if she was open to working at both places, would she consider participating in those special services?

A petite woman hurried to the bar and called out to Alex, "Alex, can you come and take a look at the strobe light upstairs? Something isn't quite right with it."

"Sure." Alex followed the woman up the stairs.

Danna knew she'd lost her opportunity for an introduction and turned her attention back to Luna who was leaning against the bar looking over the crowd.

"Hey, you don't need to babysit me. I'll have a drink and then be on my way."

"You know...with you being fresh meat...oops, sorry to be so crass. What I mean is that you might garner some unwelcome attention. You sure you'll be okay at the bar here by yourself?"

"Yes, go on. I'm sure the upstairs dance room is more to your liking."

"Not really," Luna absently answered. "There are a few friends I should say hello to, though."

A broad smile formed on Luna's face and Danna saw what had suddenly garnered her interest. Marley was walking towards the bar with her own engaging smile.

"Hey, you." Marley tilted her head. "Danna?"

"First time in Sisters," Luna explained.

Marley nodded. "Okay. Should I be keeping this little tidbit to myself?"

"Here you are. The perfect mojito. Enjoy." Chancy slid the drink in front of Danna and then placed a bottle of water in front of Luna.

Danna was glad for the interruption. She pulled a credit card from her purse and handed it to Chancy. What did she think about the fact that Luna and Marley worked for Lindy, and now Lindy might hear about her visit to the local lesbian hangout? It was one thing to have an itch scratched. She knew Lindy participated in the upstairs activities, but what would she say if Danna came out to her and admitted she was more likely than not a lesbian.

She must have worn a frown on her face because Marley quickly interjected, "Hey, don't worry. First, you being here doesn't necessarily mean you're a lesbian. Besides, I'd never out someone. It's not my place. I know you and Lindy are close friends and she's our boss. But we have as much discretion about who comes to Sisters as we do about who uses the special services we offer at TWC."

"It's okay. I never really considered this possibility until, well, until my exposure at TWC. I'm still figuring things out. Until I do, I'm not sure telling Lindy anything is appropriate. What would I say anyway? 'Hey, Lindy, thanks to you and your club, I've discovered the joys of lesbian sex and I'm pretty sure I'm a big old dyke'." Danna laughed, attempting to lighten the mood.

Marley's eyes traversed Danna's body. "Nope. Somehow dyke doesn't seem to fit. I'd say you fall squarely into the femme category, like me. Now Luna here, and oh that scrumptious new fix-it gal Janice managed to snag, they definitely fall into the butch category. For them, dyke is a fitting name. I love when those big strong butches use that term. It's been a way to reclaim a previously derogatory label. Although, labels are kind of dangerous nowadays. Everyone seems offended by something. Technically, I am a dyke, but it doesn't seem to fit."

"If you're talking about Alex, she is quite stunning. Too bad she isn't part of the TWC team." Danna took a sip of the refreshing drink. "Mmm, this is good."

"We're working on that." Marley turned her focus toward the bartender.

"Marley, what's your pleasure tonight?" Chancy asked.

"Sounds like the mojito is a hit. I'll take one of those. It looks like Danna and I have the same taste in drinks and women."

Luna grabbed her water and undid the cap, then took a swig. "I don't know if Alex will fit at TWC. She was a bit guarded when we had our little chat. She's not as open and friendly as the staff we have now."

Marley chuckled. "Don't tell me you're jealous. Competition for the tall, sexy, butch slot at TWC?"

Luna narrowed her eyes. "Envy is not a productive emotion. Nor is competition. I was simply stating an observation. You know I agreed with you that she might be worth pursuing, especially with her background and skillset."

"She seemed friendly enough to me." Marley winked at Danna. "Hey Chancy, is Janice still working that fine butch specimen to the bone? Perhaps we can offer better hours and pay."

Chancy was pulling together the ingredients for another mojito and turned around when she heard her name.

"Janice has a wicked temper; I wouldn't recommend getting on her bad side." Chancy took a step, leaned in, and whispered, "Just be patient. The way Alex has been like a whirling dervish, she'll have everything in top shape in no time. Then Janice would be more inclined to let her work for you part-time. I think she wants to keep her in Atlanta and I get the feeling Alex doesn't do idle."

"Good to know," Marley remarked. "I can bide my time and be patient, but what if Janice decides to make her a bartender."

"No way. I'm not giving up my drink-making secrets. Besides, I don't think mixologist is something she's very interested in. Sexologist is more up her alley."

Marley arched her eyebrow. "Hmm, maybe she's more open than Luna thinks. What else can you tell us about the mysterious Alex?"

Danna was particularly interested in this little tidbit and leaned in for Chancy's answer.

"I'm not sure this is giving up any confidences Alex wouldn't want y'all knowing. Don't be mad or anything, but Helena kinda let the cat out of the bag and you know it's totally cool with me. I promise I'm very discreet. Anyway," Chancy paused and then continued, "Alex used to work at some fancy spa in Nevada. She knows about this special thing called a Nuru massage. Y'all know that prostitution is legal in Nevada, right?"

Marley frowned. "I hate that terminology. Prostitution has a very negative connotation. Oh, and don't worry about giving up Alex's secrets. She already told Luna all about Nevada."

Chancy smacked her head. "Oh yeah, that's right, y'all approached her, or Luna did. Sneaky, sneaky, behind Janice's back." Chancy chuckled. "Hey, sorry about using the word prostitution. I don't know the proper word."

"Pleasure worker. That has a nice ring to it. I'll bet the professionals at the spa in Nevada never referred to themselves as prostitutes and they were undoubtedly consummate professionals. I don't even like the term *sex worker*. It cheapens the profession. What pleasure workers do is create a sensual experience. Society needs to get the fuck over their Victorian roots and stop thinking women shouldn't enjoy intimacy in whatever setting they deem appropriate," Marley lectured.

Chancy raised her fist in the air. "Speak it, sista."

"It's hard to overcome a strict upbringing. I'm working hard on it, but it isn't easy," Danna admitted.

"Sorry, Danna, we're probably shocking you right now." Luna finally entered the discussion.

"Not at all. I find this conversation refreshing. I also want to be the first one to know if you manage to recruit Alex."

Luna crossed her arms over her chest. "Will I be losing you as a client if we do?"

"Um...oh dear...I'm sorry, Luna. I think I'll shut up now," Danna sputtered.

Marley backhanded Luna. "Stop being so territorial. You'll have plenty of clients. Competition isn't always bad."

CHAPTER NINE

Danna had been back at Sisters the next night hoping to catch a glimpse of Alex and maybe garner an introduction, but she'd felt pathetic and lonely sitting on that bar stool. Getting comfortable with being around lesbians was one thing, truly fitting in was an entirely different matter.

Alex had strolled behind the bar a couple of times to replenish supplies, but Danna was too shy to introduce herself. She'd let several opportunities pass, including one where Alex seemed to look directly at her. The glorious smile transformed her face into something ethereal. A quick nod from Alex sent Danna's heart into overdrive. She was smitten with a woman who was probably nearly half her age. Age was such a difficult thing to pinpoint these days, but Danna knew Alex was much younger—maybe mid-twenties, she guessed. She had decided to leave early on that second night. Membership had its privileges, so she had scheduled an appointment for a massage and maybe more that very next morning. She hoped the spa would help her to work out the stress of coming to terms with her sexuality.

On her way to the spa the following morning, Danna spied Alex walking along Peachtree street. A healthy dose of insanity overtook her usual measured approach to life and she pulled over on the busy road. Danna didn't care when the car behind her beeped with an angry message about why her spontaneous decision was completely deranged. She hit the button for her electric window and stretched her head as she called out to Alex.

"Do you need a ride somewhere?"

Alex had turned her head when the angry blaring horn startled her as she strolled along. She appeared to size up Danna as she crouched down and peered into the car. A slow smile formed on her face. "Not really. I was checking out the neighborhood without a specific plan. I have a whole day to myself and didn't know what to do to keep from getting into trouble."

Danna made a split-second decision. If this gorgeous hunk of woman would agree, Danna would cancel her appointment at the spa and play personal tour guide. "Hop in. I'll show you around and hopefully keep you out of trouble." She quickly reached for the knob on her radio to turn down the music from the satellite station.

Alex shrugged and opened the passenger door. "Well, that's no fun. I prefer not to get in trouble by myself, but reeling someone else into the mayhem, now that's an entirely different thing." Her lips turned up into a rogue smile.

Danna chuckled. "We haven't officially met. I'm Danna and up until now I've been too self-conscious to introduce myself at the bar. I'm going against the grain today and doing something completely out of character." *Oh dear, I am making a total spectacle of myself.*

"I know who you are." Alex offered her hand. "I'm Alex and I'm very happy you decided to..." Alex swiveled her head. "Uh, you might want to either put on your flashers or pull back out into the street. I didn't realize Atlanta drivers were so impatient. I thought the South was more relaxed. I don't think they like us getting to know one another in the middle of a busy lane."

Laughing, Danna answered, "Quite right." She quickly shook Alex's hand and then instantly brought it back to her steering wheel. She flipped on her turn signal.

After Danna had eased back onto the street, Alex asked, "So where are we going?"

"I could use another cup of coffee or a latte and I have a hankering for one of the Perky Bean's heavenly scones. Shall we start there?"

"Sounds like a plan. I don't think we'll cause a ruckus getting coffee and pastries. I have a healthy appreciation for food that is not exactly good for me, so I hope this scone is filled with a grotesque amount of sugar and empty calories."

"Oh, it is. That's what makes it so delicious."

Danna refocused on driving as she continued down the busy street.

Alex interrupted her concentration after a brief lull in their surface chatter. "Can I ask you something?"

Danna nodded. "Uh, sure, I guess."

"It isn't anything too personal. Well, maybe it is, but I'll ask anyway because I've been trying to figure you out. I was wondering why someone like you would come to

Sisters. The bar doesn't seem to fit unless you're looking for a quick hook-up. I know you are somehow connected to that fancy spa Marley and Luna work at. I guessed you were a member. That fits. So why would you need to come to Sisters for a hook-up?"

Danna was glad she wasn't drinking or eating anything at that moment because she would surely have choked on any food and drink in her mouth.

"Um a hook-up. I didn't realize that women in their forties could do that. No. Let's just say I've had an epiphany since I took advantage of all of the offerings at the Trophy Wives Club."

"You figured out you're a lesbian. That makes sense. What about your husband?"

"I'm a widow. So that won't be a complication I'll have to navigate, which is a very good thing. I'm having a hard enough time trying to come to grips with this recent realization. Sisters is supposed to be my entrance into this new world in a way that won't create too much angst. But honestly, I don't feel comfortable sitting at the bar by myself while I sip on Chancy's latest creation. She really is a very talented mixologist."

"I'm sorry. I didn't know about your late husband. I hope I won't offend you with my next inquiry. Are you looking for a partner?"

"I don't know. I suppose on a subconscious level, I am. I need to get comfortable in my own lesbian skin first."

"My friend, Betty, would like to find a partner too. She's more mature as well. I don't think Sisters is the place to meet your soulmate. That's my humble opinion."

Danna groaned. "More mature. That's code for old."

"Oh, God, no. I didn't mean it like that. You're

gorgeous, but I can tell you aren't one of those twenty-something airheads who keep shoving their phone numbers into my hand. I want to tell them I don't own a cell phone to call. Instead I just smile and accept their little pieces of paper and other creative ways to give me their number. I did manage to score a baseball cap with a phone number."

"I'd recommend stopping at the 'you're gorgeous' statement and I'll forget the rest."

"Shit." Alex scrubbed her face with her hand. "Everything is coming out all wrong. I don't know how to act around sexy, cultured women, other than when I'm hired to—"

"It's okay, Alex, I overheard a small tidbit about you. Chancy was kind of bragging about your skills. I'm sure Chancy told you all about the Trophy Wives Club. Marley is very interested in employing you."

"Chancy. I'm gonna smack that girl. Not that I'm embarrassed about my work at the Ranch, but it wasn't her story to tell. Besides, I already told Luna all about it and I kind of figured she told Marley. She said she was gonna fill her in. Maybe Chancy knows who she can confide in and who she can't. If y'all want that fancy club to stay under the radar, the members probably shouldn't engage in idle pillow talk."

"Pillow talk?" Danna scrunched up her face.

"Never mind. I just think it wouldn't be a good thing to broadcast everything about TWC. Some people aren't as discreet as I am."

"Good reminder to us all. Obviously, I'm the last person to pass judgment. Honestly, if you want to work at TWC using the skills you have from your past experience at the Ranch, you should go for it."

"You are like the third person who has suggested I pursue that opportunity. I don't know. Trouble seems to follow me and I wouldn't want to bring the law to their doorstep. Hey, new topic. Are Marley and Luna a couple?"

Danna's heart sank. She'd asked the question with a hint of interest, other than idle curiosity. Danna decided to answer as honestly as she could. "No, but they haven't realized their feelings for one another yet. I wonder how they will possibly navigate those interesting waters. I do question how pleasure workers manage to have relationships without jealousy or other nasty emotions getting in the way."

"Trust. It's all about trust. A partner has to understand pleasure work is a profession and the sexual touch and satisfaction given to a client is different than the intimacy shared with a partner. I had a friend who managed to make it work, so I know it's possible. Right now I'm not looking for anything long term. I have too many other complicated things in my life to resolve, so it isn't in the cards for me until I know I can put down roots. It's not possible right now. Having to abruptly leave a place is always in the back of my mind. I can't afford the luxury of allowing myself to fall in love."

"That's sad. I suppose it isn't any sadder than my current situation. We're kindred spirits, but for very different reasons. I wonder, can you have a close friendship with one of your clients without the emotions getting in the way?"

"Yeah, you can. I have. Although, that's what has always gotten me in trouble before. I don't know you well enough to tell that story." Alex winked.

"Perhaps we can change that."

CHAPTER TEN

Alex was whistling when she walked back inside Sisters after Danna had dropped her at the front door. She'd impulsively asked the attractive woman if she would like to have dinner sometime on Alex's day off. Danna had readily agreed.

She'd started to climb the stairs to her apartment when she ran into Janice.

"You seem to be in a good mood tonight." Janice tilted her head and furrowed her brow.

"You say that like I'm some grump master normally," Alex answered.

"Oh, no, you aren't dour faced at all, just not quite as peppy. The whistling and bounce in your step screams crush, as in crushing on some woman. So, which one of our lucky regulars caught your eye? The one who gave you her phone number on a ball cap? I must admit, that was very creative."

Alex laughed. "No, but I do like having another cap for those days when I can't get my unruly hair to cooperate."

"Then who?"

Alex furrowed her brow. She wasn't sure she should be revealing the pleasant time she'd had with Danna. Somehow it didn't seem right to cheapen the day with what she considered lesbian locker-room talk.

"Hey, I thought you said I should stay clear of the customers?"

Janice laughed. "Wow, you actually took what I said seriously. I'm not sure I have the power, or right, to stop people from falling for one another. I was referring to a cavalier, love-'em-and-leave-'em attitude. That shit don't fly, but a possible relationship is fine. Who am I to dictate who someone can fall in love with?"

"Whoa, slow that speeding train down. Um, I just had a nice afternoon is all. I was checking out this new city I've landed in. I like it so far." Alex grinned.

"Well whatever is causing your new-found delight, it looks good on you. And whoever it is, she's a very lucky woman. Hey, you aren't going to move out and decide to leave Sisters, are you? I know Selene said it would be okay for you to take another part-time position because you've done an amazing job with all our fix-it projects, but we would hate to lose you. I know for a fact that having you walk through the bar and help restock gets us more business. Word is out about the hot new barback at Sisters."

Alex's face flushed. "Don't worry. No matter what, I won't forget what you and Selene did for me. Besides, no one has made me an offer of another job and I don't suspect they would want to take a chance on someone without the proper papers. I'm not expecting anything to come of it, even though I have to admit I was flattered by their interest. From what I hear, that fancy spa will have enough trouble keeping everyone happy without taking on someone who might be undocumented. If a snooty client starts doing a little racial profiling and has strong feelings about immigration...well, I'm toast and so are they. Working at a bar, no offense, seems a lot safer. The clientele here are...let's just say not the high-society types who are likely to have conservative leanings."

"True, but I know Lindy and she's not like that. I don't think she would allow...how did you describe them? Oh yeah, the snooty types, into her precious business venture. Lindy and Marley are both good people."

"Whatever you say. As tempting as it might be to work there part-time, I don't know. It seems like a risk to me. If I ever did get an offer, I'd have to think about the pros and cons. In the meantime, maybe I could learn how to mix drinks or something. That way when all the fix-it work is complete, I won't remain idle and can help out. I'm not sure how great I would be as a waitress, but I could fill in there, too."

"We better look at the waitressing gig because Chancy gets a bit territorial about her skills at mixing those fancy drinks. She's a sweetheart until you mess with that part of her job. I tried to tell her we needed a backup for when she's not here and in case she gets hit by a bus. Her answer was that she already trained Terry. Everyone knows Terry pales in comparison and the real mixologist is Chancy. The women usually order an alternative beverage like a beer or cider on the nights that Chancy isn't here."

Alex chuckled. "That sounds a bit like Chancy. I'll

bet I could get her to soften her stance on that."

"Go for it. Good luck with that, but don't say I didn't warn you. She's a little spitfire. You'd probably do well with waitressing though. The tips would be great. All you have to do is flash those pearly whites of yours and, in combination with those smoky bedroom eyes, they'll be tossing twenties your way without a second thought."

Alex was embarrassed when her boss talked about her appeal to the young women who frequented Sisters, so she changed the subject. "Do you have anything that needs my attention?"

"Actually, we do. The air conditioning unit has been making funny noises. Can you please take a look at it? I'd hate for it to go out in the middle of a busy night. I don't relish the possibility we might need to replace the whole damn thing. So, whatever you can do to extend the life of the unit, we would be eternally grateful. I know I need to budget for a replacement, but I was hoping to eke another year out of this one."

"No problem, I'm good at extending the life of various systems. Where I come from, that was the name of the game. Most people did not have the money to replace expensive equipment, so we did a good business keeping things running way beyond their normal life. Sometimes I had to get a little creative. If you don't care about how things look in those hidden areas no one sees anyway, I am definitely your gal."

"I know you are, Alex, and we really do appreciate your skills. Enough to figure out a way to keep you, no matter what that takes."

"Okay, let me change into something I can get grease on and I'll take a look."

†

Danna unlocked the front door to her beautiful Victorian estate with its lush gardens out back and the flourish of color in the front that outlined the majestic home. Although she would spend time in the garden, pulling weeds and planting new flowers and bushes, it was too much for one person. She'd given in to hiring a gardener. She felt a wave of guilt for her privileged life because she knew that was not Alex's experience. The gap between rich and poor was widening. That was a fact that left her squirming when she was faced with those realities. Most of the time, except with her work, she tended to interact with those in her socioeconomic sphere. Thus the stark differences were invisible in social settings. Today, as Alex and she had danced along the edges of their personal experiences in life, Danna needed to face those uncomfortable realities. *Am I a snob because all of my friends are exactly like me?*

Alex was not only a breath of fresh air to her mundane existence, but she was charming, intelligent, and interesting. Like a drug, Danna needed more. She'd told herself she didn't fit in with the crowd at Sisters, with her loneliness amplified when she sat on that bar stool by herself. Yet she decided she had to go back this evening. Catching a glimpse of Alex and maybe having a short conversation would be worth it. Besides, she'd agreed to dinner with Alex, and they hadn't quite nailed down those plans, leaving the date and time open.

Danna glanced at her shiny marble floor in the spacious foyer and felt a sudden wave of nausea. She didn't like this opulence she'd found herself taking for granted. Moving into the large kitchen with the sterile, stainless-steel appliances, and granite counters, she tossed her handbag on the counter and sighed. She looked at her clothes. She'd perfectly put herself together this morning in a designer outfit that probably cost more than Alex made in a month. She'd dressed to the nines for a massage appointment. How crazy was that? *Screw this.*

Danna grabbed her bag off the counter and decided she needed new clothes. Casual clothes. Jeans that weren't designer. T-shirts or sweatshirts with goofy sayings. She was going to head to a discount clothing store and find something, anything, under a hundred dollars for an entire outfit, including socks and undergarments. Or at least close to that amount. She would proudly wear those new duds, and maybe this time when she sat on that bar stool, she wouldn't feel so out of place.

On her way out, she retrieved her cell phone from her bag and called Tanya. "What are you doing right now?... I need help... I want to find an outfit to wear to the bar tonight that won't have me looking like a debutante at a pig pickin'... Oh, and I'm putting a spending limit on it... A hundred dollars... Yes, I am perfectly serious... I have my reasons... Thanks, Tanya. If you give me your address, I'll come and get you... Oh, yes, I'd love for Martin to come and help out. I might need the two of you anyway."

†

Danna crinkled her nose as she stood in front of the famous discount store. She'd never shopped here before. Perhaps she could claim a certain amount of nobility over that fact, considering the store's terrible reputation for the treatment of their workers and the fact no union had ever

111

managed to organize any of their stores across the US.

"Are you sure about this?" Danna asked.

"Well, you sort of clipped our wings a little with the spending cap. Unless we go to a second hand store, your options are limited," Tanya answered.

"What about that fruit republic store. Won't they have clothes that a respectable lesbian might wear to the bar? Have either of you ever shopped here before?"

"Uh, no, but..." Martin began.

"Okay, I'm amending the rules. Perhaps we can increase the limit, just a tad, but not to anything extravagant. I still want clothes that will allow me to fit in better with the crowd. I'd rather not look like a Goth at a pep rally."

"Impressive," Tanya noted.

Danna scrunched her face in confusion. "What?"

Tanya chuckled. "That you'd even know Goths exist."

"Funny. Okay I haven't led *that* sheltered of a life."

"Says the person who wears designer duds to a massage appointment," Tanya quipped.

Danna stuck out her tongue. "For your information, I ended up spending the day with a lovely young woman. I was grateful for the fact I'd decided not to throw on yoga pants and a sweatshirt."

"You don't own yoga pants or sweatshirts. But I must say, I do like this new playful side. And, dish please. Who is this new woman?" Tanya grabbed her arm and began pulling Danna back in the direction of her BMW.

Danna's face flushed as she sputtered, "Um, just a person I ran into that works at Sisters."

"Hmm, let me guess. She's the one you want to impress and you think that by dressing more appropriate for the venue, you'll change her perception of you. Yeah, this outfit" —Tanya waved her hand in front of Danna— "screams snobby socialite."

Danna groaned. "I know. All of a sudden, I hate my life, my clothes, and my vast resources. I would throw the whole lot away..."

"This woman must have gotten to you. Okay, listen. I know the perfect place to go, but we will need to spend more than a hundred dollars. I promise, the outfit will be something that won't have you looking like a ballet dancer at a rodeo." Tanya let go of Danna as they reached her car.

"Okay, we've sufficiently covered enough odd analogies," Danna said.

"You are gonna rock your new outfit. Tanya has great taste when it comes to picking out clothes. I must admit the very first time she shed her rich Southern belle persona and wore those tight jeans, she had me salivating. Just because we're a bit older now does not mean we have to wear grannie pannies or jeans that cover our navels." Martin opened the passenger door for Tanya and grinned.

Danna slipped into the driver's seat and looked at Tanya, then swiveled her head to Martin who had climbed into the back. "You do know that I've adopted both of you as my personal mentors into lesbianland."

"We will eagerly accept our new role," Tanya answered.

"Yes indeed. Do you think we'll get a new microwave instead of a toaster oven?" Martin quipped.

"Blender. I want a fancy new blender." Tanya reached back to her wife and patted her knee.

"I'll buy you both." Danna chuckled.

†

Alex was leaning against the bar and chatting with Chancy when she saw Danna come in with two women who were laughing while whispering in Danna's ear after a quick glance in Alex's direction. Danna's face had turned a bright shade of red, but that wasn't what caused Alex to gulp. Alex didn't have a type of woman because she thought all women were beautiful—big, small, muscular, dainty. But the way Danna filled out her jeans had Alex looking at her in a whole new light. Earlier, it had been Danna's easy way and hint of loneliness that had attracted Alex, coupled with a sense that Danna was a genuinely kind individual. Alex wanted to get to know her beyond something superficial. Trivial tended to exist when their only interaction might be at Sisters.

Danna's light brown hair sat loosely on her shoulders, touching the top of her perfectly fitted tunic. Alex liked how Danna's hair framed her delicate face. When she smiled, Alex loved seeing her laugh lines mold perfectly with the dimples on both sides. The tiny crinkles at the corners of her eyes betraying her age were something that aroused rather than turned Alex off. She wanted to map every line with her index finger and pepper her face with tiny, butterfly kisses. What really sucked Alex in were Danna's expressive green eyes. If eyes could display intelligence, she was sure Danna's fit the bill.

"Earth to Alex, earth to Alex, anyone there?"

"Huh?" Alex turned her head to Selene who, she thought, had some kind of stealth powers to allow her to sneak up on Alex unnoticed.

Selene turned in the direction of the women making their way to the bar. "Ah, I take it one of those lovely women approaching was your tour guide today."

Alex narrowed her gaze.

Selene grinned. "Janice told me about your date today."

"I better go see what they want to drink. I promise to give them extra special attention and make the best damn drinks to keep them coming back." Chancy winked at Alex.

Alex chose to ignore the comment. "Did you need me to take a look at something else? Is the air conditioner not working like it should?"

"Oh, no, nothing like that. I got a return call from Rosie, your trucker friend. She grumbled about not having your number and you leaving a message to call my phone, which was fine with me," Selene quickly added.

Selene had garnered Alex's full attention now as she reluctantly turned her gaze away from Danna and the women walking alongside her. "Does she know where Betty is?"

Selene smiled. "She sure does. Apparently, Betty did something very uncharacteristic. Some might even say swoon-worthy."

Alex arched her eyebrow. "Betty?"

"Did she ever talk about a woman she was close to that had moved away? Someone in desperate need of a new direction in life?"

"Come to think of it, she did. We talked about a lot of things. Since I confided in her, she opened up to me. I had to prod her a little. I told her about my past and how I'd gotten myself in trouble. After she asked me a strange question, I encouraged her to talk about it. She wanted to know if I thought it was wrong to break up a lesbian couple if one was beating on the other. You know, if I believed doing that was being a home-wrecker or something. I told her no, because straights don't corner the market on domestic abuse and it's always wrong. I was supposed to see if I could find out where Tam took this woman that Betty developed feelings for. I never got around to asking about this Tam person."

"Tam was a real piece of work. We wanted to ban her from the bar because she was always causing trouble, but Betty would step in and promise to smooth things over and settle her," Selene said.

"So maybe Betty found her own way to track down the damsel in distress," Alex suggested.

"Bingo. She drove cross-country to rescue this woman. The way Rosie tells it, she thinks Betty might have saved the woman's life. Punching bag was putting it lightly. Betty's with her at the hospital right now. I think she's planning on bringing her back to Atlanta after she heals enough to make the journey. If you ask me, love is in the air."

Alex nodded her approval. "Good. I sure hope so. Betty might need this woman every bit as much as the woman needs her. I do hope they are a match made in heaven. I'm going to make my way to Betty's as soon as I know she's back in Atlanta so I can meet this person. Do you think I could borrow your phone and call Rosie myself? It's not that I don't trust your information, but I'd like to talk to her."

"Sure, Alex. I just thought you'd want to hear the good news right away." Selene gestured to the other end of the bar where the three women had taken seats. "You might as well go on and say hello. One of them hasn't taken her eyes off of you since she walked in."

Alex didn't want to have the barrier of the bar between her and Danna when she approached her to say hello.

"Hey."

Danna blushed. "Hi Alex. These are my friends, Tanya and Martin. Tanya was my roommate at Wellesley and Martin is her wife."

Alex offered her hand. "Alex. Nice to meet you." She shook both their hands and then awkwardly waited for someone to say something else.

"So, I hear the bartender makes a killer mojito, we've ordered three. Too bad you can't join us," Tanya said.

"Oh, um, as good as her drinks are and how great that sounds, I can't because I'm still working," Alex stated.

Selene gracefully slid next to Chancy who was busy making their drinks and interjected, "You know, Alex, you've earned the night off after fixing our air conditioning unit and saving our bacon again. Go on, have a drink with your friends." She waved her hand in the air. "It wouldn't kill me to schlep a few cases to the bar when Chancy runs out, or better yet, get my wife Janice to do it. Might help her tone up those biceps."

Chancy turned her head and said over her shoulder, "You better not say that within earshot of Janice. She's the one with the temper."

"True dat. Go on, I insist." Selene waved her hand in the air. "One drink won't kill you and if you are hell-bent on replenishing the bar when Chancy needs your help, we'll come and get you. We shouldn't deprive all these ladies from ogling over your bulging biceps. Chancy make her a mojito. Light on the alcohol. I don't need a work-related injury."

As Alex was walking over to the table where Danna, Tanya, and Martin had settled, she saw an attractive older woman enter Sisters. She was dressed in what appeared to be very expensive designer clothes. Alex thought she looked out of place until she watched her approach the bar and saw Chancy's eyes light up. *Ah, the infamous Helena.*

†

Danna tugged on her shirt, trying desperately to pull it down so that her top would cover most of her forty-two-year-old tushy, even though it was nearly as taut as when she was in her twenties. Her time at the club and Luna's fitness routine had worked wonders on getting her back in shape. She was amazed by the quick results. The targeted exercises had made a world of difference to her most problematic spots. Danna still felt self-conscious in an outfit she was sure someone her age didn't often wear. Tanya and Martin had insisted it looked good. They'd talked her into the purchase and then waited in her living room while she showered and dressed. Tanya and Martin were not going to let her go to Sisters alone. They were dying to check out who had caught Danna's eye.

As they walked in the door and she'd reluctantly told them who Alex was, Tanya had whispered, "Jeez, Danna, you picked butch royalty. If I wasn't married, I'd ask her to lubricate my love cave."

Martin had quickly retorted, "Lubricate your love cave? Where did you hear that ridiculous saying? I'd like to think I'm butch royalty, but even I wouldn't mind if she shined my pleasure button."

They'd both laughed at their raucous jokes and Danna blushed, wondering how she thought this was a good idea. Then she'd caught Alex's wide-eyed stare and smiled. The owner, Selene, had captured Alex's attention and thankfully she'd turned away from Danna and her friends while they made their way to the bar. It didn't take Alex long to step away from inside the bar and approach her and her friends after they'd all ordered mojitos from Chancy. Danna had raved about how good the cocktail was and her friends seemed excited to try the refreshing drink.

Danna wasn't sure how everything had evolved so quickly, but she found herself sitting next to Alex with Tanya and Martin grinning like fools at her across the table. Tonight was turning into a bushel of surprises. She thought she was seeing things when she'd noticed another TWC patron, Helena, approach the bar. She nearly busted out laughing as she watched a few seconds of the interaction between the young bartender and the much-respected woman in Atlanta's high society. Now she understood Alex's "pillow talk" comment. There was no doubt in her mind that Helena and Chancy were having a torrid affair. *Good for Helena.* Danna felt a twinge of jealousy that Helena had managed to act so brazenly, as if she didn't have a care in the world. Tanya interrupted Danna's internal dialogue when she started talking with Alex.

"So, Alex, where you from?" Tanya asked pleasantly.

Alex took on a guarded look as she forced a smile. "Oh, here and there. Nowhere special really. Just arrived in Atlanta and I was happy to land a job at Sisters. I like it. As you can see, my bosses are very nice."

Tanya shared a look with Martin, but took the hint not to pursue the topic further. "Well, technically, Atlanta is in the South and lord knows the South has a negative reputation regarding our treatment of the LGBTQ community, but Atlanta is very cosmopolitan and it's home," Tanya answered wistfully.

"I might not be very cosmopolitan or have a college

education, but I do know when someone wasn't born here. Where are you from, Martin?" Alex asked.

"Paris. Tanya and I have been living in France for the past eighteen years. The officials directed me to apply for a green card, even though we are married. France does not have the same, how do you say, hang-ups as you Americans. Your immigration system is very complicated," Martin stated. Her accent grew heavier as she spit out the last part in apparent frustration. "I suppose it is a good thing I never tried to live here illegally. That would have added a whole new labyrinth to navigate."

"Nice word, honey, but labyrinth, really?"

"Is it not the correct word?" Martin asked.

Tanya leaned in and kissed her wife's cheek, smiling with affection.

"You're white and rich, I'll bet it will be a walk in the park for you," Alex stated without malice in her voice. "I hope you don't run into any problems. I'm sure Danna appreciates re-connecting with you. Now she can visit the bar more often and not feel so out of place, sitting on one of those hard bar stools, nursing a drink. She brightens up the place, so I hope she'll continue to come here."

"I'm glad I ran into Danna the other day. We had a blast shopping today." Tanya giggled.

"Ah, the new clothes. I wondered what inspired the fresh look. I like it. It suits you. Much better than...oh shit, I'm sorry. I shouldn't always say every little thing that pops in my head. It was intended as a compliment."

"No apology necessary. I guess this look" —Danna tugged on the bottom of her tunic again— "is growing on me. I'll admit to feeling like this isn't really an age-appropriate outfit."

"Screw that. Haven't you heard? Forty is the new thirty," Tanya declared. "Besides, those twenty-somethings have not cornered the market on fun, sex, or spontaneity. You are only as old as you feel. Right about now, I feel like having another drink and shaking my ass on the dance floor. I'm going to show those youngsters how to party."

"Older women have everything on these young women, style, looks, experience, you name it," Alex remarked.

"Aren't you in that twenty-something category?" Martin asked.

"Hardly." Alex grinned. "I turned thirty last month."

Twelve years difference. Okay, that isn't so bad. If Helena can do it, why can't I?

"Oh, well, then you are positively ancient." Tanya laughed. "If forty is the new thirty and thirty is the new twenty." She shuddered. "I'd hate to be twenty-something and have anyone think of me as a snot nosed adolescent."

"But, darling, is that not what the new generation is? Snot-nosed, spoiled rotten, adolescents who think the world owes them a 100-k starting salary right out of college." Martin sipped on her drink.

"You've been listening to our American friends too much. Now you're starting to talk like them," Tanya gently chastised. "Over-generalizations are dangerous. I need to remember that myself and not fall into that same trap I'm always complaining about when my mother starts on her rant about women like us."

Danna wondered what her own mother would say about her burgeoning feelings. She'd only talked with her once since the funeral and the conversation was strained and uncomfortable. Based on that conversation, she doubted her mother would embrace her recent epiphany or her interest in Alex.

"There are many things I like about America but I have to admit that I prefer France. If I did not love my Tanya so much, I would not go through all the hoopla to become a citizen. We could have easily stayed in France. I have learned much about your immigration system. Even though Tanya's mother is, how you say it, a first-class bitch, my Tanya could not stay away when she learned of her father's ailing health."

Danna glanced at Alex who looked like she wanted to ask Martin something but wasn't quite sure how to word it. Finally, her voice came out soft and hesitant. "What do you know about the hoops a person has to go through to become a citizen if they are undocumented? Is there a way to accomplish that if someone has been deported?"

Tanya gave Alex a sympathetic look. Danna recognized that look from their college days. For as brash as Tanya was, she always seemed to have a soft spot for the downtrodden or those who did not quite fit into Wellesley.

"Unless a person has a criminal record and those crimes are serious, deportation could take years," Tanya said. "The best strategy is to keep fighting until a new, more sympathetic President, moves into office."

Alex's head snapped up. "You mean people are not sent straight back to Mexico when they are caught?"

Tanya furrowed her brow. "No, of course not, but a legal defense can be very costly. For those that have the money, the hearings and process can drag on for many years before the courts make a final determination. Most of the time, the INS agents don't put a lot of effort into undocumented people who've never had a run-in with the law. Unfortunately, sometimes those folks are unwittingly caught in a snare. With the right assistance, they can manage to escape deportation."

Danna took a chance and covered Alex's hand. "Alex, do you have friends or family that are in trouble?"

Alex seemed to weigh her options and was probably deciding whether these three strangers could be trusted. Words didn't flow from her mouth, only a simple nod as her eyes glistened with unshed tears.

"I'd like to help. Will you let me?" Danna asked.

Alex opened her mouth and then stalled.

"Of course I do have one condition." Danna smiled as Alex frowned. "You asked me to dinner and I'm going to hold you to it. We can talk more about how I can help."

"I might have to work a few more shifts so I have the funds to take you somewhere nice."

Danna started to answer, but Selene interrupted the conversation when she walked up to the table and put her hand on Alex's shoulder. "Hey Alex, do you mind getting a couple of cases from the back? Chancy is swamped at the bar and I was planning to help her out for a few minutes. I hate to disturb you, but we kind of need you right now."

Alex popped up. "Sure thing, boss." She looked down at Danna and smiled. "I'll see you ladies later. Um, I don't have a phone, but I can borrow Selene's if you give me your number."

"I'll drop it off before we leave," Danna answered.

CHAPTER ELEVEN

True to her word, Danna had dropped off a card with her cell phone number on it and Alex was flipping the card in her fingers. Her head was spinning with the new information about immigration. She had assumed her parents were somewhere in Mexico, maybe living with her papa's sister whom he sent money to every month without fail. Alex had lamented over the fact that she hadn't paid closer attention to the address. After she'd found her way to the Ranch, she figured since her aunt lived in a small town in central Mexico that someday she'd find a way to bring them back. Money. Lots of money is all it took. There was a phone at the shop, but even if her papa managed to go back and keep the business open, he wouldn't be there now. No sense in asking to borrow Selene's phone to call. Besides, maybe the INS agents were setting a trap, waiting for Alex to call. She was hesitant to bring a bunch of trouble crashing down on Selene and Janice's heads after they'd been nice enough to give her a job without papers.

She hadn't promised her loyalty to Selene and Janice lightly. But now everything had changed. If her papa and mama were still in Texas waiting on a hearing and they needed money, she was determined to make some quick dough at the Trophy Wives Club. She had the skills and knew that generous tips were a walk in the park if she provided them with that extra special attention they craved.

Alex began pacing her small studio apartment. She was like a caged tiger. She shoved Danna's card in her pocket and took several long strides to her futon which she hadn't unfolded into a bed yet. Yanking open the small drawer attached to the combination side table and nightstand, Alex retrieved the card Marley had given her. It was late and she should really wait to call her. Another night wouldn't make that much difference, would it? Either they'd give her a job or they wouldn't.

She wondered if Danna would think less of her if she decided to ask Marley for a job. Could she offer Danna those special services without wanting more? It was a conundrum she couldn't worry about right now because her first priority was making quick money and traveling back to Texas to see for herself. Leaving in such a hurry had not afforded her the opportunity to learn the score and that was something she thought she would regret for the rest of her life. Eight long months had passed. What a waste of time. The excruciating feeling of loss hit her nearly every day. She missed her papa and mama. They'd been her whole world.

She was definitely out of her element when she'd jumped into the back of her neighbor's truck. They'd taken her to the main road where Alex caught a break. An almost full car of college students was heading to Las Vegas for a long weekend. She kept the conversation low key as they traveled the highway and talked about things that Alex couldn't relate to. When she'd eventually landed in Nevada, the bright lights of Vegas overwhelmed her so much she couldn't breathe. She was out of her element with all the flashiness and looked for a way to escape from something so foreign to her. It was simply dumb luck that she'd ended up at the Ranch.

The only good to come of this was learning to fend for herself and make her way in the world without the crutch of her family. She'd definitely ventured beyond her small town and the periodic trips to Laredo. Now she liked visiting new places. Atlanta was nice. She wouldn't have minded settling here, but now that was out of the question if her parents had remained in Texas.

A knock on her door startled her. Sisters closed at one, so surely Selene or Janice didn't need her. Hopefully, the fact that she'd been distracted for the remainder of the evening and had messed up a few times, didn't mean she was about to lose her job. All her thoughts about Danna, her family, and screwing up at work jumbled together. Alex was on the verge of a major panic attack. Too many important things were weighing heavily on her.

With a fair amount of trepidation, Alex pulled open her door. "Danna?"

"I'm sorry, this was probably a really bad idea. You looked a little lost tonight after you left and I...uh...it's late. I'll go."

"Wait, don't go." Alex turned and waved Danna inside. She led Danna to her futon and gestured for her to take a seat. Alex wasn't necessarily embarrassed about her humble apartment, but she wondered what Danna thought about the place. "It isn't much, but it sure beats a tent under an overpass. I don't have much to offer. Sorry about that. I know that sounds crazy, living above a bar and all. I might have bottled water. I could brew some coffee if you'd like."

She slipped Marley's card into her pocket along with Danna's. For some reason she felt guilty about the two cards mingling together. Marley was a beautiful woman and Alex had entertained the idea of asking her to go for a drink until she'd picked up on a vibe from Luna. She did not relish the idea of pissing off the other woman who might have some influence over who they hired at TWC. Especially now.

"Water might be a good idea. I'm afraid my friends talked me into a third mojito. Even though we were at the bar for several hours catching up with one another, it was still more than I usually imbibe in. I'd rather not feel the effects of dehydration from too much alcohol and not enough water. Thanks."

Alex pulled open the door to her refrigerator to retrieve two bottles of water and then handed one to Danna who had taken a seat on the futon. She looked uncomfortable and out of place as she sat on the edge and kept her hands in her lap. Her erect posture revealed a stiffness that Alex wanted to massage away. A sudden thought of giving Danna one of those sensual Japanese Nuru massages appeared without warning. "So, it must be pretty important for you to knock on my door at" —Alex glanced at the clock on the microwave— "two in the morning."

"I suppose it seems odd I was watching you so closely tonight. Close enough to determine you might need a friend. I promise, I'm not some crazy stalker. My offer to help was sincere. I had a lovely day today and feel this strange pull toward you. A tug I can't seem to control." Danna shook her head. "It's crazy. I know. When I returned home tonight, I felt this intense need to come back and make sure you were doing okay."

"I suppose it wasn't my finest hour when I dropped that whole rack of beer glasses. I told Selene I'd pay for their replacements and she just brushed me off. Said something like I'd saved them one hundred times the amount with all my creative solutions to their equipment issues."

"I've no doubt you are an extremely valuable employee."

Alex twisted open the cap on her bottle of water and sat next to Danna. "You know, you're making me nervous right now because you seem so uncomfortable. I'll get a handle on my jumbled emotions if you promise me you'll relax, sit back on this semi-comfortable futon, and we can talk into the wee hours. I'm guessing you don't have to be anywhere at the butt crack of dawn, right? No job?"

"I don't have regular hours, no. Besides, I make a rule of pampering myself on the weekends. Normally it does wonders to help relax me, but unfortunately you do make me nervous, Alex. And I didn't keep my massage appointment today. I'm not used to being in the company of someone so beautiful that isn't being paid to, uh, make me feel nice. I was beyond flattered when you asked me to go to dinner. I kind of felt like some ridiculous cougar. Twelve years is a lot, but I suppose it could be worse. I thought you were nearly twenty years my junior."

"Can I ask you something?"

"Sure."

"Do you think I would have a chance at getting

another part-time job at TWC? I could use the money and the potential at the spa is much greater than tips from waitressing. That is, if they still decide to train me after the catastrophe that happened tonight."

"I'm certain they would hire you. I can make sure that happens if you'd like. Lindy is a good friend of mine and all I would need to do is tell her they should hire you and you're in."

"I can't ask you to stick your neck out for me like that. Besides, I might have a small problem with having the right papers to work for a fancy club."

"You didn't ask, I offered. You let me worry about the finer details like proper documentation to work. Alex, I hope you know, you can tell me anything and I'd never judge you for it."

"Marley gave me her number, but I don't feel right using Selene's phone to call her."

"Oh that's right, I do believe you are the last woman on this planet who doesn't own a cell phone."

"Doubtful. You don't run in the same circles that I do."

Danna frowned. "I'm being a snob. I didn't mean that to sound so..."

"It's okay. I'd probably get one if I had a bunch of cash to throw away, but I don't and it isn't practical. I'd only ever use it to call you, Marley, my papa's shop, and maybe Betty to make sure she's okay. Oh, and Rosie, too. I'd like to keep in touch with her."

"Who's Rosie? Do I have to worry about one more woman capturing your attention? As if the beautiful Marley wasn't enough competition," Danna joked. "I could see Marley giving you her number for more reasons than wanting to hire you, even though I feel confident the lovely Luna has her attention."

Alex shrugged. "I don't know. When Marley's not paying attention, I've seen the way Luna looks at her. If given the chance, she could turn quite possessive. I don't need to buy any more trouble than I seem to get for free."

"And Rosie?"

"She's a trucker who was kind enough to give me a ride. Her heart definitely belongs to another woman. Not that I have a type or anything, but I don't think Rosie could ever be competition even if she wasn't in love with someone else."

"I...uh...I don't know what I'm doing here. I like you, Alex and it's probably no mystery I find you attractive. I've only ever dated men, so I'm not sure how this works. You asked me to dinner. Is that a date or are you being polite because I showed you the sights today? Is there some lesbian dating book I should get?"

Alex erupted in a full belly laugh. *"Lesbians for Dummies.* I'd like to see someone write that."

Danna chuckled. "If they did, I might just buy it." Danna put her hand on Alex's knee. "It's late, so I should go. But I'll swing by tomorrow morning and take you over to see Marley. Face-to-face meetings are much more productive than a simple phone call. How does that sound? Besides, maybe if I am there with you, she won't flirt."

Alex was enjoying the brief connection to Danna as her hand remained on Alex's knee. When she severed the link and stood, Alex wondered if now or ever was the right moment to capture Danna's alluring lips. Earlier, other things had distracted Alex, but with Danna so close the temptation rose to the surface. After following Danna to the door, Danna turned around and Alex decided a friendly hug was safe. She held on, not wanting to disengage and it seemed like Danna didn't wish to let go either. Finally, after she had casually run her hands up and down Danna's back, Alex pressed her lips lightly to Danna's.

"I should be up and moving about by nine. I don't think a full eight hours of sleep is in the cards for me. Feel free to come over any time after nine."

Danna sighed and touched her lips. "Sounds good. I'll bring the coffee and croissants. Remember that favorite place I took you to for the scone? Their croissants are even better. It would be a sin to keep it all to myself."

"Ah, sin, never much worry about that." Alex grinned. "Carpe diem, right? Latin for seize the day. I guess I did pay attention in high school. Although many of my teachers did not appreciate my non-stop questions about every little thing. I learned quickly to shut my mouth. Working in my papa's shop was what was expected of me. Going to college was not something anyone considered, including me."

"Did you want to go to college?"

"Honestly, no. I loved working with my papa."

"I'll bet you are his pride and joy. I can almost see you following him around as a little girl. I'll wager you were adorable." Danna caressed Alex's cheek and leaned in for another kiss. Her hand traveled down Alex's arm before she opened the door and then said, "Goodnight, Alex. I'll see you tomorrow morning."

After Danna left, Alex leaned against the door. *What the hell am I thinking? I can't be starting something I may not be able to finish.* Her blossoming feelings for Danna were a complication she didn't have time for right now. Even if Danna was willing to help her, should she involve Danna in something that could create havoc for her? That wasn't fair to Danna and her cushy life.

Her only attempt at a relationship before hadn't worked out because she wasn't willing to disappoint her parents. She saw how her mama would give her those disapproving looks when she stayed over at her lover's or remained all night with a woman. She never asked questions and Alex never offered any explanations. What kind of message would she give to Danna if she wasn't willing to introduce Danna to her parents?

†

Danna was grinning the entire time as she made her way home. Falling asleep tonight was going to take a great deal of effort in her current state of euphoria. She knew she shouldn't make too much of Alex's brief kiss. It was barely more than a peck. Danna had surprised herself when she initiated the second kiss. Sure, it wasn't anything too risqué, but she'd answered with her own quick kiss.

When she arrived home, the emptiness of her house was a stark reminder of the craving she had to connect with another person. Danna now understood that person had to be a woman. She hoped it would be Alex. A part of her knew she was in trouble. Alex would undoubtedly break her heart. She had too much going on, Danna knew that. Nevertheless, Alex drew Danna into her sphere. Danna thought of a dieter staring inside her refrigerator after someone had stowed three quarters of her favorite pie inside. Lemon meringue.

She forced herself to crawl under the covers after removing all of her clothes. Feeling the soft cotton sheets against her skin might soothe her aching need. Four hours of sleep. That was all she would allow herself before needing to get up, shower, and stop by the Perky Bean to pick up the promised coffee and croissant to die for. All the excitement and perpetual state of arousal around Alex exhausted Danna. She hoped that would help her sleep even though she was exhilarated by tonight's turn of events.

Danna was glad Alex didn't own a cell phone or she might have been tempted to text her and tell her sweet dreams. What an entirely ridiculous thing to do. Especially at her age.

After setting the alarm on her smartphone, Danna settled into her bed and closed her eyes. Sleep came quickly and all too soon her phone was blaring. The temptation to press the snooze button or change the time to the alarm was almost too great until she envisioned Alex's smoldering brown eyes and that casual grin that made Danna's heart flutter.

She groaned when she padded to her master bathroom and her bare feet touched the heated tile floor. The warmth traveled up her body. The mornings could be cold and this small pleasure, although extravagant for most people, was worth every penny. Guilt over her wealth invaded her thoughts again.

Danna pushed away her discomfort and stepped into her glass-enclosed shower. The pulsating spray from the three separate showerheads invigorated her body. Senses teased her into action, and Danna knew a strong cup of coffee would finish the job. She debated for only a second before deciding to call Lindy and grease the skids a bit. Lindy wasn't necessarily a morning person, but she was a good friend and would forgive her for calling so early.

Danna pressed the button on her smartphone and commanded, "Call Lindy." Setting the phone back on the stone counter, she forged ahead when Lindy answered. "Lindy, I know it's early, but this is important... I wanted to bring someone to TWC today that I think would make a perfect addition to your staff... Just hear me out... Yes, Marley has already met her and I believe she's interested... No, she's the new fix-it person at Sisters... Yes, the very attractive butch... Um, I've sort of befriended her, and she could use the extra cash... She's a good person. I can tell from the short time I've known her... And, yes, the women are going to love her. Plus, I understand she has experience providing those special services... So you've heard, huh... Um, no, not exactly... I don't know, early days. I'm trying not to read anything into it... Thanks, Lindy... Yes, I'll bring her with me to the club today."

Danna supposed that was the easy part. She wondered what Marley and Lindy would say when they learned that Alex was undocumented. Alex hadn't come right out and said it, but it didn't take a Nobel Prize winner in neuroscience to figure that out. Soon enough, Alex would have to come right out and say it. The other difficult piece was coming to grips with envisioning Alex's hands, mouth, and whatever else she might deploy over another woman's body. She was already having strong feelings. Would those evolve into feelings of possessiveness or exclusivity? Would she want Alex to provide her with special services and would she schedule future appointments with Luna? What an intricate collection of brambles to sort out. This was an especially thorny situation to wrestle with. There were so many societal mores to overcome, she wouldn't know where to begin.

Danna completed the finishing touches on her light make-up for the day and pulled her hair back for a simple, casual style. Fortunately, she'd purchased several informal outfits yesterday and proceeded to snip off the tags before slipping the jeans and fitted shirt over her body. The buzzing of her phone startled her. It was a little past eight when she pushed the button to answer the call from an unknown number.

"You're still coming over this morning? Right?" Alex's hesitant voice came out through the tiny speaker.

Danna smiled to herself. She wondered who Alex had tracked down this early to borrow a phone and took that as a good sign. She'd gone out of her way to make this call.

"I'm about to walk out my door right now. Be prepared to taste Nirvana. I swear the butter coats the inside of your mouth for the most sensual morning experience a person can hope for from a mere croissant. It's almost better than sex."

Alex's chuckle echoed against the walls of her bathroom when she'd put the phone on speaker. The sound caused a warm feeling to seep deep in Danna's soul.

"I seriously doubt that, so you better hurry if you have any chance at changing my perspective. Now my mouth is watering. I'm looking forward to seeing you and tasting Nirvana."

"I'll be there shortly before nine, I promise. Goodbye, Alex. See you soon. I've got a tight schedule to keep."

"Bye, Danna."

Alex had ended the call and Danna's smile overtook her as she grinned all the way to her BMW. Fiddling with the dial on her radio, she decided to find the NPR station. Keeping up with the morning news was something she looked forward to, even if the ride to Alex's place was short and might not allow her to satisfy her need.

CHAPTER TWELVE

After Danna rapped on the door twice, Alex stood there leaning casually against the wood frame, grinning and letting her eyes roam over Danna. Since Danna had the coffee and croissants in her hands, she couldn't absently smooth down her clothes. Danna knew the nervous habit was her tell. Alex looked confident as her intense eyes made their way to Danna's and held her gaze for several seconds, making the flutter in her gut do a double-time dance.

Alex must have realized she hadn't invited Danna into her studio apartment yet and moved to the side. After Danna took a few steps, Alex offered to help with her morning gifts.

"Sorry, I'm not being very hospitable. Let me take the coffee. You seem a bit possessive over the pastries, so I'm not going to take a chance that you'll slap my hand for taking that bag from you."

Danna laughed. "Sorry, I did say they were positively delectable and the best you'll ever put in your mouth, but I didn't mean to be all territorial."

Alex smirked. "Hmm, the best I'll ever put in my mouth, I seriously doubt that. I can think of a few other things I've put in my mouth and intend to do so again that are ambrosia to a dyke like me."

A rush of arousal traveled down Danna's body, but the flush to her face revealed the newness of flirtation with a woman. "Oh, um..." Danna set the bag on the tiny counter in the compact kitchen.

"I'm sorry that was rude and crude." Alex placed the coffee next to the white bag that Danna had deposited on the Formica. "How about an innocent hello hug?" She opened her arms and Danna folded her body inside, drowning in Alex's tender caress to her back.

After the two women separated, Alex placed a gentle kiss on her lips and then pulled back to study Danna.

"I'm not going to go running for the hills if you deepened the kiss, you know?" Danna smiled.

"I haven't had a whole lot of experience with a high-society lady before, except to, uh..."

Danna shook her head to get that mental picture of Alex pleasuring another woman and decided to put another picture in her head and have her actions match that visual. She reached up and placed her own hand on Alex's cheek and leaned in for a kiss while pressing forward with a compulsive need to thoroughly explore Alex's full lips. Her tongue pushed inside Alex's welcoming mouth as the kiss took on a life of its own. Passion sparked between the women and left Danna breathing heavily after the kiss ended.

"Mmm. Now that was definitely ambrosia. I don't think the pastry you brought is going to come close to what I just experienced."

Danna smacked her arm. "You can't help yourself. Charm oozes from every pore. You better try the croissant before making that bold pronouncement."

"Are you saying you prefer a croissant over—"

"Now don't twist my words." Danna pulled the napkins from the bag and set them on the counter. She laid one croissant on each napkin then sat on one of the stools. Gesturing to the croissant in front of Alex, she commanded, "Eat."

Alex chuckled and took a large bite. "Mmm." After chewing she exclaimed, "God, you weren't kidding. This is positively orgasmic."

"Told you so." Danna pulled off her own small piece and popped it into her mouth, wiping her fingers on her napkin as she chewed and swallowed. The flaky crust melted in her mouth and coated her taste buds with the buttery flavor. "I called Lindy this morning and she's expecting us today. I don't know if they'll do a formal interview or not. I suspect not."

Alex sipped her coffee. "This is pretty good, too." She glanced down at her clothing. "Do you think what I'm wearing is okay?"

Danna let her eyes drink in Alex in her snug jeans and tank top. The muscles in her toned arms flexed whenever she moved. Even the slightest movement to pull out a stool, showed her assets. "Oh, I think what you're wearing is perfect. The place is air conditioned, though, so you might want to grab a jacket in case you are easily chilled."

"Nah, I tend to run a little hot."

"Mmm, yes I can see that." Danna offered a seductive smile.

"Nicely done and a bit out of character. You're flirting," Alex stated and then her face adopted a serious expression. "Danna, I don't know what's happening here between us. I'm a little concerned this might be a runaway freight train that'll—"

"It's okay, Alex. I know the score. Settling down is probably not in the cards for either of us. I get it."

"That's not exactly what I meant. I don't know how to act or what to do with these sudden emotions, but I do know I have a lot going on that needs resolution. I might not be the best person to try out your newly discovered lesbianism."

"Can we not analyze this to death and simply let each day unfold organically?"

"Sure. I just didn't want you to get the wrong impression. I like you and I'm attracted, that's not the issue..." Alex sighed. "Okay, not picking things apart and placing them under a microscope. Carpe diem."

†

Prior to Danna knocking on her door Alex had found Selene in her office and borrowed her phone. She'd wanted to try to contact her parents at her papa's shop, even though she knew it was a long shot this early in the morning on a Sunday. She'd rationalized that certainly she wasn't important enough for the INS agents to trace a cell phone that happened to call the shop. After she'd let the phone ring over a dozen times, she'd given up and found herself picking up Danna's card and calling her to make sure she was still planning on coming over.

The flirtation they'd engaged in earlier was both welcome and unwelcome. It was a distraction. The raw sensuality in the kiss that Danna had initiated had completely blown Alex away. She didn't think the high-society woman had it in her. The kiss had affected her more than she wished to acknowledge.

On the drive over, the silence was a telling sign to how both women remained deep in thought. The low rumble of the newscaster's voice filled the void, even though Alex hadn't focused on the words. Alex didn't believe she could keep her distance, as her mushrooming feelings grew with each minute she spent in the company of Danna.

"Here we are," Danna announced as she parked the car and unclasped her seatbelt.

"Wow. It's huge." Alex emerged from Danna's car and took in the buildings and obviously newly landscaped grounds.

She had been used to an upscale place when she'd worked at the Ranch, but this was something way beyond the Nevada brothel. This place reeked of money. She took in the exquisite details of the club, right down to the polished marble floors and solid cherry-wood desk in the reception area. The modern lighting created a soft glow with the artistic blown glass hanging from the ceiling. She was sure a local artist, well known for his or her work, had specifically crafted each lighting fixture. These were not factory made, but rather unique, one-of-a-kind lights.

Alex whistled. "Wow. This place is amazing."

"Wait until you see the Roman bath," Lindy and Marley said in stereo.

Alex was so excited she barely contained her

childlike enthusiasm. "Can we? Take a tour of the Roman bath. I don't even know what a Roman bath is," she admitted.

Alex followed Lindy and Marley down a hallway and absently took Danna's hand as they walked along the corridor with the tasteful artwork on the walls. The wall art was a stunning combination of landscapes and beautiful women in sensual poses. Marley pushed open the door to reveal the room where the sauna and Roman bath were located. She looked around at the intricate tile work with designs unique to Georgia. Beautiful flowering trees created the subtle, yet strong, essence of the South. A continuous spray of water cascaded into the large pool from all four sides in much the same way a waterfall might fill a natural body of water.

"Is this just for the guests?" Alex asked.

"No," Marley answered. "But obviously we want the staff to only use the facilities after hours."

"Oh, yeah, of course. I wasn't asking about the times the club is open." Alex looked at her feet avoiding eye contact with Lindy and Marley.

"What about if I want to bring Alex as a guest on her day off?" Danna squeezed her hand and Alex realized she'd laced her fingers together with Danna's and in embarrassment, she let go. If this was an informal interview, she didn't want to get the job solely because of Danna. Marley had seemed interested in hiring Alex but she wasn't sure if that interest would wane when they found out about her immigration status. Maybe they'd already figured that out, none of these women were stupid. It was a good sign they were showing her around. Thanks to Danna.

"Well then, that's a different story. Guests can bring

whomever they want. We won't question that. Ever." Marley winked at Danna. "Shall we go to the juice bar and grab a fresh smoothie? Alex, would you have a few minutes to talk with me in my office while Lindy and Danna visit with one another?"

"Um, sure." Alex glanced at Danna who nodded her head and smiled. She found that she was very nervous since there was a lot riding on this job.

A perky blond woman efficiently produced four fruit smoothies and set them on the fancy stone counter. Marley grabbed one for herself and then picked up a second glass and handed it to Alex. Gesturing with her head, she directed Alex down another corridor to a decent-sized office with modern, solid-wood furniture and comfortable leather chairs for both the office occupant and any guests. There was a round conference table and Marley set her drink on the table waving for Alex to sit in one of the tall chairs.

"Look, let's cut to the chase. We wanted to recruit and hire you before Danna made the call to Lindy. I've watched you at Sisters and I've no doubt you could be an asset to TWC, but we have a small problem. I'm hoping Danna can work her magic on Lindy to allow us to ignore a few things that might be required for you to work here. I know you don't have legal immigration status and that's not an issue for me. I'm betting this won't be a concern for Lindy either, considering the services we offer upstairs aren't exactly legal. The South is a funny place, though. They might be willing to turn a blind eye to pleasure work, but immigration can sometimes be a sticky issue for the old guard like Lindy's husband, Judge Freemont. I know that if he ever found out about our 'special services,' he'd gladly grease a few palms or do whatever was necessary to make sure his wife stays out of trouble, but he'll likely have a double standard for other less than legal activities. If you get my drift?"

"Yeah, I do. Wouldn't want to stick your neck out for us Mexicans," Alex remarked with an edge to her voice she hadn't intended. Her body became rigid in irritation.

"I get it. I can't possibly walk in your shoes, but believe me, I'm on your side, Alex. Danna is a good friend of Lindy's. Let her handle things. In the meantime, tell me when you can start and how I can avoid Selene and Janice tearing me a new butthole."

Alex relaxed her posture and chuckled. "Don't worry about Janice and Selene. If I can work part-time for both of you, they won't care. I've already been given the go-ahead. Not to be ungrateful for this opportunity or anything, but can you tell me the pay?"

"Good maintenance folks are hard to find. How does thirty dollars an hour sound? Time-and-a-half on weekends. Oh, and if you want to participate in the special services, you'll definitely make very healthy tips that will ensure providing those services are worth your time. I don't think I need to tell you that discretion is very important here."

Alex grinned and stuck out her hand. "You got yourself a deal. I'm very discreet. I'd worry more about some of your members."

"Yeah, I know all about Chancy and Helena. Hopefully that won't be an issue for any of us. Lindy is going to talk with Helena. Perhaps you can emphasize the importance of prudence with Chancy."

Alex nodded. "I'll have another conversation with her. She might even be someone to consider recruiting. She has a certain charm that at least one of your members finds irresistible."

"Hmm, I guess that is an option to consider. Regarding your other duties, everything is new right now, so besides a little tweaking to get the settings correct, you shouldn't have to do much. Keeping the Roman bath and sauna in tip-top shape will be a big priority, but there are a lot of systems to attend to in a large facility. I'm sure you'll need to spend at least twenty hours a week here."

"Preventive maintenance is key. I'll put everything on a schedule. That should keep you running without any issues. Maintenance should be invisible to guests."

"Don't be too invisible. Those guests are going to love seeing you in your tool belt." Marley winked. "Come on, let's go back to the juice bar and see if Danna's worked her magic on Lindy yet?"

Alex felt like she was doing the walk of shame, and on the other side there would either be cameras with blinding white lights or confetti when she reached the bar. She held her breath as Danna tossed a reassuring smile in her direction. Lindy's expression was harder to read.

"Relax, Alex. Danna has managed to convince me that the pros outweigh the cons. Speaking of pro, I understand you have as close to professional training as we are likely to get based on your experience at the Ranch in Nevada. Is that correct?"

"Yes ma'am," Alex added.

"Don't force me to fire you already. Marley has barely hired you. If you ever call me ma'am again, I won't be as forgiving. Call me Lindy, please. Ugh, I'm at the age these young'uns have started calling me ma'am. I'm not going down without a fight," Lindy joked.

"She's never called me ma'am," Danna said quietly.

Lindy pushed Danna's shoulder. "You shush, you little braggart." Lindy held out her hand to Alex. "Welcome to the Trophy Wives Club, Alex. I trust that Marley offered you a satisfactory wage. I've done a bit of research on this Japanese technique called Nuru massage. Do you think you can show me your technique? Marley knows a little about this because I think I've been the lucky recipient. Between the both of you, perhaps we can ensure that at least the two of you have this respective technique in your tool belts."

Alex accepted Lindy's outstretched hand and gave it a quick shake. "Thank you, Lindy. You won't regret giving me this opportunity."

Lindy gave Alex an appraising look. "I don't suspect I will. I'd like very much to schedule a private session with you. What are you doing later this afternoon? A Nuru massage sounds delicious to me."

Alex glanced at Danna who nodded. "It would be my pleasure to introduce you to this erotic massage technique. What time?"

"Shall we plan on two?"

"That should work."

Alex began to fret a little. The only small problem with her working at TWC was a lack of transportation. She couldn't depend on Danna ferrying her back and forth to work. She'd have to try to resolve that hurdle and quick. Alex wondered if asking Danna to help her shop for a cheap motorcycle or bicycle would be too much.

"I suppose your official start date is today. Do you wish to orient before two, or come back for orientation at a later date?"

"Um, if it's okay, I'd like to see about obtaining transportation. I've never had to consider that before," Alex answered.

"I can take you car shopping. I'll be able to get you special pricing at one of my late husband's dealerships." Danna stood and looped her arm through Alex's.

"I was thinking more along the lines of a bike, either human powered or a used motorcycle. I don't have a lot of cash to throw around at the moment."

"Marley, give Alex here a sign on bonus of say, five thousand. I have a feeling she'll be worth every penny," Lindy directed.

"I can't accept—"

"Nonsense, I never offer money without good reason. This is a business decision and I don't make poor decisions when it comes to business," Lindy answered.

"Thank you, I don't know what to say."

†

Danna was securing her seatbelt when she asked, "Auto row or somewhere else?"

"I've always wanted a motorcycle. Do you think I can get something decent with the sign on bonus?"

"Yes, you might even be able to purchase a Harley." Danna pulled her smartphone from her purse and began typing. After scrolling through the craigslist site, she looked into Alex's anxious face and smiled. "There are multiple postings right here in Atlanta. With your mechanical skills, I'm sure you can decipher what would be a good buy."

"True, I can fix most anything, but engine repair is a bit specialized. I might have to study up on it."

"Have you ever driven a motorcycle?"

"Nope. How hard can it be?"

Danna threw her head back and laughed. "Nothing fazes you, does it?"

"I wouldn't say that exactly. You unsettle me." Alex shifted nervously in the soft leather of Danna's car.

"Well, I'm not quite sure how to help you with a crash course in riding a motorcycle, not to mention getting a motorcycle endorsement. By the way, do you even have a driver's license? I never asked. I'll bet Texas had very stringent laws."

"They did. I used to have a valid Texas license until they decided to tighten the laws. I had to be very careful when I couldn't renew it anymore without providing proper documentation. I admit I drove without one for a long time. Fortunately, California was close to Nevada and I managed to put a friend's address down as my own so I could get one there. So yeah, I have a driver's license, but no, I don't have an endorsement to drive a motorcycle." Alex frowned.

"Maybe you should consider a top of the line scooter. To tell you the truth, I don't know what the laws are like in Georgia. That could pose an additional problem for you." Danna began a search for the license requirements related to scooters and motorcycles. With her focus on the search she almost didn't hear Alex's response.

"I'll look like an idiot on a scooter. How in the world can my tall frame not look ridiculous on some tiny scooter? That's the opposite of big bad butch. Nope, I want to learn how to drive a Harley."

Danna looked up. "You don't need a license for a scooter that is under 50cc's and the best part is that you can buy a brand new scooter for less than a thousand dollars. A top-of-the-line scooter doesn't go very fast, though. The small motorcycles cost a little more, but might give you extra speed. They don't require a license and enhance the big-bad-dyke cool factor a smidgen."

"I'd still probably look like a clown on one of these smaller bikes. But I suppose being able to send four thousand to my family right away makes it a lot easier to endure the ribbing I will surely get. That is, if they're still here in the States. I haven't managed to connect with them." Alex seemed to melt back into the seat and a sadness developed in her eyes as Danna looked in her direction.

"We can keep trying. You can borrow my phone anytime you want to call. So, what will it be? A used Harley that you won't be able to drive away? And, you'll have to take a driving test to use legally, or a brand new 50cc bike?"

"I'll take door number two. Pride has no place when my family's ultimate survival is at stake. Thanks for the offer of your phone, but I can't keep depending on you. Even if they're still in Texas, papa's shop isn't open on Sundays, so I'll have to try again tomorrow."

"Sick of me already?"

"No, no, that's not what I mean. God, I don't know how to..."

"I was joking. I'll drop by tomorrow before I start my workday and you can try calling. Since I set my own hours, I'll come by around nine. Is that okay? You'll have to let me know where you'll be, Sisters or TWC."

"You really work?"

Danna chuckled. "Of course I do. I'd go batty if I was all alone with my thoughts for the entire day."

"I'm sorry. That was rude again. I assumed you were independently wealthy and didn't have to work."

"I don't. I choose to work."

"Can I ask what you do?"

"I'm an attorney. I do pro bono work for people who can't afford legal services. Mostly for women who need to navigate the legal system related to anything from uncontested divorce to more complex cases involving Family Court. The custody issues can generate a whole host of complications. The assistance I provide to those struggling with domestic violence doesn't even scratch the surface. Lately, I've wondered if I should branch out to LGBTQ legal aid. I haven't done a lot of that unless it has been related to family issues such as adoption."

"Wow! Beautiful, smart, and kind. That's a lethal combination."

"David, my husband, wasn't in favor of me working, but I put my foot down."

"Good for you. That's why you said you were going to help me. Do you think you can?"

"I'm not an expert in immigration but I do have a network of attorneys I can contact. I'm sure I can get you one of the best to start working on your legal status as well as your family's."

Alex took Danna's hand and squeezed. "I don't know how to thank you for all you've done for me. I'm a virtual stranger to you. I think I may have several guardian angels. People keep popping into my life to provide the exact thing I need at the moment. First, there was Henry, then Rosie, Betty, Selene and Janice, and now you, Lindy, and Marley. I haven't been all that great at letting people get close. The jury is still out about Luna. She sees me as her competition. Which I swear, I am not. Someday Marley will wake up to the woman standing right in front of her and then I see great things for those two. I'll admit, Marley did ring a few bells for me at first, that is, until I met you." Alex brought Danna's hand to her mouth and kissed it. "I don't know what our future will look like, but I'm at least open to exploring something."

"That's enough for me. There is one tiny request I have."

"Anything."

"Will you accept a small gift?"

Alex's brow furrowed in an adorable signal of trepidation. "I like to make my own way in the world and you've already pushed the envelope regarding my personal rules on life."

"Well, I do want to hear more about those rules. But for now, I'd simply like to get you a cell phone. This is for selfish reasons. I can't ask you to move in with me, I know that would be crossing the line and violating one of your rules, so the next best thing is to be able to connect via modern technology. I know you aren't the last woman on earth not to have a cell phone, but you're damn close. I promise putting you on my family plan will be nothing. A very small cost."

Alex chuckled. "Okay, I'll get the damn cell phone, but I am buying it with all the money I'll save from not purchasing a Harley. Also, I insist on paying whatever extra monthly costs you incur to put me on your family plan."

"Deal." Danna leaned over and sealed the pact with a light brush of her lips against Alex's. She readily agreed to the bargain. She desperately wanted to be able to call, if for no other reason than to continue to slowly get to know everything about Alex. What compelled her to get up in the mornings? What brought a smile to her face? What made her angry, sad, and discouraged? What caused her joy, pleasure, satisfaction, contentment? She needed to know the intimate details of Alex, the things she had yet to share with another single living individual. Putting the car in gear, she eased out of the parking lot and headed in the direction of the first place that she knew would have exactly what Alex had compromised on regarding her choice for transportation. Danna decided she would subtly influence Alex and encourage her to buy the best helmet manufactured. She did not want anything to happen to that beautiful head of Alex's.

"I suppose I should also look for a helmet, huh?"

"You just read my mind."

†

Alex was frustrated. She needed to find reliable transportation so that she wouldn't have to depend on anyone to travel back and forth from Sisters to TWC, but her choice was limited if she wanted a 50cc motorcycle. The places they had checked out either had 50cc scooters, dirt bikes, or motorcycles that exceeded the limit for a street-ready vehicle that wouldn't require a motorcycle license.

"This is getting us nowhere," Alex exclaimed in exasperation. "I need to be at TWC in little more than an hour and I've no way of getting home. What can you tell me about the bus system? I suppose I could use that method of transportation.

Lines formed on Danna's forehead. "I don't know. I suppose MARTA would work for you. There's bound to be a route that will get you close enough to commute. Don't give up. This calls for some in-depth Internet research."

"I don't have a computer or a cell phone yet."

"I'll do a search tomorrow. Maybe there is a dealership that specializes in small motorcycles. Will you let me help you until we can get you set up with a phone?"

"I don't have much of a choice, do I?" Alex grumbled.

"You could borrow David's car, until you have your own transportation," Danna suggested.

"No."

"Stubborn woman. I understand your need to be independent, but this would simply be a temporary solution. David's not going to crawl out from the grave and demand to have his car back."

"Morbid."

"No, practical. Sometimes the easiest solution is the one that nearly nips at our nose. I should have thought of that before."

"Or the one that will bite us in the ass."

"So cynical for someone who hasn't quite hit middle age." Danna smiled and Alex began to lighten up.

"If I borrow your car, then maybe I can take my time, learn to drive a motorcycle and get a real one instead of some clown's tricycle with a motor." Alex grinned.

"We can learn together. Ooh, I can ride bitch in the back."

"I am a bad influence on you, Danna. You're starting to talk like a gutter rat. It doesn't fit."

"No, you're a good influence. I'm tired of doing exactly everything expected of me. Tanya would be proud."

"I like her, and Martin. They both seem so...down to earth."

"And I'm not?" Danna wrinkled her nose.

"That's not exactly what I meant. Shit. I always seem to say the wrong things. Let me clarify. You're not really stuffy, but you don't seem to be very comfortable in your own skin sometimes."

"See, I need you to help me find my inner home girl. Now, how about taking a look at David's old Porsche. It probably needs a new battery or something. I've left it alone in the garage. I didn't know what to do with it. The car was never my style."

Alex choked. "A Porsche? I'll bet it's a stick shift too. I can drive one, barely."

Danna's face scrunched again in confusion. "It is. David tried to teach me how to drive it, but I wasn't interested in learning. See, it'll just sit idle in the garage because I can't even drive the damn thing. How about if I take you to TWC today and then hang out for a bit while you do what you need to do. After, I'll pick you up and you can take a look at the car. You'll probably be able to figure out what the car needs."

Alex sighed. "I don't like that plan, but I suppose the carrot that is dangling in front of me is too irresistible. I'm warming to the idea of owning a real motorcycle. Although I'd rather look for a used one. A lot less money. There aren't too many things I've bought in my life that were new and there's no sense in starting that trend when I've done fine up until this point."

Danna glanced at her expensive watch. "I better head in the direction of TWC. I wouldn't want you to be late for your first day at work. Ugh, that sounded so...maternal. And I definitely don't have maternal feelings for you. In fact, I'd kinda like it if you wouldn't enjoy your job so much. I know it's important to like what you do for a living, but I've got to admit to trying to work through you getting too much joy from giving Lindy that Nuru massage. The mental picture is all wrong in my head. Lindy is one of my oldest and dearest friends and you are...well...someone I'd very like to share a Nuru massage with."

Alex winked. "You could also book an appointment with me."

Danna lost all the color in her face. "I really hope you were joking."

Alex banged her head against the backrest. "Oh my God. I was. I'm such an idiot. We haven't had enough time to process things. And when I say we, I mean me. I'll admit that what's going through my head right now is what appointment you might book while I'm giving Lindy her massage. If I'm one hundred percent honest, I would admit I don't like the thought of Marley or Luna giving you a special treatment. No, I don't like that at all. Yet, I have no right to dictate anything to you."

"Hmm, I like the idea of you not wanting me to seek comfort in the arms of another woman. I suppose you providing that service is very different from me scheduling a pleasure session with another person. I believe I can compartmentalize this enough to view what you do as legitimate work that makes a difference to women. It sure made a difference to me. It opened my eyes to something I hadn't been willing to face before David passed away."

"Does that mean we've officially started dating?"

"I'd like that."

"So would I. I still can't promise much until things settle in my life, but I'd like to try dating. That works."

"Exclusive dating? I'm a lawyer after all. We always examine the fine print."

"It's not that I'm opposed to..."

"Too soon. I understand. Just so you know, I won't be scheduling any special sessions and I don't plan to date anyone else. That's just me. I won't hold you to the same standards."

Alex frowned. "I'm not sure I like that. Already you and I are so unbalanced. I don't want there to be another level of disparity. Can you give me a couple of days to think this over? I like to take my time to process the big things. I didn't get the chance when I went on the run and I've been off kilter ever since. I feel like everything in my life is out of control and this is the one area where I have the ability to manage things."

Danna reached across the console and grabbed Alex's hand. "I want you to take all the time you need. Hey, since we missed lunch, I know of a great take out place. I'll call ahead and Tony can prepare our order. That way we won't have to set aside any manners trying to eat in a short amount of time. I'm still trying to impress you and snarfing down barbecue while the sauce trickles down my chin is not the way to do it. I should make sure you like barbecue before I call in the order."

"I'm not picky. Barbecue is fine with me. As far as that sauce thing dribbling down your chin, I might like licking it off you. No need to display exceptional manners for my sake."

"I can see I'm going to have my hands full with you."

"Hands, mouth, whatever you like. I hope you don't mind a little harmless flirting. I learned at the Ranch, it tends to ratchet up the excitement. I do believe I'd like to take my time with you. Getting you to that point of no return is going to be so much fun."

Danna gulped. "Um, pulled pork, beef, or chicken?"

"Nice diversion. I'll take the chicken. Can I buy, please? I want to at least make an attempt to fool myself about this not being a completely lopsided relationship."

"You do owe me dinner. I'll tell you what, let's count this as the dinner date you owe me."

"I'm not sure I like that. Are you saying you aren't interested in going to dinner with me?"

"Absolutely not. That came out all wrong. You're rubbing off on me. I don't know how to act around a sexy, confident lesbian who has women tossing their phone numbers every which way at her."

"Relax. No, I don't want to consider this dinner, so you aren't getting out of me taking you to dinner. I can afford both now, considering the big sign-on bonus that's burning a hole in my pocket."

"Yes, but even though I'm not an expert on immigration law, I doubt resolving those issues will be cheap. And you still have to obtain transportation. Don't go throwing all your money away just yet."

"Good point. Okay, I'll consider your proposal. I can see now how good a lawyer you are."

Danna grinned. "Oh, you ain't seen nothing yet. I've been taking it easy on you so far."

CHAPTER THIRTEEN

Alex was no fool. She knew her good fortune could turn on a dime. The scheduled Nuru massage was a test. An interview of sorts for pleasure workers. Either she would pass and secure herself a position with TWC, or she would fail and need to think up plan B. She wondered, if she bombed, would the five thousand be refundable to Lindy? Alex was not going to fuck this up. If it was the last thing she did on earth, she was going to make Lindy scream in pleasure. She knew just how to approach the massage. Controlling the pace was key.

Marley had directed her to this private space and told her to wait for Lindy who would enter when she arrived. Alex looked around taking in the details and planning her seduction. The lighting in the room was perfect, a soft, almost rose-colored haze. Alex flipped through the collection of music and wondered which Lindy preferred. At the Ranch she'd known such a range of tastes when it came to music. Some of the women wanted hard and fast with an almost ear-splitting backdrop to enhance the thrill. Others gravitated to soft jazz or the sultry music from a range of popular female musicians. Alex suspected Lindy would choose the latter, but she'd learned never to judge a book by its cover. Since Lindy owned the place, she would have knowledge of the different choices regarding a specific playlist.

She was delighted TWC had purchased the special, waterproof mattress necessary for a proper Nuru massage; one that would allow Alex to slide her body along Lindy's easily without friction or rubbing. Marveling at how thorough the owner of TWC was with every detail, Alex found the thick gel and heating element for the warm water she would mix with the authentic Nuru massage gel to achieve the perfect viscosity for two bodies in motion. She doubted that TWC needed any of her assistance with this special technique. All the evidence pointed to the fact they had already researched this erotic Japanese massage. Her performance today would demonstrate her knowledge and expertise in executing the technique with precision and flair.

Alex had changed into one of the thin silk robes. The robe looked a little out of place on her tall, muscular frame since silk robes were designed for petite women. She'd go with the flow. The soft material rested well above her knees showing off her toned thighs. She was thankful she had shaved her legs this morning because nothing was worse than stubble to ruin the effect of two bodies gliding smoothly over each other.

Not that Alex had expected Lindy to knock, but she was still startled when the woman appeared and shook her from her thoughts.

"Hello, Alex. I see you found the robe already." She leaned in close, giving Alex's senses a treat as she pointed to the specific playlist displayed on the device that piped music into the room. "The female artists, please."

"Mmm, you smell nice." Alex breathed in and let the aroma flow over her. After working at the Ranch, Alex had come to understand that more expensive perfumes lacked an overly sweet smell. She'd come to appreciate the light, somewhat flowery scent. Alex remembered those summer evenings when she'd breathe in the blooming jasmine. "Would you like to put on a robe? Or shall I undress you?"

Lindy tilted her head. "I'd like to put on a robe and see how you decide is the best way to approach this."

"Perfect. I generally recommend that," Alex answered.

Gleaming brass fixtures adorned the master bath that was attached to the suite. The same marble as in the front room and a claw-foot tub made this room perfect for seduction. Maybe she would have another chance to impress Lindy and show her how well she knew how to incorporate this old-fashioned tub into sex play that would have her begging for release. Lindy shut the door and Alex gathered her strength as she prepared to make Lindy the center of her universe for the next couple of hours.

Five minutes later, Lindy emerged from the bathroom in a similar style robe and smiled with confidence at Alex. The soft music began to play in the background after Alex pushed the button to begin Lindy's preferred playlist. So far everything was going smoothly. Turning the dial on the wall, Alex dimmed the lights further and gently tugged on Lindy's belt to pull her close. Alex had learned that even the women who were paying for her services wanted intimacy. Beginning with a kiss was one method of starting the experience in a way that didn't scream professional. Some of the pleasure workers at the Ranch refused to kiss their clients. Alex never had that rule.

She let her fingers caress the side of Lindy's face before slowly trailing down Lindy's neck, then onto a cavern between her breasts, which were much firmer than Alex anticipated. Lindy clearly took care of herself. After allowing the tips of her fingers to gently brush across Lindy's skin, Alex brought her lips to Lindy's and started an excruciatingly slow exploration. Her tongue lazily entered inside Lindy's mouth as she sucked lightly on Lindy's bottom lip. She unhurriedly mapped every single inch as Lindy started to moan her response. If a person could make love to another by kissing only, Alex had nearly perfected that technique.

Lindy was breathing heavily when Alex paused on her assault of Lindy's swollen lips. "Oh my God, I could come simply from your kisses."

"You are an exceptionally beautiful woman, Lindy, and I have no intention of stopping before we experience the true beauty of the Nuru massage. This technique was made for women and only women. Let me help you de-robe and then I'll take you to the bed and begin coating your body with the gel." Alex tugged playfully on the belt, pulling Lindy to the bed. She let her fingers hover over the tie, making brief, deliberate contact with Lindy's stomach as she released the belt to let the robe hang slightly open. She imagined she was blind as she let her hand travel inside reading Lindy's body as if it were one large, braille manuscript. Eventually she pushed the silk robe off each shoulder and let it drop to the floor.

Alex let Lindy decide whether it was more arousing for her to help Alex remove her own robe or watch as Alex slowly removed the last barrier to her full nakedness. There was always a signal for a client's preference, no matter how subtle that might be. She usually knew without asking. Sometimes it was a slight bending in Alex's direction or a twitch of the hand. In this instance, Alex let the two to three seconds pass, before determining that Lindy preferred for Alex to strip without her assistance as her eyes hungrily watched. Lindy's gaze was almost too penetrating in its eagerness to see Alex without clothes.

Smiling when she heard the slight hitch in Lindy's voice, Alex finished removing her robe with a cat-like grace. She moved toward the bowl of gel and idly dipped her fingers inside.

"Gorgeous. You are like a Greek statue," Lindy exclaimed.

"Similar skin tone, maybe, but us Latinas are much better lovers than the Greeks," Alex quipped as she smoothly maneuvered Lindy on top of the mattress.

Alex smirked as she noticed Lindy's eyes ravenously devour the scene before her. She took extra time running her hands over her own body, massaging the gel onto her firm breasts and flat stomach. Alex created a visual display worthy of an experienced stripper or pole dancer. Preparing the scene was partially a theatrical experience, and Alex had learned her part long ago.

Soon enough she was sliding her hands along Lindy's body, creating a healthy coat of gel before adding more of the odorless and tasteless substance to her own tall form. She kept a connection to Lindy at all times, not wishing to break the spell. She could tell Lindy's arousal was continuing to climb with every new development. Soon she would be sliding her body on top of Lindy's in a practiced method of teasing until Lindy could take it no more and begged for release.

When Alex had enough of the gel distributed on both of their bodies to begin her seduction, she flipped Lindy onto her stomach and began the massage at her feet. At first she was using only her hands and she could see Lindy quivering with expectation. She could almost hear Lindy's question about when Alex would choose to use another part of her body. Alex would make her wait just a little while longer as she moved her hands up the inside of Lindy's thighs without ever coming near to her center. Lindy began squirming on the mattress so Alex climbed on top and used her generously gelled pussy to glide over Lindy's ass.

A Nuru massage was not for the faint of heart or for anyone not in excellent physical shape. She would be using all of her muscles and nearly every part of her body as she made creative connections to Lindy while gliding on top. Alex sensed Lindy was ready for Alex to turn her over, allowing a breast to breast connection. Using her breasts and her entire body, she planned to stimulate every erogenous zone on Lindy's hypersensitive skin. She knew she might have to slow the experience down or Lindy would explode in ecstasy far too soon and well before she had planned. Edging was another technique that combined with Nuru massage could achieve a kind of pleasure women rarely experience. Based on Lindy's gyrations as she attempted to seek more contact to her core pleasure center, Alex knew she was on the verge.

Carefully repositioning herself by moving slowly

down Lindy's body and not stopping on the way to her pussy, Alex concentrated on Lindy's sensitive feet. She sucked each toe and began to pepper all ten with small kisses. Although Alex could tell this was arousing, she managed to slow things down and carefully brought Lindy back from the brink.

With the back of her hand she brushed along one side until she reached Lindy's mouth and traced along the edge. Capturing Lindy's mouth, she began to deepen the kiss and then directed Lindy to a sitting position so she could straddle her from behind. Her long legs wrapped around Lindy and she pushed Lindy's thighs apart while she used nearly the entire length of her arms to stroke on the inside. The pleasure workers at the ranch had taught her many exercises that allowed her to stimulate Lindy in new and different ways. Alex was very limber as a result of her dedication to those exercises.

Lindy lifted her ass from the mattress seeking greater contact in an area Alex knew was pulsating in anticipation. "Mmm, please touch me."

"I am touching you," Alex whispered in her ear, reducing the tone in her voice to a sultry teasing.

Lindy laughed. "You know what I mean."

"All in good time. Surely I have at least another hour to give your velvety lips the attention they deserve."

"You know, I'm not that stuffy, you could've said clit or pussy."

"Good to know," Alex answered as she surprised Lindy by sliding her hand along the soft curly hair on her pubis.

Seeking more contact Lindy bucked to meet Alex's touch, but Alex moved away and began massaging her legs while subtly moving behind Lindy. Alex was sure Lindy could feel the silky hair on her own mound as it made contact against Lindy's cheeks.

"As your employer I am begging you, no, I'm ordering you to place your mouth on my pussy and then fuck me with at least three fingers."

Alex was lightning fast in swiveling Lindy around. With her legs still spread apart, she brought Lindy's center on top of her own, positioning Lindy's legs around her waist. Alex held Lindy securely allowing her to lean back as Alex did all the work by licking and sucking each breast while continuing to slide their pussies against each other. Alex was bucking at the same time she was forcefully moving Lindy's core against her own.

As Alex recognized that Lindy was nearing the point of no return, she gently pushed Lindy on her back, once again sliding up and down, this time using her breast as a stimulator. She began to rub one breast against Lindy's clit as Lindy writhed in ecstasy. Finally, Alex repositioned herself one last time and took the sensitive nub in her mouth, sucking lightly while she thrust one, then two, then three fingers deep inside. Pushing her fingers all the way back she reached Lindy's A-spot. It became hard to distinguish between the gel and Lindy's natural lubrication from her heightened arousal. Having found Lindy's A-spot, Alex knew she could tease out several orgasms in a row without an inconvenient rest period.

As the contractions pulsed around Alex's fingers an almost guttural sound erupted from Lindy.

"Ahhhhh, so fucking good."

Alex removed her mouth and continued to fuck Lindy pulling out several orgasms, one right after another. Lindy's arms flopped to the side and Alex knew she'd achieved her mission. She let Lindy rest for a few more moments before she began touching her again and offering at least one more orgasm for good measure.

†

Danna did not want to be that woman: the jealous lover who spent an inordinate amount of time wondering what her girlfriend was doing at that exact moment. With her head between the cushion of the massage table she sighed. It wasn't Marley's fault she couldn't relax enough to enjoy the treatment. She'd told Marley not to venture into any erogenous zone and to stick with a back and leg massage. Her ass was strictly off limits today. She could feel her taut muscles as she tried to relax on the soft cotton sheet. She was like a newly strung guitar before the strings have had a chance to stretch out.

"Something has you all wound up. I don't think I've ever tried to massage someone who is so tense." Marley continued to dig her fingers in Lindy's shoulders.

"Sorry, Marley. You're doing a great job. It's not you, it's me."

Marley chuckled. "Thankfully, I've never heard that one before. Usually my girlfriends say something more direct and have no compulsion against blaming me for not taking the relationship to the next level."

"I don't know how to have a relationship with a woman. In some ways, men are much easier. Give them sex two to three times a week and they're happy. I am in way over my head."

"Look, I know you realize this in your beautiful head,

but what Lindy and Alex are doing is merely business. Honestly, I see the sparks between the two of you. Sure, when Alex first met me there was an attraction of sorts, but with you it seems a little different. A bit deeper, I guess."

Marley put more pressure on a particularly sore spot and Danna concentrated on letting go of some of her worry. "Thanks for that small bit of reassurance."

"That's a bit better. Keep thinking positive, relaxing thoughts while I work out these knots."

"You don't think I'm too old and inexperienced for Alex?" Danna mumbled through the open head pillow.

"You're only like, what, ten years older, right?"

"Twelve, actually. Besides my session with Luna, I've never slept with a woman. Even though I wanted to touch Luna, something felt off about it and I was only a recipient. Alex has a lot of experience; how will I possibly be able to please her?"

Marley continued to move her hands up and down Danna's back and pressed her thumb at the dip above Danna's ass in the place that often gave Danna fits. Her hunched-over posture at work created tension in both her shoulders and lower back. Marley paused while still maintaining a connection to Danna.

"In my experience, Danna, perfect technique is only a small part of the equation. Whenever I listen to an artist, like a musician for example, the person may have perfect pitch, but if I don't sense any passion or emotion behind the voice, the music will never touch my soul. I believe making love is a bit like that. No matter how green a person is, they can make up for that inexperience with genuine feelings. Does that make sense?"

"Yes, it does. There is something about Alex that

draws me in. I'm not talking about her exquisite physique or that face that could give Helen of Troy some serious competition."

"She's a hottie all right." Marley continued the massage and started making small circles with her thumbs, increasing the pressure incrementally.

"Oooh, that's good. Yeah, that spot is very tender right now. Any chance you can slip some pointers to me on how to please a woman? You know, sexually."

Marley chuckled. "Everyone is different, I like the direct approach of asking if it isn't apparent from your partner's reactions. Of course, there's always YouTube."

"You're kidding, right?"

"Nope. How do you think we learned about Nuru massage? I've also done a little research on a new technique I'd like to offer here at TWC. I meant to ask Alex about it because she might already know."

"That sounds fascinating, what is it?"

"It's called a Yoni massage, and basically it's a vaginal massage. Apparently, some women get stuck down there and a Yoni massage releases the emotions."

"Oh brother, now I've heard everything. New age sex where your energy is released through vaginal massage."

"Hey, don't knock it 'til you've tried it. I'd be happy to set you up with an appointment after I do a little more research. You can be a test client and we'll give you one for free."

Danna laughed. "I'll pass. I don't think I'll be continuing with the special services anymore."

"Well, hell, why would you? You'll have your own personal sex slave to give you anything and everything you want."

Danna's body tensed again. She didn't think of Alex in that way. She wasn't some play toy intended to help Danna release her pent-up, sexual energy.

"Hey, I'm sorry. Sometimes I take joking around with my favorite clients too far. Now I'll have to start all over after causing you to tense up. Do I have to get Chancy to deliver some mojitos and pour them down your throat for you to relax?" Marley joked.

"Taking a few deep breaths right now. I'll be fine as soon as Alex is finished with Lindy and I have a chance to spend a little time with her."

"Mmm mmm mmm, you do have it bad. Okay, can I get you to flip over and I'll massage your front. By the time we finish, you won't have to wait too long. I want you to replenish your body with some water and sit for a spell anyway."

Danna grabbed the sheet, suddenly feeling too exposed and turned over while keeping the sheet tightly against her body so that her breasts and other intimate parts remained covered. "I don't suppose I have time to run out and purchase a cell phone, do I?"

"Probably not, but don't you have an assistant or something that helps you with things like that?"

"I'm not calling my assistant on a Sunday to purchase a phone for me. Besides, she'll get nosy and ask questions I'm not prepared to answer yet. It's not that I'm embarrassed by my attraction to women, and specifically my fascination with Alex, I just don't think it's anyone's business who I choose to sleep with."

"Uh huh, still coming to grips with all of this." Marley moved her hands down Danna's arm and began massaging each finger in her hand.

"Maybe. Oh God, I'm one of those closet cases, aren't I? Does it get easier to admit you're a lesbian?"

Marley shrugged. "For me, it was never an issue. I knew I liked girls as far back as I can remember. I wanted to kiss my best friend at five, so I'm not the person to ask this question. Different era, I guess. Maybe it was easier on me because I don't come from one of those Old South families with more money than God."

Danna groaned. "Sometimes I hate coming from that privilege. It seems to drive an automatic wedge between myself and people I genuinely wish to form friendships with."

"You like slumming with us poor folk, huh?" Marley chuckled. "Hey, for what it's worth, I don't see either you or Lindy as one of those uppity women who are threatened by anyone not of your socioeconomic class."

"That's good, but does Alex feel the same?"

"I'm pretty sure she does. She doesn't act uncomfortable around you. That's a sure sign she feels the same."

†

While Alex proceeded to clean the room after the messy massage, Lindy decided to take a quick shower to remove the remaining gel. She smiled and reached into her purse, extracting a small white envelope that she opened and added another bill to, before handing it to Alex.

Alex hadn't expected Lindy to tip her for their session. When Lindy handed her an envelope filled with three crisp one hundred-dollar bills, she tried to hand the envelope back to Lindy. "I know this was really all part of the hiring process. Besides, you've already given me a hefty sign-on bonus."

"You earned every penny, darlin'. Tips are how you can earn a decent living. You're going to make us a lot of money, so please take this. When word leaks out about our newest staff member, this will undoubtedly lead to a swell in club membership. Buy Danna a nice dinner tonight." Lindy winked. "I'll let her know you'll be down shortly after you've had a chance to shower. Next time, if you don't leave me completely knackered, we can shower together. I'm not sure how I managed to get my legs to move. By the way, we do have other staff that could have taken care of turning over the room, but I do like your initiative. It's nice to know you'll never have idle hands. Let Marley know when you'll be able to officially start. I assume you'll need to make some arrangements with your bosses at Sisters." Lindy gave Marley a small wave as she exited the room.

Alex hadn't ever seen the kind of luxury this suite provided and mentally chastised herself for basking in the shower as three separate showerheads pulsed soothing water over her exhausted body. The Nuru massage was hard work. Although she deserved the extra few minutes in the shower to let the water cascade over her body and perform a bit of magic, she didn't want to keep Danna waiting. Her need to rejuvenate her energy won out.

Alex hadn't planned far enough in advance to bring a second set of clothes, so she put her jeans and tank top back on and hoped the day's sweat hadn't caused her shower to be for naught. At least she'd washed away the heady aroma of sex. That would not be something to place her in Danna's favor when they had their dinner date tonight. The smell of sex from another woman was a surefire way to blunt the evening. She'd been careful not to agree to what Danna had proposed and was hoping Danna wouldn't throw up too much of a fuss. She chuckled at how cute Danna was when negotiating the dating rules.

Before opening the door that led to the corridor and hopefully down the hall to Danna, Alex sniffed her armpits. She was glad the private suite was equipped with deodorant. It wasn't her normal extra protection stick. Alex reeked of that femmie flowery odor she didn't particularly care for, but it would have to do. The alternative was *eau de naturale* and Alex didn't think a musky scent was appealing.

When Alex reached the juice bar, Danna swiveled in the stool, and she saw the special smile that Alex was convinced Danna saved specifically for her. Alex knew Danna was glad to see her when she saw the tiny crow's feet make an appearance on Danna's face.

"Hey, you," Alex said.

"Freshly showered, I see. Would you mind terribly if I took a shower? We can swing by my house and I can show you the car. I promise to be quick."

Alex placed her index finger on her chin and pretended to consider this. "Well, I don't think it's fair you get to change clothes and use your own grooming products. I had to put on some perfumey deodorant and the clothes I've worn all day, but I suppose so. Although, you should have to wear the same clothes. No changing to some wickedly sexy dress that will distract me all night. It'll be hard to pay attention to any meaningful conversation when I'm trying to figure out a way to remove said dress."

Danna stood and closed the distance as she barely brushed her lips against Alex's. "Come on, I'm starved and your flirting is only delaying my gratification."

Alex pulled the money that Lindy had given her and held it in front of Danna. "I've got more cash that I'm dying to spend on you tonight. Pick out a nice place, not some dive, please. We both deserve to celebrate. I've considered your earlier proposal and I have to decline. I'm buying."

Danna frowned and Alex nearly smacked herself on the head for saying, yet again, something so stupid. Flashing the money was sure to remind Danna of what she'd just done with Lindy. Alex wondered if she would ever learn the subtleties of courting a high-society woman. She looked down at her feet and mumbled, "Sorry, I just meant to remind you that this dinner's on me. I asked, you accepted before trying your earlier fancy lawyer maneuvers. In my world, that means I pay."

Danna looped her arm in Alex's. "Stop beating yourself up and thinking that you're always saying the wrong thing. You couldn't be any more adorable if you tried. I like you just the way you are. I don't want you to change one single thing. I'm the one who needs to have an attitude readjustment at times. Green does not look good on me, so I refuse to buy that color. I've discarded the green blouse and decided blue or red is a much better choice. Don't you agree?"

"Okay, I amend my earlier comment. Feel free to slip into a sexy red dress."

"Hey, by the way, Marley and I were talking about another kind of massage called a Yoni massage. Have you ever heard of it?"

Alex grinned. "As a matter of fact, I have." She wiggled her eyebrows. "I could show you tonight."

"I can already tell you are a temptation I won't be able to resist. Honestly, I'm at the age that I don't give a shit what people think. Adults can decide to sleep with a person on their first date without guilt. Hell, I'm a member of TWC, playing coy or hard to get doesn't seem to match up, now does it?"

"Thank God for the women's revolution and changed perspectives on sex." Alex raised her fist in the air.

†

Danna suddenly felt awkward as she drove them up the winding driveway to her home. She was embarrassed by the ostentatiousness of her residence that would undoubtedly be perceived by Alex as one more reason the two of them might not work. She snuck a glance at Alex whose eyes grew wider as she rolled up to the four-car garage. She and David hadn't needed all that space because there were only two cars in their family, but the house came equipped in case they wanted to add more extravagance in their life. It was wasteful and unnecessary. That thought pierced Danna's heart as she realized how utterly pointless all this wealth really was. In her mind, the divide between her and Alex grew wider.

Alex put her hand on Danna's thigh and squeezed before removing the hand Danna was using to grip her steering wheel as she tensed. Alex gathered her hand and began making soothing circles with her thumb.

"Don't you dare apologize for your wealth. You run a pro bono legal clinic. You have nothing to be sorry about. I'm not letting our diverse backgrounds push an unwelcome wedge between us. If you can let it go, so can I."

Danna sucked in a deep breath before turning to Alex. "Thank you. I don't know how you can so easily read people, but I am very relieved to hear you say that."

"I may have lived in a town with less than a thousand people, and I probably seem very naïve to you, but my mama and papa both taught me to pay attention. I think for us, survival depended on it. Although papa was a bit too kind sometimes and wanted to trust people he shouldn't have. You haven't judged me for my near poverty status, so why should I hold your vast financial resources against you. Being rich isn't a crime, you know." Alex chuckled.

Danna pressed the button above her mirror to open the garage door and the soft whir of the motor interrupted their conversation.

Alex whistled when the cherry-red Porsche 911 came into view. "Wow, I'm not really a car junkie, but that is a very beautiful car." She squirmed in her seat. "Um, I'm not all that comfortable with using it. Maybe checking out the MARTA would be a better thing to do. Besides, walking a little bit to get to and from the bus stops might keep me from getting flabby from all this luxury."

"Seriously, someone should enjoy this thing. I certainly don't appreciate her. She's feeling abandoned and it is a crying shame to neglect this beautiful girl." Danna pulled into the space next to the cherry-red sports car.

"Okay, true, you have a point. Still...I'm not sure my tall frame would fit."

"Only one way to find out. While I'm taking a shower and getting ready, you can check the car out. Maybe see if it needs anything else besides a new battery. I don't know a lot about cars, but I do know enough to realize if a car hasn't been run for months, the battery goes dead." Danna unlatched her seat belt and then grabbed her purse. "First let me settle you inside and offer you a drink or something. One thing us Southern ladies know how to do properly is offer Southern hospitality. Ready?"

"Although I was kind of kidding about the red dress, you should feel free to change into anything you like. If you don't mind, can we swing by my place and I'll at least put on my one good shirt?" Alex followed Danna into the spacious garage running a hand along the sleek car before they entered the house.

"Deal. Does that mean I can impress you with something a little sexier than what I'm wearing right now?" Kicking off her shoes in the mud room, Danna moved inside her house and tossed her purse onto the massive island counter in her kitchen.

Alex sat on one of the stools butted against the granite counter and propped her hand against her chin. "Oh, Danna, everything you put on that body of yours is sexy to me. You could be in a ratty old T-shirt and sweats and I'd still probably want to rip your clothes off and taste every inch of your body."

"God, you are good for my ego. What would you like, beer, wine, coffee, tea?"

"I'll have some water if it isn't too much trouble. I'm saving myself for tonight. We'll order a bottle of wine. You'll have to pick the wine out, because I know nothing about fine wines. I hate to admit this, but they all taste the same to me. I wouldn't know the difference between a five-dollar bottle of wine and a hundred-dollar bottle."

Danna smiled. "Have you ever had a hundred-dollar bottle of wine?"

Alex chuckled. "Well, no, but..."

"Don't worry, I can't tell the difference either. I was sick and tired of all the wine snobs my husband always hung around with when we would go wine tasting, so one night I pulled a trick on them. I got the winery to go in on the hoax and took all the dump bucket contents and had him pour those into an empty bottle. He presented the bottle as their very finest special reserve wine for the year. Do you know what happened?"

Alex looked at Danna with rapt attention. "No, what?"

"All those blowhard wine connoisseurs swooned over the wine. David was so angry with me for embarrassing him and his friends, but honestly, I'd had enough of their snobbery."

"Oooh, I better watch out, you have an evil side to you."

"Only when I believe people are behaving badly and need to be taught a lesson or two. Honestly, they've done experiments before and proven that no matter how much you protest to know the difference, many don't. I did my research before pulling off this stunt. There are so many examples of similar experiments conducted as proof of the power of suggestion. Sometimes marketing trumps quality. I suppose it all started when an upstart California wine maker fooled a bunch of Parisians into choosing his wine over their own Bordeaux's with their century-old grapes."

"Well that makes me feel better. I'll admit I was worried, but I'll still let you choose."

"Maybe we should simply ask the waiter or waitress for their recommendation. I swear, I read all about the various tests between cheap and expensive wines with similar results. There was another experiment with a bunch of wine snobs who chose one wine over another with absolute confidence they were picking the better wine when in reality the only difference was either food coloring added to one, or a slightly higher or lower temperature. I honestly don't believe it will matter. I generally like a sweeter wine, but you might prefer something completely different."

"It's all new territory to me. I'll let you lead the way."

Danna leaned in to gently kiss Alex. "I won't be long." She allowed her hand to caress Alex's face and down her arm before she left the room to take her shower.

CHAPTER FOURTEEN

Danna strolled into the garage while Alex's head was under the hood of the Porsche. She'd turned toward Danna when she heard the tapping of Danna's heels on the concrete, and her eyes had nearly popped out of their sockets. Bumping her head on the metal, she rubbed it in embarrassment. "Wow, you really do have a sexy red dress."

Looking around in the pristine garage, Alex couldn't find a rag to wipe the dirt and grime from her hands. She didn't have another nice pair of jeans to change into so she had to be careful not to soil her only clean pair. Danna walked to a built-in cabinet in the garage and pulled out a white cloth, handing it to Alex. She quickly wiped her hands.

"Um, do you mind if I go back inside and do a more thorough wash before we leave. I wouldn't want to inadvertently deposit grime on that very tempting dress.

Avoiding all touch is going to be nearly impossible."

Danna chuckled. "Go right ahead. There's a bathroom to your right in the mudroom."

"Thanks."

Danna had assured Alex the restaurant she had in mind wasn't too far from Sisters and Alex could take her time changing. She had promised to introduce Alex to traditional Southern cooking with a flair. Alex had worried the venue wouldn't appreciate her casual attire and hoped it wasn't some stuffy five-star restaurant that required jackets and ties for men or had a no-jeans rule.

When Alex and Danna pulled up to South City Kitchen, Alex pushed out the breath she was holding in. Danna had assured her they were going somewhere that she would be fine in with her jeans and button-down shirt. The place had a modern feel to it with gleaming wood and shiny black accents. White tablecloths provided an elegant touch, but as Alex looked around, she saw others in a wide range of attire.

The hostess led them to a table and then Alex held out Danna's chair. After Alex sat in the chair opposite from Danna, she looked into Danna's worried face.

Danna was biting her bottom lip. "Can we talk for a few minutes about your immigration status? I did a little research while I was, uh, waiting for you today."

Alex nervously grabbed the white linen napkin and placed it over her lap. "Um, sure. I suppose moving that big elephant before getting to know each other might be the thing to do."

"Sorry, but I had hoped if I shared what I learned it would help us with a plan. Basically, the first step is you have to obtain a green card. There are two ways to do that.

I'm assuming you can't claim fear of persecution and you haven't served in the military, right?"

"Yeah, neither of those options are available to me."

"Okay, so either you need to accept a job offer from an employer who is willing to sponsor you because no U.S. worker is qualified, willing, or available to take the opportunity. Or, you have at least one million dollars to invest in the creation or expansion of an existing business. Um, there is one more option that I should share." Danna wouldn't meet Alex's eyes.

"Well, I don't think door one or door two will work for me. So lay it on me, what's door three?"

The waiter approached the table with a wide smile on his face. "Welcome to South City Kitchen. Can I start you ladies off with a drink, or perhaps you'd like to order a bottle of one of our fine wines?"

Danna looked up at the waiter. "We haven't quite decided yet on dinner, but when we do, perhaps you can suggest a wine that would go with our main entre choice."

"Shall I tell you our specials for the evening?"

"Sure," Alex and Danna answered in unison.

"We have a Caroline trout with braised artichokes, swiss chard and burnt orange vinaigrette, and our bone-in strip steak is guaranteed to melt in your mouth. Of course the steak is cooked perfectly to your specification."

"Which is more traditionally Southern?" Alex asked.

"Probably the trout."

"Sold." Alex flashed the waiter a genuine smile.

"I'll have the same, and go ahead and choose a bottle of wine that will go well with the fish."

"Very well."

"Rieslings are sweet, right?" Alex asked.

"Yes ma'am, they are."

"Can we get one of those?"

The waiter nodded. "Yes, I have the perfect choice for you."

After the waiter walked away, Danna took Alex's hand. "You are too kind. You remembered when I mentioned I liked sweet wines. Nothing much gets by you, does it? I feel like I am the center of your universe. You pay attention like no one else ever has. David couldn't be bothered to remember what I was allergic to."

"You're easy to focus on. Paying close attention is a necessity in my line of work. Sometimes the subtle cues are all you have. The women who came to the Ranch wouldn't always say out loud what they wanted. I developed a skill for being a mind magician."

At first she wanted to suck the words back into her mouth because once again she was reminding Danna about what she would be doing at TWC. Then she noticed Danna's relaxed expression and the absence of a tightening in her body. She was thankful that it appeared as though Danna was settling into a kind of comfort with talking about pleasure work. She looked down at their hands.

Danna was stroking Alex's hand. "I'll bet these hands are pure magic. Not to embarrass you or anything, but I couldn't help noticing how long your fingers are. Is that beneficial?"

Alex threw her head back and began laughing. "I used to hate my big hands when I was younger, and my gangly limbs. Now, all I can say is thank the good lord that he decided to bestow on me that particular gift. Yes, in answer to your question, the ladies do love my long fingers."

The waiter returned with the wine and a bucket filled

with ice that he placed on a stand next to the table. After opening the wine and pouring a small amount into Alex's glass, he waited.

Alex was confused and looked to Danna for help.

Danna whispered, "Take a sip and let him know if the wine is okay."

"Oh, why don't you do the honors?" Alex pushed the glass toward Danna.

"Nope, I wouldn't know a good wine from one of those boxed varieties." Danna winked. "Just tell him if you like it or not, and if you do, I'm sure I will as well."

Alex brought the glass to her lips and took a small sip. The aroma was very pleasant, a little bit perfumed but not in an overpowering way. "This makes me think of apples or pears. It's fruity. Yeah, I like it."

Danna beamed at Alex and nodded to the waiter who proceeded to fill both glasses.

After he walked away, Alex captured Danna's eyes. "Thank you for not laughing at me and my inexperience."

"Oh, Alex, if this is the first time you've ever been offered a small pour to ensure it has not gone bad, I feel so blessed I get to experience that with you. I'm sure there are so many firsts I won't be able to share with you. I'll take every single one I can."

"Before we were interrupted by the waiter and this wonderful new sensation, you were about to give me my third option for legal status."

"Oh, yes, um..." Danna looked away for a moment. "You can also get what's called a K1 fiancé visa if you are engaged to marry a U.S. citizen."

Unfortunately, Alex had taken another sip of wine while Danna provided the third alternative and choked on the mouthful that didn't quite make it down her throat. "Oh, um, I didn't know that applied to same sex couples," she managed to say despite choking her words.

"It's legal in all fifty states now whether the conservatives like it or not. Yes, that's an option," Danna answered quietly.

Alex leaned back in her chair. "Well, then I'm screwed. I suppose if I have any chance of helping my parents, I have to find a way to change my own legal status first."

"I was assuming you've never taken advantage of DACA. I could do some more research on that specifically."

"Okay, that would be good. I may not have the morals of a nun, but I wouldn't dream of asking some woman to marry me just to obtain legal status."

"I've married for far less scrupulous reasons. If it comes down to that being your only option, Alex, I would readily offer my hand in marriage." Danna picked up her glass of wine and took a sip avoiding eye contact with Alex.

Alex wasn't sure if Danna looked away because she felt obligated to offer herself up for this ruse or if there was some other reason for the discomfort. "You really are something special."

†

After dinner, Alex had invited Danna to come inside although she didn't have much to offer in the way of drinks. Danna had hesitated and Alex wondered if she'd come on too strong with her flirting and sexual innuendos. It wasn't like her to read the signals wrong.

"I'd like nothing better than to make love with you

tonight, Alex. In fact, it's all I've been thinking about all night long. But I'm wondering if that happens, will I disappoint you and then this will only be a memory I get to pull from a tiny box and look at every once in a while. I don't quite know where to get the experience I'll need..." Danna trailed off.

Alex tugged Danna inside. "Danna, there's one thing I haven't shared with you yet. Have you ever heard the term *stone butch*?"

"I've heard it, but I don't know what it means."

"It's a term for someone who is on the masculine side, like me, and doesn't enjoy reciprocation or being touched sexually by their partner. I hadn't heard that term either until my friend, Ariel, at the Ranch told me the best workers at the Ranch, who specialized in women, were stone butches like me. I learned a lot from her."

Danna chuckled. "I suppose we're all lucky you did."

"Ariel told me there are some theories about butches not being comfortable in their female bodies and that being the reason." Alex shrugged. "I don't think that applies to me. I'm not saying I'm one hundred percent stone butch, but a lot of stone butches get their pleasure from touching another woman. They'll touch to the point where they can become aroused enough to have their own orgasms. I'm one of those women. I can easily achieve satisfaction when I know I've pleased someone. Does that make sense and, more importantly, will that bother you?"

Danna frowned. "Will I never be able to touch you?"

"No, no, that's not what I'm saying. I'm only helping you to understand it isn't a requirement. I've not let too many women touch me, though. I've no doubt that with the right person, I will want to travel that path, but for the moment, I'm not quite there. I'd very much like to make love to you, if you'll let me."

Alex wove her fingers into Danna's hair and brought their lips together. Sucking on her bottom lip with reverence and care, she sought entrance inside with her mouth and when Danna opened to her, the kiss heated and caused a flood of moisture to her jeans. Today was one of those days Alex wished she'd put on underwear.

"I hate that I live in this tiny studio and have to interrupt what we've started, but unfortunately I need to make up the futon. Shit. That is the clumsiest thing I've said all night. Will you please just hold that...um...feeling while I make up the bed? I know this isn't what you're used to, but I'd also really like you to spend the night with me. Sometimes I like to wake up to a beautiful woman. That luxury was not something I got to experience very often. Is that too much to ask?"

"No it's not. Let me help you. It will give me something to do rather than explode in anticipation before your very eyes and before we have a chance to, uh..."

"Make love," Alex answered with a smile.

Danna nodded and then blushed.

†

Danna was at the point of no return now. She'd opened to Alex like the petals of a flower blooming in the springtime. The interruption of making up the futon with the clean sheets Alex had pulled from the small closet did not pour cold water on her arousal like she'd thought it would. Alex seemed almost shy now as she clasped both of Danna's hands and led her to the edge of the futon.

186

"I've been salivating over the thought of slowly pushing down the zipper on this smoking hot dress. May I?" Alex asked.

Danna gulped air and nodded. Alex's long fingers moved to the back of Danna's dress as she took her time to push the zipper down while lightly caressing Danna's back. She felt the slight coolness in the studio as Alex pushed the dress from her shoulder. Goosebumps erupted all over her body.

"Cold?" Alex asked. "I can turn down the air conditioning."

"No, just a bit frenzied right now by your touch."

After the dress slipped to the floor, Danna stepped out from the possible entanglement at her feet and removed each high heel tossing them both far from the bed. She'd carefully picked out the lacy lingerie that nearly matched the color of her dress and Alex was now staring appraisingly at her with a sort of raw hunger.

"I cannot even describe how unbelievably turned on I am by your..." Alex ran her finger down the center of Danna's chest and hovered in the cavern between her breasts before bringing her finger back up to push each strap to the side. Soon she was undoing the clasp in the back. The lacy bra joined Danna's red dress on the floor and Alex's hand slowly made its way to the edge of Danna's lacy thong.

At first, Danna thought the impulse purchase was ridiculous for a woman her age. But, she'd worked hard on her body for the last several weeks, attempting to sculpt it back into something resembling what she had looked like in her twenties. The personal trainer she had hired before joining TWC hadn't done nearly as much as her last several weeks with Luna. The emotions and loneliness after David's passing had wreaked havoc on her body. She wasn't where she wanted to be yet, but she was a lot closer with the help of the club and Luna's personally developed routine for her specific goals. Alex's reaction was all she needed to confirm the thong was not a frivolous purchase that would never see the light of day.

"Hmm, I can't decide if I should keep these on or take them off." Alex slipped her finger under the top band and then moved her hand to cup Danna's cheeks, letting her finger sweep over the bare skin in a way that sent new shivers down Danna's body and created moisture below. "Off, I think."

"Will you please get naked with me? I know you don't want to be touched, but I would feel too vulnerable being the only one without clothes."

"Your wish is my command, but first let me help you out of these."

Danna was sure she had never been undressed by someone in quite the same way that Alex was proceeding. The teasing approach only added to her excitement and she was ready to burst. Alex moved the thong down her legs inch by excruciating inch until a gentle urging to lift one foot at a time left the panties pushed to the side along with everything else.

Alex moved Danna to the futon and kissed her once before she quickly divested herself of her own clothes. Although Danna was bereft at the loss of Alex's expert touch, she thought it might have been a good thing because she was already so close to climax. She watched as Alex's sinewy form flexed and moved with such a catlike grace, and Danna wondered if somehow there was an invisible airbrush to remove any imperfection. Of course there was imperfection in every body, but all Danna could see was the flex of muscles and how they created a kind of symphony of form. A canvas of elegance.

"Will you let me show you the Yoni massage? I hope you won't think of this as something completely devoid of emotion. That isn't what I want for us. It's very intimate and I want to share that with you. I want you to be the center of my focus. Is that okay?"

Breathing heavily, Danna nodded. "Where do you need me?"

"I'm going to sit on the bed in a butterfly position. I'll position your legs in a way where you can straddle me so I have easy access to your, um, I don't want to be crude, because this is a beautiful experience, so may I use the clinical term?"

Danna's mouth was so dry. She licked her lips. "Yes."

"So, I'll be touching your vulva, clitoris, and vaginal opening. I'm going to use a natural almond oil, all right?"

"Okay."

Alex retrieved a small container of almond oil from the drawer in the side table by the futon and then moved quickly into position. She sat on the bed with her legs folded in front of her and took Danna's hand first as she effortlessly brought each leg around her body leaving Danna's center open and inviting.

Danna tried not to think about how convenient it was that Alex had the oil in her nightstand. She wondered who else Alex might have invited to her studio apartment, but quickly divested herself of those thoughts as being unimportant. Right now she felt like the only person who mattered to Alex.

Alex kissed her once again, lightly, with a small amount of pressure, before asking, "May I touch your lips?" She chuckled. "I mean, the ones quite a bit lower. Not the ones you're nervously licking right now."

"Oh, God, yes. Please do."

Alex dripped oil onto her long slender fingers and then moved to Danna's vulva and began sensually massaging. At first she used both index fingers as she rubbed down the sides of Danna's labia, then she used both thumbs as she let her fingers caress other parts of her sensitive center above the hairline. The whole experience was an erotic journey like none other. By the time Alex asked for final permission to proceed, Danna was squirming and seeking greater connection.

"May I go inside now?"

The air in the room suddenly felt ten degrees warmer as Danna answered with a breathy, "Yes."

Nothing could have prepared Danna for Alex's long, slender fingers as they moved inside and pressed against a place she was sure no person, man or woman, had ever touched before.

"Danna, will you do something for me?" Without waiting for an answer Alex continued, "Will you contract your muscles around my finger while I press inside?"

"I can try."

Alex continued to stroke the outside while pressing on the inside. Her gentle touch created an ever-increasing wave of pleasure and Danna leaned back pressing her hands flat against the bed. She moaned loudly and was surprised by her outburst. But this felt so damn good.

The building sensations took her to the edge and she tumbled over effortlessly as Alex managed to catch her as she fell into the depths of a euphoric coma of blessed release. Satiated beyond the point where she'd ever thought it was possible.

"Wow. That is the only word I can think of because uh...I can't think of a less crude way to say this, but you've fucked me stupid."

Alex roared with laughter. "God, I am so glad I can tease such a crude response from you. It's better when you're not so high up on that pedestal."

"I wish I could keep this Yoni massage all to myself. Is it terribly mean that I don't want you to do this to the other clients at TWC?"

"Done. I will save this for you and you alone, but can I at least teach the others this skill. Some of the women will greatly benefit from a Yoni massage."

"Sorry, I'm being selfish. I would not want to completely deprive them of this wonderful technique. What about you? Can I do anything for you? I must admit I've been aching to touch a woman and perhaps after I'm not feeling like a noodle."

Danna had thoroughly enjoyed the experience and Alex was no doubt a talented lover, but something was missing. She didn't want to be like one of Alex's clients. Even though Alex had described this as intimate and she had clearly treated Danna with a kind of reverence, in some ways their love making lacked the intensity of emotion she craved. Did it mean something to Alex?

"I'm good. Come lie next to me, please. I'd like to wrap you in my arms. If something further transpires in a little bit, we can just go with it. For right now, what I'm longing for is the kind of closeness I only get when I'm holding another woman; one I care deeply for. I had that once in my life and I let her go without a fight. We were young and I wasn't ready to introduce this part of my life to my mama and papa. I miss that."

The magic words penetrated Danna's ears. She wasn't simply a woman needing an orgasm. Alex told her she cared. Perhaps this stone butch thing was something she'd have to learn more about. She didn't wish to lessen the intensity of making love with Alex with her insecurities. Climbing under the covers, Danna nestled against Alex and the last thought she had was that a piece of her soul might be lost if she never got to feel this again with Alex. The absolute perfection of how her body molded to Alex was something she didn't think she'd ever experience with anyone else and she selfishly wanted Alex all to herself. At least all to herself at night. She'd have to get used to Alex giving a piece of herself to the needy women at TWC during the day. It was too early to speak of love, but Danna knew she could easily fall in love with Alex. If Alex's only option to stay in the country was to marry, becoming Alex's wife would not at all be a sacrifice.

CHAPTER FIFTEEN

Despite the warmth and pleasantness of waking up with Danna beside her, something was nudging Alex's barely conscious mind. She needed to do something very important this morning. When she realized her evening with Danna had completely taken her focus away from trying to connect with her papa and mama, she mentally kicked herself. She looked toward the small window and guessed it was about six in the morning. Still too early to call. Alex didn't know if she should wake the sleeping woman. She'd caught the hint of disappointment in Danna and knew it was because she always held a part of herself back. Without meaning to, she might have reverted to treating Danna like one of her clients and that was the very last thing she'd wanted to do. Danna was special.

Danna stirred and opened her sleepy eyes. "Good

morning." She smiled lazily and stretched.

"Good morning, beautiful. Did you sleep okay?"

"Never better. What time is it?"

"I'm guessing around six."

"Oh, I better get up. I need to head home, shower, and change before I make my way into the office. I've got a busy day," Danna said.

"Oh? What's on your docket, anything you can talk about?"

"Well, the most pressing thing is to score some coffee and croissants for this beautiful masseuse. Then, I have to buy a cell phone and a new battery for the Porsche."

"Oh, no you don't. I'm buying my own phone and getting a new battery. I took note of the right kind when I was under the hood. And, yes, I know it won't be cheap, but I can afford it now. I don't want you to be my sugar momma. I need to be an equal player. I will let you buy me some coffee and another of those buttery croissants that literally melted in my mouth." Alex grinned.

"Well, I feel a bit lopsided about last night. I thought I might get a second wind then try to...um...give you pleasure, but I promptly fell asleep." Danna blushed.

"I told you I was good and I really was. If I let you touch me, it will be much further down the road. And, all the stars will need to line up perfectly. I've no doubt they will, because you mean that much to me," Alex replied seriously. "Remember, mostly stone butch."

Alex was glad to see Danna emerge from the bed and not try to cover her naked body. That was a good sign. Despite Danna's newness to admitting she was a lesbian, she wanted Danna to feel comfortable the morning after. She hated any awkwardness, even a discomfort over a partner seeing their lover naked in the light of day. That seemed ridiculous to Alex given whatever had transpired the night before when either her mouth or hands had explored every part of her lover's naked body. She never could understand the need to cover up the next morning.

"I'd like nothing better than to lay around all day in bed, but I should go now. Seriously, can I bring you coffee?"

"Yes, I wasn't joking about that."

"Okay. I'll swing by before work. Um, what do you think about getting together tonight for dinner? Unless you have something else going on today. Then you can put in the battery and take the Porsche with you. Would that work, say 5:30ish?"

"Sounds perfect. I'll cook for you. Mama taught me how to make a mean tamale. I'd love to introduce you to a different kind of spice."

"It's a date. Should I bring a bottle of wine? I'll have to research what goes best with tamales."

"Corona and lime or maybe margaritas would be best. I'll bet Chancy would fix us up, so no, don't bring anything but your gorgeous self."

†

After Danna had dropped off the coffee and croissant, she'd only spent a few minutes with Alex before leaving for her office. Although Alex wished she would have been able to stay a little longer, she knew the day was packed with talking with Selene and Janice, finding the closest stores to purchase a new battery and cell phone, and most importantly, borrowing Selene's phone again to make the call to her papa's shop.

Alex jumped into her tiny shower. After toweling off, she brought her jeans to her nose, and took a quick sniff. They would have to do until she could do laundry. Galloping down the stairs, she found Selene in the office and decided of the two, Selene would be the better person to talk to about working through a schedule where she could maintain both jobs. She poked her head inside the office.

"Hey, Boss, got a minute?"

"Sure, but you can save the big speech. We'd be crazy if we tried to make you choose between TWC and Sisters. You let us know how you want to work things out and we'll make whatever adjustments you need us to. Honestly, you can do repairs at any time. Well, except when the bar is hopping. It would be better if you fixed things after hours or on the days of the week when it's slower."

"What if there's an emergency?"

"We could get you a pager or you could join the twenty-first century for shit's sake and get a God-damned cell phone."

Alex grinned. "Shush. I am getting a cell phone. As a matter of fact, unless you need me to attend to anything today, I was planning on going shopping and picking one up. Danna offered to add me to her family plan."

Selene raised her eyebrow. "Family plan, huh? So she's officially family?"

Alex laughed. "Yes, I can attest to the fact that she's pure lesbian."

"Is this serious?"

"We're dating. I like her. A lot. I know we come from very different worlds, but somehow we fit. I'll need to work through a few things. I'm not used to heavy emotions."

"Hey, I'm not judging. Maybe she'll be the answer to

your little immigration status problem. Get married and bam, automatic citizenship."

"It isn't that simple. Even if it was a good idea to marry Danna, there's a whole complicated process to go through. Although the other options don't seem plausible. But, I'm not roping in Danna to a marriage of convenience or whatever the hell else you might call it. I'll figure something out. Speaking of which, the other reason I needed to see you this morning is to borrow your phone one last time."

Selene picked up her cell phone sitting on the desk and handed it to Alex. "Here you go."

"Thanks, Boss. I'll bring it right back." Alex turned to leave.

"Don't leave the office on my account. Listening to phone sex might be the highlight of my day."

"Ha ha ha. I'm not calling Danna. I need to try to track down my papa and mama."

"Sorry." Selene waved her hand in the air. "Go on, I don't think anyone will be at the bar this early. Janice doesn't move until at least ten."

Alex shuffled to the empty bar with the cell phone in her hand. She wasn't sure what outcome would surface from her call to her papa's shop. If he answered, what would she say? How would she explain that she hadn't known they would still be in the country? How could she tell them she'd met someone? Someone who mattered. If she was completely honest with herself, she didn't want to leave Atlanta. Before her internal struggles got the best of her, Alex used the keypad on the phone and entered the number she knew by heart. Her nervous energy jostled around in her stomach causing an unpleasant feeling. The phone rang three times before her papa answered.

"Juan's Fix It Shop. What can we fix for you?" Her papa's thick accent floated through the tiny speaker. Alex thought she'd never heard a happier sound.

"Papa," she whispered.

"Mija, is that you? Oh, Alex, your mama and me were so worried for you."

"Oh, Papa. I am so sorry. I didn't know you would still be here or I would have never left. I swear, Papa, I was going to get enough money to bring you and Mama back."

"Mija, don't you worry about us, we have many powerful friends in community help us. The lawyer, he say it take years for process."

"I have money, Papa. I will send it now that I know you're still here."

"When you coming home, Mija?"

Alex hesitated. She didn't know how to honestly answer her papa. The silence was deafening.

"Mija? You still there?"

"Yes, Papa, I'm here." Alex thought it was now or never. "I've met someone, Papa."

"Good, that is good. Your mama and I so worried about you. Maybe you come home and bring this young woman."

Alex choked and began coughing. She couldn't speak through the air that caught in her throat from her papa's response.

"Oh, Mija, you think we blind to your love of women? I understand. Women are tempting creatures. Your mama capture my heart very first time I saw her. You love this woman?"

"I don't know, Papa. I think I could, maybe."

"You have job?"

"Yeah, I have two. I work at a bar and at a spa. It turns out all my years under your tutelage taught me how to fix just about anything. That's a skill needed in both places."

"Tutelage?"

Alex relaxed and laughed. "Yeah, it means you took me under your wing and taught me everything I know."

"I teach you how to charm ladies, too, huh?"

"Oh, Papa, I miss you. I'll talk with Danna and maybe we can visit. I just started the jobs here, so it won't be for a while. I'm making very good money and received a big sign-on bonus, so please don't let that big macho pride of yours get in the way. You need money for proper legal fees and I have it."

Alex could hear her papa sigh on the other end of the phone. "I not like this."

"I'm sending the money and if you do not take it, I will track down your lawyer and give it directly to him. I am my papa's daughter and just as stubborn as you, old man."

Her papa's laughter was a welcome sound. "I am getting too old to fight with strong-headed daughter. You come home soon. I not fight you on this."

"Deal. I'll call again soon, Papa. I love you. Please give Mama a hug and kiss for me. Maybe she can come to the shop in the mornings and I can talk to both of you."

"Si, si. I tell her. When you call again and I bring Mama?"

"Is it too soon to call again tomorrow?"

"Will call cost you much money?" her papa asked.

"No, Papa. These cell phones have plans with unlimited time that allow me to talk as long as I want. I'm borrowing one right now, but I'll have my own after today."

"Good, I bring Mama tomorrow. I love you, my

precious Mija."

"Love you too. Bye, Papa."

Alex pressed the button to end the call and with a spring in her step returned to the office to give Selene back her phone. Life was finally going her way. She chuckled to herself at how wrong she had been about her mama and papa. Of course they knew. How could they not? She'd never shown any interest in boys or men and they never asked. Besides, one look at her and anyone with eyes would have screamed, *dyke.*

She thought back to her mama's disapproving looks when she'd strolled in the next morning looking like the cat that ate the canary. She'd assumed her mama wouldn't have approved if she'd known. Maybe she wouldn't have appreciated her cavalier attitude toward sex, but a steady, loving, relationship with a woman was probably fine and dandy. It was possible her mama simply wanted her to share that part of her life rather than keep it secret. She was waiting for Alex to open up to her. And she was waiting for Alex to settle down. How wrong she was to not introduce her girlfriend to her parents.

Maybe she did get a few more traits from her papa besides the ability to fix anything. She'd certainly heard about his exploits with women before he'd met her mama. Mama would tell the stories of how she rebuked him for many months because he was a terrible prospect for a husband. Papa had persevered and shown he could be the man Mama needed him to be.

Although it was a relief for her parents to know about her loving women, she didn't think they would ever understand her other job at TWC. There was only so far she could push her mama's deep Catholic faith. Need-to-know basis. That would be her mantra. Her papa and mama did not need to know that, so she would never tell them. No person ever shared everything with their parents, like she was sure parents did not tell their children all their secrets. Some truths were best left locked away.

Alex needed to step up her pace. She had things to do today, people to see, places to go. She needed to find the ingredients for her mama's famous tamales. Maybe the way to a woman's heart was not through her stomach, but it couldn't hurt. Could it?

†

Alex was humming and swaying her hips to Gloria Estefan. The lively beat was hard to resist. She'd made a lot of other purchases today besides the cell phone, the ingredients for the tamales, and the battery. She needed music while making the famous dish, so she'd purchased a portable CD player and some used CDs. Finding the second hand store had been a godsend as she picked up the basic kitchen items not already in the small cupboards. A Dutch oven was essential to cooking the meat to tender perfection. She'd rushed around like a crazy person and had to phone Marley instead of stopping by to talk about her hours. The meat would take at least two hours to cook and she wouldn't have time to adequately prepare the meal if she made an appearance at TWC.

Alex needed at least four hours to make the homemade tamales and she was running behind. She had wanted to start the meat by no later than one and it was already close to two before she had the chicken cooking in the Dutch oven with the onions and garlic. Next on her list was preparing the chile sauce. Alex hoped Danna liked spicy food or else she was totally screwed.

Her mama had taught her to carefully remove the stems and seeds from the chile pods. This was a painstaking process and more difficult with gloves, but a young Alex had learned her lesson one day when helping her mama. She'd forgotten her gloves. When she went to rub her eye, it was one of the few times she had cried as a young girl. Alex never made that mistake again. Adding the chicken broth, garlic, Mexican oregano, sea salt, and cumin, Alex brought the mixture to a boil. She reduced the heat and let it simmer for an hour. Although her mama had said that traditional red sauce does not use chicken broth, she added that because for some people the sauce was too bitter. She didn't think it was wrong to lessen the bitterness and make a more robust flavor.

Alex kept returning to those fond memories with her mama. She had delighted in Alex's desire to learn how to make the homemade specialty since it was the one thing Alex had shown an interest in that was traditionally female. Her mama had not let the initial disasters sway her from teaching her only child how to cook this special meal. Her mama understood how she gravitated to other activities more like the boys in the neighborhood. This was the only way her mama could spend quality time with her. Her mama always let her make the big mistakes and learn from them. She chuckled to herself when remembering the catastrophic blender event, which she later called the Mija Volcano.

"Mija, do not fill the blender too full," her mama warned.

Young Alex did not heed the warning and placed all the boiled red chiles into the blender nearly filling it to the top. She saw her mama smirk before she hit the button and red chile sauce splattered over almost every inch of the counters and a large area of the floor. It took Alex nearly two hours to clean the kitchen and then she had to repeat the painstaking process of preparing the chile sauce for the blender.

Her mama had only said one thing after she'd cleaned up the disaster. "You must listen carefully in life, Mija, or the best parts of that life will splatter all over like the chiles. Then you must start over again. Paying attention is important."

This was a lesson in life young Alex never forgot. She laughed to herself as she wondered what her mama would think of how she had used that advice. Alex always paid close attention to her lovers, and that was what made her such a talented pleasure worker.

Cleaning up as she went, Alex looked around her small kitchen. There was one last item to cook and then she could jump in the shower and get ready for her date. She needed to prepare the corn husks. To soften them with warm water. She would then combine the lard, salt, masa harina, and baking powder until the consistency was a spongy dough. Spreading the dough over the husks and adding the meat filling combined with the red chile sauce was the last step before placing the tamales into the steamer to cook for one hour.

The whole process was very labor intensive but the end result was divine. She hoped Danna would appreciate the effort, but even if she didn't, Alex enjoyed preparing the meal as it had brought back so many fond memories of her mama.

†

Danna had rushed from her office excited to see Alex. She lightly rapped on the door to the studio and Alex answered with a brilliant smile on her face. She wrapped Danna in a hug before kissing her. The kiss danced along the edges of an R rating, but Alex broke the embrace, pulling Danna inside.

"Come on in, the tamales are almost done. I got a bit of a late start. I'm sorry."

The smells inside tickled Danna's senses as she detected garlic and other spices. "Oh my God, something smells heavenly. My mouth is watering."

"I haven't had a chance to run downstairs and ask Chancy to make up some margaritas."

"I'll go. You attend to the final preparations, because I don't want anything ruining what I am sure will be an orgasmic explosion to my taste buds."

Alex chuckled. "I think someone has something else on her mind besides enjoying a home-cooked meal."

Danna felt her lips tug in a shy smile. "Maybe. I'll be right back. I want to hear all about your day and I'll share some more of what I've learned."

Danna was excited and terrified to talk with Alex, but determined to be honest with her. She ran down the stairs and came to a breathless halt in front of the bartender. "Hey Chancy, any chance I can get you to make a pitcher of margaritas to go? Alex made homemade tamales for us."

Chancy quirked her eyebrow. "Of course. Hmm, homemade huh. You must be special. I dated a Latina woman once who made them for me. You know they take like four hours to make. She's trying to impress you."

Danna grinned like a fool. "I know and I love it, but she doesn't need to do anything but stand there in front of me and smile and I'm impressed. God, I have it bad. I am positively giddy around her and that's so...oh I don't know...completely out of character for a middle-aged woman."

"Hey, the love bug knows no boundaries. I've heard it can even bite someone in their seventies or eighties if only we would allow that bug inside."

"Ew, don't know if I like imagining a bug biting me while I sleep."

"Figure of speech."

"Let's think of a different one. I suppose an arrow piercing the heart isn't any better."

Chancy turned around and began mixing the drinks. Her head swiveled back as she said, "Let me ponder that, and I'll get back to you. I'm really happy for both of you. Alex is the best."

"I know." Danna sat on the stool and waited patiently for Chancy to finish.

With the pitcher in hand, Danna resisted the temptation to take the stairs two at a time. She didn't want to spill any of Chancy's special margaritas. After letting herself back inside the studio, Danna spied what she suspected were two salt-rimmed glasses sitting on the counter.

She lifted the pitcher in the air and gestured toward the empty glasses. "May I?"

"Yes, please."

Danna filled the two glasses. Alex lifted one and paused, holding the margarita in the air. Danna followed and lifted her own glass.

"To the beginning of a beautiful relationship." Alex touched her glass against Danna's and then took a sip. "Mmm perfect. Just right as a pairing for the tamales. Can mixed drinks be considered pairings like wines?"

Danna took her own sip and smiled as she noted the toast mentioned a relationship and not a friendship. "Mmm hmm. Why not."

Alex pointed to the dinette that contained two plates, silverware, napkins, and a small vase with flowers. "Have a seat while I pull out the tamales from the steamer. If you wouldn't mind, bring over the plates first."

As they sat at the table, Danna's nerves began to overtake her.

Alex tilted her head. "Okay, spill. What's got you all nervous?"

"Nothing gets by you, does it? First, I want to thank you for preparing this lovely meal I know will far surpass anything I've ever had before, because I know your loving hands made it."

"It was actually a joy to do this. Made me remember all those times I cooked with my mama. I know you have some things to share with me, but after, I want to tell you what happened this morning. I called my papa's shop and he was there. He answered and we talked," Alex said excitedly.

"Oh that is so good, Alex. I want to know everything. What I have to tell you involves your parents."

"I told Papa I had met someone important to me and before I confessed it was a woman, he said 'come home and bring this young woman with you.' I was floored. All this time I have been fretting over a way to tell them I'm a lesbian. We joked a bit about that and had a debate about money. Papa is a proud man. I had to play hardball to get him to accept money to help change their immigration status if possible."

"Um, so you didn't tell him how old I was." Danna

frowned.

Alex shook her head. "You are never going to let me live it down when I used the word 'mature.' Danna, you have to know how beautiful you are. You *are* young in both outward appearance and where it really counts—in your spirit and quest for life."

"When I'm with you I do feel young again." Danna took a small bite of her tamale. "Mmm this is positively divine. Am I in heaven right now?"

"Flattery will get you everywhere, but honestly I'd ravish your body even if you hated the tamale. Stop stalling now and spill about what's got you so worried."

Danna set down her fork. "There is no good way to tell you this so I'll just blurt it out. Even if you become a U.S. citizen, and you sponsored your parents, the waiting list is so long for individuals born in Mexico that it will undoubtedly take twenty years to accomplish. This is assuming we are able to achieve legal status for you."

Alex slumped in her seat. "Okay, give me the rest. I know you have more bad news."

"At this moment DACA is not an option for you because INS is not accepting any new requests under the current White House policies. Your two best bets are moving to Mexico for a short while, then getting engaged and filing for the K1 fiancé visa, or letting me loan you a million dollars to establish a business. Although Lindy could potentially create a position and go through obtaining a green card for you, I think this might be challenged. I'd like to suggest holding that particular option for when we can use it for your papa. There might be a bit of subterfuge when we create the position, so it would be best to not have more than one employer sponsor. Hopefully they won't look so close and her husband might be able to help keep your parents off the radar if we pursue that path." Danna took both of Alex's hands in her own. "I know you won't accept a large sum of money from me, and this is probably the most unromantic way to propose, but Alex, I would like you to consider becoming my wife. I know I could fall deeply in love with you, I'm already halfway there."

Alex opened her mouth to respond and Danna placed her finger on Alex's lips. "Please, don't answer yet. I want you to think long and hard before you reply to my question, and I want an answer to this second question. Do you see yourself ever falling in love with me?"

Alex stood and leaned over the small table. She cupped Danna's face and brought their lips together. "I will honor your request, but I do want to say how important you are to me. Okay? Can I say that?"

"Yes, now let me eat this wonderful meal."

Alex's joyous laughter settled Danna's nervous stomach as she took another bite, enjoying the spicy treat.

†

After dinner, Alex proudly presented the cell phone she'd purchased and Danna quickly went through the activation procedure. She had assured Alex she had previously arranged everything with her cell phone carrier to make the process smooth once she had the phone in her hands. They'd both let the meal settle and some of the effects of the alcohol dissipate before Danna drove them both to her home and prepared some coffee while Alex installed the new car battery.

Danna had given Alex the key to the vehicle and she

was pleased when the Porsche purred to life. Running her hands over the soft leather, Alex sighed and tried not to let her thoughts about Danna's marriage proposal completely overrun her and ruin their evening. She knew without a doubt she could fall deeply in love with Danna. If she were honest with herself she would admit she was already all the way down the track. The fact that she'd told her papa about Danna and wanted to bring Danna to meet her parents was all the evidence she needed. But marrying Danna was an entirely different thing.

Alex could continue to do what she'd been doing for the last thirty years—stay under the radar and remain undocumented. Would it hurt Danna's feelings if she turned down her generous proposal? Yeah, Alex knew it would. She'd paid attention to the hopeful, pleading expression on Danna's face; the one she'd tried desperately hard to hide. *Fuck, I can't turn her down. I'll crush her.*

What Alex could not accept was making a commitment to someone when she wasn't one hundred percent sure it was the right decision to make. Weren't her doubts the answer? If she couldn't say yes right away, did that mean she should never say yes? Shutting the door to the shiny red car, she went back into the house and attempted to school her expression. She didn't want Danna having any inkling about the war raging in her mind over what answer to give.

Danna was waiting for her with her head propped on one hand as she sat in one of the tall chairs in front of the granite Island. When her face fell, Alex knew she hadn't been successful at keeping the expression from her face. She set the cup in her hand on the counter and closed the gap between them. A gap that Alex had surely created.

Danna placed her hand on Alex's cheek and Alex melted into her touch. "Please don't answer me right now. I shouldn't have asked; that's all on me. If you answer now, I know it will be no and I'm not prepared for that answer yet. Alex, in life there are no guarantees. I came to you with my heart in my hand, offering you something I knew would be difficult to accept. My heart will be there, in a month, a year, however long it takes. I can wait. Because the last thing I want is for you to be unsure about your answer. Women have been known to change their mind in a heartbeat and sometimes when they do, the moment passes and the damage is done. I don't want that happening to us. Okay?"

"Okay."

"Now will you do me the honor of spending the night with me and if we venture into naughty territory, all the better. Maybe you will let me touch you tonight. Baby steps, Alex, baby steps."

CHAPTER SIXTEEN

A week after Danna's proposal, Alex had called Rosie to see if she'd heard anything about Betty. Betty had apparently returned to Atlanta with her friend and Alex was anxious to talk with her. She wanted to get Betty's perspective on Danna's marriage proposal because she trusted Betty's friendship and her wisdom. Since Alex didn't have her mama here to confide in and see her facial expressions which told the whole story, Betty was the next best thing. And Betty was a lesbian so she would understand her dilemma that things were moving too quickly even in lesbian land.

Alex picked up her new phone which had come to be something she wasn't sure how she'd lived without in her past life. The phone kept her connected to both her parents and to Danna. She could also keep in close contact with

Marley to ensure she was meeting the needs of TWC, especially when Marley would call for last minute appointments. Those phone calls were becoming increasingly more frequent as her reputation grew and the elite members of TWC would ask specifically for her.

"Hey, Betty. It's Alex. I hope you don't mind that I'm calling. Rosie gave me your number. She said you were back in town."

"Hey, Alex. How are you?" Betty sounded like she'd won the mega million-dollar lottery. Her voice had a kind of spark Alex had never heard from Betty before. Granted, she hadn't known Betty long, but Alex paid attention to cues and Betty sounded genuinely happy.

"I'm good. Listen, do you think you would have time to meet for coffee or something. I need to talk to you."

"Sounds serious."

"No, I just need some advice."

Betty chuckled. "You need someone who is older and wiser, huh? Met someone special did you?"

Alex felt her face flush. "Yeah, how'd ya know?"

"I can hear it in your voice. Just like I'm sure you can hear it in mine. Why don't you come for dinner and you can meet my Alice? Dinner ain't gonna be nothing special. We can cook up some burgers on the grill and chill with a few beers."

"That sounds perfect. I look forward to meeting Alice."

†

Alex carried the three four-packs of Torched Hop Brewery's Pale Ale. She didn't want to arrive on Betty's doorstep empty handed. Her mama had taught her better. She thought she especially owed Betty something more than a few tasty microbrews, but this was a start.

Betty opened the door and Alex could see her peering over her shoulder. "Is that a fucking Porsche?" She grabbed Alex's arm and pulled her inside. "I see we have a shit ton of catching up to do."

Alex laughed as she allowed Betty to lead her to the small back patio. "It's not mine. It's my...shit...I don't know what to call Danna. Girlfriend seems sophomoric. Lover is limited."

"Soul mate?"

"Whoa, that's what I need the advice for. She's very important to me. That's the best I can do right now."

"Well, I will say if she is anything close to what my Alice is to me, don't let her slip through your fingers. No matter what. Biggest mistake of my life was letting Alice move away without me fighting, and I mean fighting hard, for her. All the years and months wasted." Betty shook her head. "Not to mention what I allowed to happen because my lazy ass wouldn't do what I knew was right. I shoulda pounded that no good bitch into the ground when I had a chance."

"Betty!" a tiny woman with short gray hair exclaimed. She was sitting in one of the lawn chairs with a T-shirt and loose-fitting khaki shorts.

Betty beamed. "That's my Alice. Alice, this is Alex. The young stud I was telling ya about."

"Oh, she was going on and on about this hot dyke and if she'd been twenty years younger. I would have been jealous had I not seen the look of love in her eyes. Then when she confronted my ex and threatened to chop her into little tiny pieces and feed her to the fishes, I swooned." Alice giggled. "I'd never been so turned on in all my life. And when we made love after I got out of the hospital, I knew what real love was." Alice pointed to the chair next to her. "Come sit and tell us what's causing those tiny lines around your face. You're too young for frown lines."

Alex held up the beer. "You got a cooler or a fridge for these?"

"Ooh...coming up in the world. A Porsche and fancy beers. I'll take one and my Alice will probably have one too. Gimme the rest and I'll put them in the fridge." Betty pulled two from the four pack and handed one to Alice.

Alex grabbed one for herself and gave the remaining beers to Betty to stow away for later.

When Alice accepted the beer, she reminded Betty, "Don't forget about the burgers, dear, nothing worse than crispy overdone meat that don't have no juice left."

Betty pecked Alice on the lips and hurried back inside.

"So, Alex, you got woman trouble?" Alice asked as Alex slid her tall, lean body into the empty chair.

"I wouldn't exactly say that. But I do have a dilemma I don't quite know how to work out. My heart and my head seem to be at odds. Or maybe I'm a little confused by stuff I've never felt before."

Alice nodded. "Love can be very confusing."

Alex popped the top. "It's not that I don't trust you or anything, but maybe we can wait til Betty gets back."

"I understand. My Betty, she has a heart of gold, and if I wasn't such a stubborn cuss thinking once you make a commitment, no matter what you gotta live with it, I'd have been with Betty long before now."

"Hmm, maybe I should be asking you instead of Betty."

"Lay it on me young'un."

"Did Betty tell you I'm not in this country legally?"

"Nope, she wouldn't break any confidence. That's my Betty. Loyal to the very core."

"Well, I'm not legal. I'm one of those evil undocumented immigrants wreaking havoc on this great America. Even though I've lived here in the states practically all my life, I wasn't born here. I met a woman a few weeks ago who is special. Real special. I've never met anyone quite like Danna, but I don't know her all that well. How could I? We've only known each other a few weeks. Anyway, she proposed. She did it because it's one way I can achieve legal status. I take my commitments seriously and I don't know how to answer her. I'm thinking that if I'm hesitating right now, maybe I can't give her the kind of commitment she needs. She deserves someone to worship her, love her without conditions, and make sure her needs are met before my own. I don't know if I can be that person."

"Do ya love her?"

Alex lifted her beer to her lips and took a long draw. "You know if you'd asked that question a week ago when she'd popped the question, I would have said I don't know, but I think I could, given time. Now, I'm pretty sure the answer is yes. Is that crazy?"

"No, not at all. Everyone falls in love in different intervals. And nobody has the right to judge how long it takes. Sometimes it's instantaneous and other times it takes years. There ain't some specific formula you gotta follow, you know."

The sliding glass door squeaked open and Betty

walked to the patio and lifted the lid to the grill, flipping over the burgers as she glanced their way. "You ain't getting into the juicy stuff without me are ya?"

"Sorry, Betty. You've managed to woo the last perfect female on earth. I couldn't help myself. Spilled my guts in less than a minute." Alex settled back in the lawn chair.

"The burgers are almost ready, unless you like them well done." Betty waved her spatula in the air.

"Nope, I like a little red juice oozing from mine if you don't mind," Alex answered.

A small table was already set with ketchup, mustard, mayonnaise, salt, pepper, and a container of potato salad.

"Hon, will ya get the tomatoes and lettuce for the burgers out of the fridge and put them on the table? Oh, and I think I left a bag of chips on the counter, too."

Alice got up and slowly made her way into the kitchen. Alex noticed the slight limp and her heart went out to the woman who had probably endured a great deal of pain in her life by choosing the wrong partner and sticking to her. Danna was nothing like Alice's ex, Alex knew that. There wasn't a cruel or possessive bone in her body.

"Alex, will ya get me one of those paper plates on the table and I can pull the burgers from the grill. Shit, I forgot to tell Alice to grab the buns."

Alice limped outside with a Tupperware container in one hand, a bag of chips under her arm, and a package of hamburger buns in the other arm. She pushed the sliding glass door shut with her foot. She was laughing as she reached the table. "I didn't need you to remind me about the buns. I ain't senile yet, ya know."

Alex stood and walked over to the table to grab a

paper plate that was sitting in the center with the salt and pepper holding it down. She strolled over to where Betty was grilling.

Betty chuckled. "Okay, just put them on the table please." Betty flipped the three burgers onto the paper plate Alex held out for her and they both joined Alice at the table.

When all three had settled at the table, Betty lifted her can in the air. "To love."

The three clinked cans and laughed. As all three women prepared their burgers to their individual liking, Betty started the conversation. "So, what'd I miss?"

"Your young friend here managed to get herself a marriage proposal to make her legal, and she ain't sure, but she thinks she loves the woman."

Betty stared at Alex and spoke with an air of sadness. "Alex, you grab this woman and don't let go. Tell her you love her and accept that proposal. Don't be a stupid clod like me. Sure, it worked out, but look what she done to my beautiful angel? Alice has a limp she ain't ever gonna lose, and all because I was too insecure to do what I knew all along was in my heart. Sometimes the universe gives old dykes like me a second chance, but it ain't without its price. Don't let the woman you love pay the price for your stupidity."

"It isn't like she has to be saved from an abusive husband. He's dead," Alex argued.

"You don't think you have the power to hurt her with your words? Sometimes words cut more deeply than a knife ever could." Betty took a large bite of her burger and a glob of mayonnaise stuck to the side of her mouth.

"Yeah, but people shouldn't get married because they're worried about hurting the other person. That isn't right either. Getting married under false pretense is just as wrong."

Betty set the burger on her plate and finished chewing. After Alice pointed to her mouth, she grinned and wiped off the mayonnaise. "Alex, why you lookin' for excuses not to accept her proposal? People who are in love get married every single day. What's really behind your reluctance?"

That was a very good question that Alex wasn't sure she had the answer to. It was on the tip of her tongue, but wouldn't surface. And then it hit her like a cement building crashing down. She wasn't sure if Danna loved her. She'd only said she could see herself falling in love.

"I don't know if she loves me or is simply very fond of me and my uh...skills in the bedroom. I'm her first lesbian relationship and that's bound to be intense. Sometimes that intensity is misunderstood. It's easy to mix up love and lust or sexual gratification."

Betty nodded her head. "Okay, well you're a smart woman. You pick up on things that no one else would. Look for the clues and when you think you've uncovered the key to the mystery, there's your answer. If you determine she loves you, marry the woman and live happily ever after."

"Thanks, Betty. Can I say that love looks especially fine on you? I'm real happy for both of you. I want to have you and Alice over for dinner so you can meet Danna."

"We'd love to," Alice and Betty answered together.

†

The days turned into weeks and Alex and Danna settled into a routine. On the weekdays they stayed at Alex's

218

place. It was more convenient for Danna since her office and favorite coffee place were close by. On the weekends they enjoyed Danna's sprawling estate, complete with heated pool and all the privacy they needed for their active exploration of each other. The sex was always exemplary, but thankfully, Danna began to feel like Alex's lovemaking was less about ensuring Danna felt good and more about a special connection.

Alex still had not let Danna touch her more intimately than soft caresses to her breasts, stomach and other parts far away from her center. Usually it happened after Alex had made love to her and they were relaxing in one another's arms, basking in the afterglow. But she was getting close. Danna was venturing into new territory every night. The previous evening she had stroked Alex's behind and moved her hands along Alex's hips and down her legs. She had almost reached the apex with a daring brush of her fingertips to Alex's inner thighs.

Alex had growled and flipped her over, grinding her body against Danna's until she climaxed with her head thrown back in a throaty moan. To Danna, it was the most beautiful sight she'd ever seen and she had toppled over soon after. That's how she knew her touches were arousing and Alex was on the verge of completely letting her inside. She was determined to demolish that final barrier. When she'd uttered those three small words after climaxing, the shock must have been evident on Danna's face.

"I mean it, Danna. I do love you. I want you to come to Texas with me. My papa and mama ask me nearly every day when I will bring you to meet them. I'm ready. Marley, Selene, and Janice have given me Friday and Monday off. Will you come with me?"

Danna had wrapped her arms around Alex and screamed, "Yes." Then Danna had stiffened as she worried what Alex's parents would think of a woman twelve years older than Alex.

Alex had squeezed and said, "They are going to love you as much as I do."

Danna had wanted to say those three words back, but something was stopping her. Alex hadn't said a word about the proposal. Sometimes she felt like she was under a microscope with Alex and she was being judged or evaluated for something that was elusive. Danna had gotten the feeling over the last four weeks that in some strange way she was in the middle of one big long interview. The results would determine her future with Alex. It was unnerving. Alex hadn't reacted poorly or given any indication she needed to hear Danna declare her love, but still Danna was waiting for something. She'd know when the time was right and then she could declare her feelings without remorse.

When she had sensed what Alex's answer would be to her proposal if she pushed her for an answer right then and there, she had known it would have been a resounding no. The simple knowledge that Alex didn't want to marry her had pushed Danna back into a protective shell. She kept a piece of herself and a large part of her heart behind a locked door. She knew Alex had the key, but would she use it? Would she try a bunch of other keys before the right one slid into the lock?

"I've never been on an airplane before. Laredo isn't far from San Ygnacio—maybe thirty miles or so. I should know, I went there often enough for...uh...you know. I'm pretty sure they have a small airport there. I'm not sure if it's better to rent a car or make some other arrangement."

Danna chuckled. "I think a rental would be good. Let me make the travel arrangements."

Alex began to protest and Danna shut her up with a kiss. "You can pay half, that's my last and final offer. Such a stubborn little shit," she grumbled.

CHAPTER SEVENTEEN

When Alex walked up to the security checkpoint she tensed. Danna quickly took her hand and squeezed it for assurance. She whispered, "He just needs to see your license, hon. Easy peasy. I have all the information on my phone for him to scan. If you act nervous, they'll pull you aside. Be that confident woman I've come to adore."

Alex turned her head and smiled at Danna, squeezing her hand back as she reiterated the words that began to melt Danna's resolve to keep her slightly at arm's length. "Thanks. I love you."

The TSA agent impatiently waved them through. Having pre-check status normally meant the agents didn't give the travelers a second glance. They barely lifted their heads from the focus of scouring bags for dangerous objects. Having only brought a few outfits, minimal electronics, and a paperback, there wasn't a lot to hide or cause concern. The carry-on luggage sailed through the conveyor belt and they were on the other side of security in a matter of minutes.

Danna had insisted on Alex taking the window seat so she could experience the view. There was a childlike joy emanating from Alex as she squirmed in her seat. At first, she'd staunchly refused to fly first class, even though her long legs would not fit comfortably in coach. She'd carefully explained how the extravagance of flying like she was a rich person was 'not her thing.' Danna pretended to agree and booked the tickets for coach, knowing she'd have the option to upgrade when they reached the airport. She would have the airline customer service agent carefully explain that with her miles, there wasn't an additional cost to the upgrade. The perk would go to waste if she didn't use them. Alex abhorred waste. David had racked up the gazillion miles that Danna would never, ever use.

The car she'd rented was nothing special; a compromise to knowing she would get her way in the end with the first-class upgrade. Alex approved. She still wasn't comfortable using the Porsche, but it gave her more time with Danna. She reluctantly agreed to maintain status quo until she was able to learn how to drive a motorcycle and, hopefully, obtain the endorsement without risking her immigration status. Danna had arranged for a car with GPS. She hated getting lost in a strange place, and even though Alex had made the trek from Laredo to San Ygnacio rather frequently when she lived with her parents, Danna didn't think she'd ventured too far from home other than going to the bars in Laredo. Danna wanted to possibly explore the area a little.

Alex took the key from the clerk and announced she

would drive since she knew how to get to her parents' small home. There was a bounce in Alex's step and she grinned when she pressed the button on the key fob and heard the double beep as the sedan's doors unlocked. She tossed both bags in the back seat and they were on their way.

Danna clasped her hands tightly in her lap, keeping herself from biting her nails. This was a habit she'd not completely left behind during times of high stress. Alex glanced in her direction and placed her large hand over top of Danna's white knuckles.

"I know you're nervous, but I promise, Mama and Papa are the salt of the earth. They are generous to people who don't deserve their kindness. Papa and Mama are both so excited to meet you. They know I would not bring just anyone to their home. They'll be far more nervous than you. They know you come from money and I'll bet Mama has scrubbed our tiny home until her fingers are raw. I told her to make tamales and you'd be duly impressed. She'll probably have a feast laid out for us—all homemade traditional Mexican dishes. Papa will pull out his special tequila." Alex turned the dial on the air conditioner to increase the amount of cool air blowing inside.

They pulled up to a small white house with a carport that covered her papa's old truck with the large rust patches along the edges. The faded blue paint no longer glistened in the sunshine, but instead revealed a dull patchwork of color. The truck might not have been much to look at, but she was as reliable as they came. Her numerous trips to Laredo had proved that.

Alex unclipped her seat belt and reached over to caress Danna's cheek. "Ready?"

Danna nodded and when she opened the door, she felt

the blast of heat. "And y'all think Atlanta is warm. How do you possibly do anything in this heat? This is almost worse than the dry heat in Arizona and Nevada. And don't give me that crap about it being a dry heat. Lordy, I know this has been said before, but I really do think you could fry an egg on the blacktop in those horrid places."

Alex chuckled and opened the back to grab both bags. She tossed her backpack over her shoulder and lifted the handle to the expensive bag with Danna's clothes. With her free hand, she took one of Danna's hands, leading her to the front door.

Before they made it all the way, a dark-haired woman with streaks of gray rushed from the house, wiping her hands on her apron. She turned her head back toward the house and yelled, "Juan, they come." The woman shuffled quickly in their direction. Danna could see some of Alex's more delicate features in this woman. When a handsome man with graying temples emerged from the house grinning, Danna knew where Alex got the rest of her striking good looks.

Gathering Alex in her arms, the woman crushed her with a warm hug and then turned her attention to Danna whom she embraced a little less enthusiastically. As she stepped back, she took both of Danna's hands in her own and declared, "Muy bella. She is very beautiful, si? You pick a good one. My Mija always had the eye for the best fruit."

"Mamma, Papa, this is Danna."

"Juan, what you wait for? Go hug our Mija and her friend."

Juan dutifully embraced both Alex and Danna. "You see who wear long pant in family, eh?" he joked.

"Bueno, bueno, now you come in from hot sun before you dry up like hot chile pepper. You call me Mama and he is Papa."

Papa raised his eyebrows as if to say, "see, she is the boss."

Danna's eyes nearly bugged out of her head at the amount of food on every square inch of the counter and center of the table.

"We eat now." Mama bustled around the small kitchen, putting food on the four plates and directing the others to sit while she dished everything up.

†

Alex was happy to see how her mama and papa were continuing to warm to Danna. She knew her mama had liked Danna right from the start. Her papa seemed more reserved and she wondered why until he gradually loosened as the evening progressed. He was watching her carefully and seemed to finally come to the conclusion that Danna fit. Even though her mama was a perceptive woman who paid close attention, it was her papa who had the exceptional observation skills. He picked up on subtle clues not evident to most people. Alex had been his shadow for as long as she could remember. When he taught her something, the lesson was generally more insightful and profound than that of just about any other person she knew.

When her mama began clearing the table, Danna piped up, "Mama, may I please help you with the dishes? This was such a lovely meal that I know it must have taken days to prepare. We should send Alex and Papa outside so they won't get in the way. Then I can pick your brain about all these wonderful foods I've had tonight so one day I may attempt a few of the easier entrées."

"Si, si, but only because I love to teach the young ones. We must not forget our...how you say...?"

"Culture, Mama," Alex interjected.

Alex was relieved because she desperately wanted to have a talk with her papa and get him to share one of his hidden cigars her mama pretended she didn't know a thing about.

"Go now and smoke your stinky cigars."

Alex raised her eyebrow. "Mama is acknowledging your vice now? What happened to blissful ignorance?"

"She say she too old for secrets." Papa opened one of the cabinets and pulled out a bottle of tequila. The amber liquid sparkled in the light as the last rays of sunshine finally dipped into the horizon, leaving a small flicker of warm light before the deep red appeared.

"Now he brings out the good stuff, while we're slaving away in the kitchen cleaning up," Danna joked.

"You like tequila?" he asked in surprise.

Danna laughed. "As a matter of fact, I do, so save some for Mama and me. Maybe one day I'll even try one of your stinky cigars. I've got to make sure I keep up with that one." Her head nodded in Alex's direction.

"I try stinky cigar. Tequila is better," Mama added. "Go on before we make you clean and I take the bottle from you, and Danna come with me for drink instead."

With the sun finally setting, the temperature was tolerable in the back patio. A light breeze added to their comfort as Alex sat on the cheap second-hand lawn chair next to her papa. The edges of the crisscrossed material were beginning to fray. Alex wondered when it would completely give way and no longer hold a person's weight. She looked around and, for the first time, saw the near poverty of her papa and mama's house compared to what she was used to. Everything was either covered in rust or bore the signs of incredible wear and tear. And yet she knew both her papa and mama felt blessed to have a small business and a home to go to every night. This was a happy life for them.

Papa pulled a cigar from his breast pocket and handed it to Alex as he began rolling the second one in his fingers before lighting it. "What you do to cause your Danna to hold back a tiny piece of her heart?"

"What makes you think I did anything?" Alex lit the cigar in her hand and took a small puff, immediately blowing out the smoke.

"She love you, I can tell, but she is, how you say, walk the egg shell."

"She wanted to offer me a path to citizenship with a marriage proposal. I couldn't accept. She told me not to give her an answer right away because I think she knew it would be no."

"Why no? You love her? She love you. Why you make this hard? The big court say you can marry now."

Alex sighed. "I know, but I hurt her and now it's complicated. I told her I love her. She didn't say it back. But I know she loves me. I've held back a piece too, Papa."

"What piece?" Juan grinned and toked on his cigar.

Alex blushed. "I can't talk about that with you. God, Papa don't make me."

"Ah you like big macho man, you make her scream, but you not let her touch you?"

"What?" Alex choked on the smoke from the second puff on her cigar.

"There is girl, she come round the shop to learn. She tell me stuff. I no ask, but she think I know things. I see little bit of her in you. I tell you what I tell her. Man does not have to be in control in bedroom. Sometimes it is nice to let woman drive. Otherwise they think you not respect them as equal. You let this Danna drive and touch you. It is nice feeling when woman get pleasure from touch. You listen to your papa on this."

Alex stuffed her fingers in her ears. "Ew, stop. Besides, I'm a woman not a man."

Juan waved his cigar in the air. "Bah, you think like stupid man. You ask her to marry. That is only way you knock down fence. But you let her make you scream first."

"Okay, stop. I don't think I need advice from my papa on how to satisfy a woman."

Her papa's deep laughter made Alex smile. "Big fence to climb. I think you do need advice from your old papa."

Alex smacked her papa. "You are such an exaggerator. There's a tiny two-foot fence I need to hop over."

"You have money to get nice ring?"

"I honestly don't think she cares about that."

"True. Your mama did not mind. You ask while you are here and then we celebrate with tequila."

"Maybe. Don't push. Okay, Papa?"

"Okay, Mija."

"Papa?"

"Yeah, Mija?"

"Why does love have to be so damned hard?"

Juan shrugged. "When love is easy, sometimes, not so good because we take them for granted. Hard is okay, but not too hard. Make it simple, Mija, let her in all the way."

"Papa?"

"Yeah, Mija?"

"Open the damn tequila already."

Juan chuckled, opened the bottle, and handed it to Alex who took a swig and grimaced as the amber liquid burned all the way down.

"I think, maybe time to go back inside before Mama start talking grandbabies."

Alex popped up and nearly ran back into the house, catching her mama and Danna sitting with coffee and laughing like old friends who had just shared a naughty secret.

†

The four days flew by and Danna wished her own family was as loving as Alex's. It had nearly broken Danna's heart to learn Alex's mama had desperately wanted more children but couldn't have them. She'd not been very subtle with her hints of desiring grandchildren. Danna was a little worried that perhaps Alex's parents did not realize the age difference. Alex had deftly changed the subject anytime her mama had steered it in that direction and that wasn't a good sign. Did Alex not want to have children? Or did she not want to have them with Danna? Danna shook her head. Cart. Horse. The whole train of thought was skirting that dangerous edge. They hadn't spoken of the proposal since Danna had unwisely placed that option on the table. Prematurely, she realized, but she couldn't push the toothpaste back inside.

As they rode in silence back to Danna's house each woman was immersed in her own thoughts. Danna turned to look at Alex. Her beautiful profile caused a rush of emotions in Danna, but she couldn't bring herself to say those three words. She squirmed in her seat.

As if Alex realized Danna was staring, she turned her head and met her gaze for a second before refocusing on the road. "Danna, I love you and I promise everything is all going to work out. Papa says sometimes it's good when love is hard. I never want to take you for granted. When we get home, I promise to help you relax in the most delightful way."

Danna laughed. "Oh, well, that is a promise I'm going to hold you to." Alex had said "home" and that had settled Danna more than the quick squeeze to her thigh and the loving look Alex had casually tossed in her direction. It was as if the feelings came easy to her because they were real. The feelings of love were genuine. Danna was on a mission. She desperately wanted to touch Alex. She needed to penetrate the stone butch persona, and reach deep inside to give her the same pleasure Alex offered to her almost every night they'd been together since that very first time. They'd even managed to make love in Alex's small bedroom at her parents' house. She'd had to temper her reactions to Alex's touch and a few times Alex had captured her lips in an attempt to stifle the loud moans. Giggling afterward, Danna knew she wasn't acting her age and wondered if the love bug that had bitten her had injected a rush of stupid into her veins. She wasn't sure she would ever tire of that, even though she knew it was inevitable for that part of the relationship to change. The heat would reduce and they would revert to a simmer, cooking over low heat, until the next time they were prepared to boil over again.

Simply thinking about moving her fingers over Alex's slick center and managing to taste a woman for the first time was making Danna squirm in her seat for an entirely different reason than earlier. She wanted that more than anything she'd ever wanted in her whole life. She wanted to delve inside. To feel Alex's muscles contract against her fingers and hear her call her name in pure ecstasy because Danna was touching her heart, her soul. This was the very essence of love and intimacy.

Alex glanced again at Danna. "You have a different kind of antsy going on with you now. I think I like this one better than before." Alex grinned.

"I sure hope so," Danna whispered. Tonight she would not take no for an answer.

CHAPTER EIGHTEEN

When Danna had looked at Alex beseechingly, asking if she could be the one to pamper Alex after the long trip. Alex had offered to drive again and they'd gotten caught in the middle of rush-hour traffic because a particularly nasty accident had created a two-hour delay.

Alex surmised the Jacuzzi tub hadn't been used very often. When Danna suggested she draw up a bath for both of them, Alex had agreed that sounded nice and it was. She had even allowed Danna to be the big spoon as she washed Alex's back. Danna had used her hands, rubbing a generous amount of soap over nearly every inch of Alex, including her breasts. Alex had leaned into the touch and kept reminding herself of what her papa had told her. She needed to allow Danna this honor. To Alex, it was an honor. She was going to give a part of herself she had not allowed to others. She would work very hard to relax and let the feelings flow over her.

With the soft white towel wrapped around her body, Alex sat on the bed waiting for Danna. Vulnerable and exposed Danna walked toward Alex completely naked as she towel dried her hair. Alex had never been self-conscious about her body before, so she suspected the towel was symbolic as the last barrier to shed. After the towel was gone, there was no turning back. She would give Danna what she most wanted and then she would ask that very important question.

After Danna tossed aside the towel, she ran her fingers through her wet hair and, damn, that look of hunger on her face was sexy. She stalked toward the bed and ran her finger over the top of the towel where the two ends were folded together holding the towel in place and covering Alex's naked form. Alex had given Danna a silent acknowledgment that she would allow Danna to be the aggressor this evening. She was thankful Danna knew this without a lengthy discussion, but she did need to set some boundaries. Ones she didn't believe she could ever push aside, even for Danna.

"No toys," Alex stated.

"I wouldn't dream of putting something between you and me that, in my opinion, would not satisfy my craving to touch and taste you."

Alex merely nodded in acknowledgment that they were on the same page this evening.

Danna's hand found the top fold of the towel and gently removed the fluffy barrier to skin on skin contact. After the towel landed close to the other damp twin, Danna straddled Alex and began to kiss her neck. Soon enough her mouth found its way to Alex's and both women moaned together as the kiss deepened. Alex was still on the edge of the bed when Danna pushed her back onto the mattress. Alex's legs remained draped over the lip of the bed. Danna quickly repositioned herself and hovered over the top of Alex. The raw expression ratcheted up Alex's arousal as she eagerly waited for Danna's next move. Alex could not believe she was beginning to enjoy being the recipient of this woman's total control and masterful seduction.

Danna placed her hands on the mattress and pushed herself up. She planted her knees and curled up her legs on each side of Alex's hipbones, allowing their centers to touch. She leaned down and began kissing and nibbling, tweaking Alex's nipples with her teeth and alternately sucking her breasts as Danna held herself over Alex, giving her the leverage for total assault on Alex's willing body. Alex could feel her moisture mingle with Danna's, increasing wetness in her own center.

Alex allowed her voice to provide Danna with clues to how well this new intimacy was going so far for her. "Oh, God, yes, that feels so nice."

When Danna let her mouth slide down Alex's torso, she also brought her hands down as well and began caressing and touching Alex's skin, increasing her pleasure. She was causing Alex to move her hips in a kind of syncopated rhythm to the rise and fall of her chest as her breaths became more rapid and desperate.

Alex wanted to let her lover know everything was good and she was not only choosing to allow this, but at this point she needed Danna to touch her and taste her. She craved it as much as Danna.

"Danna, I want you to touch me. I want to feel you,

all of you. Make love to me."

With that final declaration, Danna's fingers moved rapidly to Alex's pussy lips and she parted them as her tongue moved languorously up and down brushing against her clitoris with each long stroke. Alex began to buck with vigor as the intensity grew. She felt a slight hesitation as one of Danna's fingers circled the entrance to her vagina while Danna began to suck on her clit, biting down gently in between her sucking.

Alex gave Danna permission to broach the final barrier. "Yes, go inside, please. One finger, just one."

When Danna pushed a finger inside, slowly moving it in and out, Alex knew she was close to exploding. The final moan from Danna as she continued to suck, caused Alex to climax with a force she'd only experienced once or twice before while making love with a woman. She felt herself contract around Danna's finger and when her contractions finally stopped, Danna carefully pulled her finger out. Moving slowly up Alex's body, Danna kissed her again and declared, "I love you too. I have for a long time now, probably since the first time we made love."

Alex tasted herself on Danna's lip and answered Danna with a question, or some might have said it sounded like a desperate plea. "Marry me, Danna, or ask me the question again. I'm ready to answer."

"Yes," Danna declared and a bruising kiss followed.

†

"What?" Alex set down her fork on the breakfast nook in Danna's kitchen and began shaking her head. "No, no way, I'm an American. They'd never let me back in and

I'm not going to live there for however long it takes for them to decide we can marry."

Danna finished chewing her delicious tortilla filled with eggs, avocado, cheese, and homemade chile sauce. "We can open another high-class spa and I'll move my office there to work remotely. We can make this work."

The defeated look on Alex's face was heartbreaking to see. "My parents, what about my parents? They'll never let me back and forth across the border to visit them. From what you said before, it's a minimum of two years and that's if everything goes smoothly. I can't live in Mexico for two years."

Danna pinched her nose. "Okay, okay. I can't believe I'm going to suggest this. There's no point in us getting married if we don't play by their rules and you remain in the states illegally. If, however, we find someone who can be your body double and set them up in Mexico at the new spa, when the two years are over, we bring her over and make the swap. She gets to come to the U.S. and then disappear and we get to marry as if you'd been living in Mexico this whole time."

"I don't like involving others. Too much risk. Especially a total stranger. They'd have leverage on you and it would be far too tempting to blackmail you after she knows how much money you have."

Danna pushed away from the island and began pacing. "Your damn pride and stubborn insistence on tossing out the only other option without breaking the law..." She was getting frustrated with Alex and was about to release her anger toward the situation on the woman she loved. She took a deep breath. "You asked me to marry you and I said yes. I don't believe you put any conditions on that. When people marry, their finances co-mingle. That's what happens in a true marriage."

"Not if there's a pre-nup."

"God, you're impossible. I would never sign a pre-nup. That is the most unromantic thing I've ever heard." Danna threw her hands in the air.

"More unromantic than proposing to me to keep me legal," Alex retorted and then immediately said, "I'm sorry, Danna." She stood and pulled Danna into a long embrace. "I love you. Okay, tell me what other options we have."

"Invest a million dollars into a business that will bring jobs to the US. I know an attorney who could easily set up the business in your name. We would still have to take a little vacation to Mexico and establish residence until they finalize everything. Maybe we could also find a way to make your parents legal with the new business. Lindy knows a lot of influential people. I honestly think this would be the best and most expedient option. I'm still going to marry you because you can't take back your proposal, but I won't be marrying you for all the wrong reasons."

Alex sighed. "Well, then I better think up a way to invest in a business that's going to make us a shit-ton of money."

Danna kissed Alex and began jumping around in excitement. "Really, you're honestly willing to do this?"

"I love you and sometimes love requires compromise. It's a lesson I'm slowly learning. Remember, any new ideas have to somehow penetrate this incredibly thick skull of mine. Hard-headed is an understatement."

"I always wanted to be co-owner to something."

EPILOGUE

Slowly opening her eyes, Danna placed her hand on the empty spot next to her. It was cool to the touch. As she groggily pushed away the covers and padded down the stairs, she found her wife in the kitchen. The large table was littered with various pieces of metal, nuts, bolts, and other things Danna had no idea about.

"Really, honey? You have a perfectly good shop and yet here you are getting our dining room table dirty." She pointed to the disarray in front of her. "What is this anyway? And, why could this not have waited until a reasonable time? It's not even five yet."

"There was a problem with the automatic tap cooler and I got an idea. I couldn't let that float away without trying something out."

"How do you even have the tools necessary to work

on this?"

Alex grinned. "Papa and me are like inspired artists. Ya gotta go with the flow and make the best of those ideas when they come. I can't afford to drive to the shop while the inspiration is pounding at the door and insisting I open up."

"Fine, but you owe me breakfast and don't even think about waking me before seven."

"But you're already up. How am I going to show you how it works if you head back to bed now?"

"You know I don't understand a single thing about your mechanical inventions. Besides, I thought the patent was pending on this. Can you change the design mid patent?"

Alex shrugged. "I don't know. You're the lawyer in the family. Isn't that what I pay you for?"

"I do family law, you know that. Okay, maybe I also ventured into immigration law too. Granted, I do enjoy your form of payment." Danna smiled. Alex had joked about making sure she provided appropriate remuneration for everything Danna had done to set up the business. Payment came in the form of equally inventive ways to make Danna scream. Alex wasn't only an artist in her shop, she was a virtuoso in the bedroom.

Danna had made it possible for her papa to receive a green card by insisting there was a need for a design engineer to bring to fruition the products their new company would provide. Mechanical Solutions, Inc. was born based on the creative approaches Alex's papa and Alex had designed over the years to resolve various problems. They'd received considerable acclaim when Alex had designed a tap that would cool a keg and keep the beer cold without needing to place it on ice or in an expensive refrigerator. It was an ingenious invention, but apparently still had a few bugs she wanted to work out. Sisters had been using it for the last year with minimal problems.

Danna took a seat at the table and propped her head in her hand, giving Alex a bleary look. Her wife's hair was sticking up, messy from sleep, as she concentrated on the parts and pieces on the table. A tiny bit of her tongue protruded from her lush lips.

"See the problem was this little..." She looked up and smiled. "Okay, I'll spare you the excruciatingly boring explanation."

"Hey, do you have any appointments today at TWC?"

Alex frowned. "Damn, I'm not sure. I better call Marley."

"I wouldn't call yet. She doesn't do well with morning calls when you forget the time and aren't aware that the rest of the world actually sleeps."

"Funny. I sleep. I might have an appointment with Mrs. Prince."

"Oooh, she is getting to be quite the regular," Danna teased. "Should I be worried she might try to steal you away?"

Alex scoffed. "Ha ha. She's like seventy. Be nice. You know TWC provides a very valuable service. It may seem silly to some people, but I'm making a difference in those women's lives. You don't have to do pro bono work, but you do. I don't have that skillset or education. I can open women up to their full sexual potential and that's important."

"I know, I'm teasing. I'll admit, at first I had a hard time realizing why you'd want to continue, but I do understand it now. You're right, neither of us have to work. We do it because we contribute something important to society. If Luna had not opened my eyes, I never would have met you or found the life I was intended to live. I love and trust you. You know that, right?"

"I do." Alex leaned over and kissed Danna.

"I almost forgot, there's a letter on the credenza from Henry. Someday we have to make some time to go visit. Hasn't he mentioned wanting to meet me?"

Alex chuckled. "He has. In every single letter he's written to me after the first letter I sent where I might have mentioned I'd met someone."

"You know, I do want to meet the man who picked you up and was a key person to lead you to me. If he hadn't brought you to Rosie whose route ends in Atlanta, we might have never met. And that would have been a crying shame."

"Okay, okay, I'll make sure to write him back and ask him to give us some dates. I would love to reconnect with him and meet his wife."

"I can't believe you never call," Danna said.

"Henry's old school. You'll never get him to use a smartphone. Not like me. I was a total pushover when you batted those beautiful eyes at me. Speaking of phoning someone, last time I talked to Rosie, she was making considerable progress with Maria. They went on their first date last month. I haven't heard a peep from her and I'm wondering if she finally got lucky." Alex wiggled her eyebrows.

"Stop. Don't you go teasing her. I'm happy for them both. Not to speak ill of the dead, but I am glad her husband isn't in the picture anymore." Danna shook her head. "Heart disease makes a widow out of a lot of women. I feel a real affinity to Maria. I suppose we were both in similar situations. A tragic loss led to a happy ending for both of us. Well, I hope it's a happy ending for her after she lets herself develop those feelings for Rosie."

"I'm not so sure her bastard husband's death was a tragedy. He wasn't like David from what I hear. At least David was kind and loved you. Rosie told me she brought him fatty foods all the time, hoping he might croak."

"That's terrible."

Alex shrugged. "You know it's ironic, I might have liked David. Envied him, maybe. It doesn't sound like he was as down to earth as you, but I get the sense he was a decent guy."

"He was. Sometimes I feel a little guilty for being happy he passed. I suppose that's as awful as Rosie feeding Maria's husband all that greasy food." Danna shook her head. "Hey don't forget that Betty, Alice, Tanya, and Martin are coming over for dinner tonight. I'll pick up some steaks and chicken to toss on the grill. Betty and Alice are such a sweet couple. I sure hope when we get to their age, we'll be just as happy."

"We will. Honey, I couldn't be happier. And that won't change over the next twenty to thirty years. Mama could, though. Be happier, that is. She still wants grandchildren. I might be warming to the idea now that everything is settled. What do you think?" Alex asked. Her serious tone caught Danna by surprise.

"I gave up when I learned David and I couldn't have children. I'm not a spring chicken anymore, but I suppose a little one who looks like you, well, let's just say it has a lot of appeal. Can you give me some time to process this?"

"It wouldn't be fair if I didn't remember how you gave me plenty of time to process your marriage proposal. God, I love you more every day." Alex looked directly into Danna's eyes with such love Danna thought she could

literally feel the warmth envelop her.
      "You took the words right out of my mouth."

ABOUT THE AUTHOR

Annette is an award-winning author, published by Affinity Rainbow Publications, who lives in the beautiful Pacific Northwest with her wife and their five furry kids. With seventeen published novels and one Goldie Award for her fourth novel, *Locked Inside*, she finally feels like a real author. Annette is as much a reader as a writer and is always looking for the next lesfic novel to queue up. She came up with the One Fan at a Time tagline, because it rolled off the tongue much better than One Reader at a Time. After pondering who she was at her core, it was all about connecting to each reader on a personal level. Annette would be the first to admit she doesn't do well with the masses. If someone picks up her book and it touches them, she believes she has achieved what she wants with her writing by reaching each reader. It is who she is at her core.

Drop her a line, she loves to hear from readers:
annettemori0859@gmail.com.

Sign up for her mailing list
Check out her blog: Everyday Occurrences

Visit the Affinity Rainbow Publications website for her books and many other outstanding authors:
https://www.affinityebooks.com

OTHER AFFINITY BOOKS

The Trophy Wives Club by Ali Spooner
What happens when under-appreciated professional women are offered their dream jobs? When one of Atlanta's elite businesswomen and wife of a prominent judge sets her sights on a goal, life begins to change for these women. Friendships and romance bloom in a unique fitness club on the outskirts of Atlanta, where more than a workout is offered.

Unknown Forces by Samantha Hicks
Jennifer Wilson spent the last seventeen years raising her younger sister, Kelsey, after a boating accident killed their parents. Riley hasn't had an easy life either and her friendship with Kelsey is the only thing steadfast in her life. When tragedy and secrets emerge, Jennifer and Riley must learn to lean on each other. The growing attraction between them only complicates matters. When events conspire to

keep them apart, will they trust the unknown forces that keep pushing them together, or hide from their feelings forever?

A Window to Love by Annette Mori
Two life events, two paths colliding, two souls destined to meet. Mandie Carter lives an uninspired life. No passion, no romance, and just when she thought things couldn't get worse, life throws her a curve. Gail Forrester is barely hanging on. Buried under mountains of debt, only her much in demand architectural designs keep her afloat. Now, they must find a way forward together through what life and destiny has in store for them. Only then can they hope to step into that window to love.

Free Spirit by Erica Lawson
Priory McAllister has fought off boardroom sharks, handled high-pressure jobs, and thought she'd seen it all. She found her dream home and couldn't wait to move in. Unknown to Priory, two ghosts...Rhee and a mischievous Dylan...have inhabited the house since 1935. They have no intention of leaving. Jacey Ryder, Priory's long-suffering secretary, gets to play referee between her boss and a bossy ghost, as each side try to lay claim to the house. What can she do when an unstoppable force, (her boss) meets an immovable object, (the ghost) besides hope for a peaceful solution? They are like two peas in a pod—two *angry, stubborn* peas in a pod.

Addicted to You by Erin O'Reilly
Elin Prescot's dream to be a top fashion designer is finally within her reach—then Marissa Banks enters her life. Snared by her first taste of passion, Elin is consumed by desire for more. Her life spirals out of control until she meets Doctor

Aimee Sullivan, who understands all too well what Elin is going through. Can Elin let Aimee into her heart? Or will her addiction keep her enthralled with Marissa? This story explores first love, intense passion, manipulation of emotions, and the gentleness of real love and true romance.

At Last by JM Dragon
A perfume company in trouble, leading to a town in peril. Old Loves. Unrequited Loves. New passions. Can the reclusive Gene Desrosiers save her family company and the people she cares for, even though some are not aware of it yet? Will an ultimate sacrifice win the day, or will Grady end up a ghost town of unfulfilled lives? This love story will warm your heart.

Deuce by Jen Silver
When Jay Reid was in her twenties, she had it all. A professional tennis career, Charlotte, the love of her life and a new baby. Charlotte's research vessel, *RV Caspian*, was lost at sea, leaving Jay to raise their child alone. Rescued by a local fisherman, with no memory of her life before, Charlotte lives on the Faroe Islands as Katrin Nielsen. Seeing a beached seal one day triggers her memory. Twenty-three years is a long time. Is the love they once shared strong enough to be rekindled or have too many years passed eroding all hope of a happy ever after?

After Dark by Samantha Hicks
Can a love that starts out in terror be real or last? Meredith Ashcroft disappears on her way to a client meeting. Five months later, art gallery manager Stephanie Edwards is also held and tortured by the same sadistic man. Thrown together

trying to overcome their shared ordeal, they find themselves falling in love. Is it true love or just an attachment to each other born out of fear for their lives?

<u>The Book Witch</u> by Annette Mori
What if someone had the power to bring characters from a book to life...should they be allowed to glimpse reality? Imara is that person, a book witch who is convinced of her superiority, especially over book magicians. Join award-winning author, Annette Mori, and the gang from Asset Management, The Organization, and the colorful women in The Book Addict to bring you this delightful, magical romance.

<u>Calling Home</u> by Jen Silver
Sarah Frost, director of the Frost Foundation makes her home at a writers' retreat—The Lodge on the Lake. Galen Thomas, who is taking a break from her vet's practice goes to the island to fill the post of handy person. A revelation of events from forty years earlier, threatens what they now call home. Will the lives and loves of Sarah, Berry, and Galen survive the disturbing past legacy?

<u>Reach of the Heron</u> by Angela Koenig
After an automobile accident takes the lives of her parents and nearly her own, Arkadia O'Malley faces a painful recovery. She also seeks custody of her younger sister, Rini, and contends with Irish law. Arkadia's efforts to reunite with her sister are aided by powerful women from this reality as well as from Elsewhere. Will they find her in time to save her?

<u>From Wind and Water</u> by Laura Kovack
Surrounded by the Lands of Earth, Fire, Water and Wind is the Seventh Kingdom. All but Earth have rulers. A new enemy threatens all Lands and it is imperative to find the last ruler of Earth. Morgayne, ruler in Land of Water and Ventus, ruler of Land of Wind, form a tentative relationship in this quest. Will they allow or deny their feelings in this fantasy adventure?

<u>The Book Addict</u> by Annette Mori
This is a captivating story of Tanya, a young woman whose life is without any friends or lovers. When she meets Elle, the alluring owner of the new bookstore. Tanya is immediately infatuated with the mysterious woman. Maybe, the books won't be the only thing enchanted if Elle allows the magic of love to enter her heart.

<u>Colors of Rage</u> by Nanisi Barrett D'Arnuk
Dr. Kailyn DeKendran, head of the Acoustic Research Department, and her sister Jayanta, are drawn into a fray of unrest. When Kailyn disappears, family and friends band together to find her. Time is running out, and the riots are getting more violent. Will they find Kailyn before it is too late to put an end to the madness that has overtaken them?

Affinity
Rainbow Publications

eBooks, Print, Free eBooks

Visit our website for more publications available online.

www.affinityrainbowpublications.com

Published by Affinity Rainbow Publications
A Division of Affinity eBook Press NZ LTD
Canterbury, New Zealand

Registered Company 2517228